Class Act

Also by Kelsey Rodkey:

Last Chance Books

A Disaster in Three Acts

Plus One

Class Act

KELSEY RODKEY

HARPER
An Imprint of HarperCollinsPublishers

Library of Congress Control Number: 2023948449
ISBN 978-0-06-324377-4

Typography by Jessie Gang
24 25 26 27 28 LBC 5 4 3 2 1
First Edition

To my first critique partner, Carlyn Greenwald,
We could fill a library with just our stories—okay, mostly yours.

One

We might as well be at a funeral with how dead the restaurant is.

Sunday nights are notoriously slow, practically reserved for just the Ashes regulars, which is probably why my parents assume I can multitask well enough to waitress *and* watch Connie. Tonight I almost had the guts to remind them that they had no problem leaving me alone—to watch Connie—when I was her age, but instead, I accept the challenge they don't realize they've issued and threaten my sister within an inch of her life if she dares to move from her booth without my permission. Not that she even noticed. She's been staring at a blank Word document on her laptop screen for . . . about three months now. I've discovered that writer's block has a lot of the same symptoms as depression, but it's a thing that's hard to bond over, so I keep my observation to myself and instead play a game to see how many straws I can sneak into her drink whenever I pass by. I'm up to *nine*.

A little after eight o'clock, I begin wrapping up my five-hour shift by counting my tips. It takes all of about three seconds, sadly. I start kneading away the migraine that has been slowly forming behind my eyes all day when, across the restaurant, my sister stops glaring at her computer and reaches for her drink. It's down to the dregs, but she doesn't realize or care and only snaps out of her daze when she struggles to get her mouth around any of the straws I placed in there. She blinks at her glass, confused. I pocket my cash and refill her soda from a can I grabbed out of the staff refrigerator.

When I set the new cup down in front of Connie, she pulls the drink closer without thanking me or asking about the straws, but that's no surprise. Being an older sister is often a thankless job, and one where my attempts to amuse the both of us go unnoticed. At least until the younger sister is, like, twenty-three, I've heard.

Almost immediately after taking her first sip, she recoils, holding the glass at arm's length. "What is this?"

"Caffeine-free. We have school tomorrow and, at this rate, you're going to be awake until you're old enough to vote."

I don't really want to think about school, but its looming presence is hard to avoid this close to the first day. The entire past week has been dedicated to getting our uniforms in order, making sure we have the right supplies and rented the correct digital textbooks. I can't walk into my bedroom without smelling fresh erasers and being reminded of the ticking clock. And it wouldn't be a big deal if it weren't Connie's freshman year or our first year going to school together since elementary . . . or an entirely new school for the both of us.

There's so much extra pressure this year that I'm ready to snap.

Table eighteen bursts into laughter, grabbing our attention. It's the last of three remaining tables in my section and seats a few kids around Connie's age. She tenses.

"Do we know them?" My eyes focus on the table, and the panic starts first. It's what always starts first.

Then the resentment, building deep in my gut, only to be slashed by—

The guilt.

All the usual feelings Connie brings. Being an older sister is not only thankless, but it comes with a lot of emotional baggage that absolutely no one warned me about. The biggest bag—it absolutely has to be checked preflight—is the one that holds everything bad that happens to your younger sibling that makes you feel like you could have stopped it and it's all your fault that you didn't.

"You don't," she says quietly. She places her fingers back atop the keyboard but doesn't type. "They're from school."

My heart jumps in my throat. That's all she really needs to say. I focus on the three of them: one girl and two boys, all white, and all smirking in my sister's direction.

"I'm going to say something."

"No," Connie whispers, her hand lashing out to circle my wrist. "No. It's fine."

"It's not. They're—" They're laughing at her. But she knows that, obviously.

"They're paying customers, and Dad will kill you if you upset them."

"Technically, they haven't paid yet."

Her eyes plead just as much as her voice. "*Ella.* Leave it."

I will. For now.

I shake it off and head into the kitchen to officially close out the remaining tabs and catch the tail end of another "disagreement" between my mother, Ashley, the main attraction here at Ashes, and her two protégés, a.k.a. Taylor and Andrew.

"That is *not* what I meant," my mom says exasperatedly to Andrew. She uses the backside of her hand to push a stray piece of blond hair away from her eye. "You're overcooking it. Taylor, do you see?"

They both lean over a pan and then stare blankly at Mom.

"*Hello?*" she says heavily. "Anyone home?"

My mom is not an unkind person. She's under a lot of stress—even more so in the last few years, as she has dedicated a lot of time to mentoring two apprentices per year to learn under her—and it doesn't always come out in productive ways. Ashes is my parents' third child, as they annoyingly like to say, and definitely their most problematic. It wasn't until recently that the tides turned in their favor and gluten- and nut-free and vegan foods became so popular (in Pennsylvania). It's my mom's whole Thing in the culinary world, and she refused to change even though everyone told her to branch out into a broader space, at least at the beginning of her career. She demanded the world change for her instead.

It's admirable but has always felt a little far-fetched and risky, and a *lot* exhausting. When I'm old enough to have a full-time job, I want it to be something I can leave at work by the end of the day, not something that becomes my whole entire life. Plus, I'm much too unmotivated to pave a way instead of taking the road that's already traveled.

"I see," Taylor says, while Andrew nods.

"Sorry," Andrew adds.

As gently as possible, my mom tosses the pan to the back burner, metaphorically and literally. "Clean up, please."

As they do, she passes behind me and mutters, "—in over my head. I can't do this again. I'm *not* doing this again."

In the past, the chefs who have left my mother's care have gone on to great things. While it's clear that won't happen this time, I guess it's an honor in its own for Andrew and Taylor to leave next summer having destroyed my mother's will to go on (or ever teach again, apparently). Andrew, a cousin's cousin or something of my mom's, is especially terrible at all things food. He's only here because he refused to go to college and this was some compromise he came to with his parents. I'm not sure how my mom got roped into it, but she swore off all distant family favors after Andrew's first week.

I snatch the printed receipts and watch as my mom pulls her famous Have It Three Ways Cake out of the oven. Physical presence in the restaurant might be on the lower side right now, but we always get last-minute take-out orders for this on Sundays. If they add ice cream to the order, I personally refer to it as the Sundae Scaries instead of the mouthful that is Have It Three Ways Cake. It was the first thing my mom ever named herself, and it sucks like it. She really hasn't gotten any better at naming things since then.

Back in the dining room, I intend to drop the receipts off, first to the family of three having a late dinner that another waitress served before her shift was over, then to the older couple whispering to each other in the corner, and then to the little douchebags from Connie's school, but I notice that their table is empty.

They're surrounding Connie's booth.

Before I realize what I'm doing, I clench the receipts in my fist and march over.

"Something I can help you with?" I ask without waiting to hear what they're saying.

The girl turns to me, her copper hair in stark contrast to Connie's and my pale blond. "No. We're just talking to a friend."

The two guys start laughing again, this time clustered around me—douchebaggery in surround sound. One has freckles across his cheeks and nose, and I want to punch him once for every single one.

I offer their receipt instead. "Here you go. You can pay by scanning the code, or I'll take payment as soon as you're ready."

I hate how polite my voice is, like I'm still hoping to get tips from them, but it's just that this politeness has been ingrained in me from three years of working here. I'm actually *pissed*.

"Sure," the girl says, taking it. "We'll get to it."

She and the boys turn back to Connie, who doesn't even shoot me a glance, and says, "Please? We're big fans of your work."

Your work.

My insides chill.

I'll give them the benefit of the doubt, just this once, and assume they are not total assholes. Positive, peppy, delusional Ella can convince herself that these three are actual fans of

Connie's work, that they follow her on whatever fan fiction sites she not-so-anonymously-anymore publishes to, and they are not being *antagonistic little shitheads*.

"Connie," I say loudly, pushing through the barricade they've formed around her booth, and smack my palms against the table. "Do they like *Avenged*?"

Connie's favorite ten-seasons-and-counting show, *Avenged*, is about all the fridged significant others and family members who died to further superheroes' character development living in the same alternate reality and becoming superheroes themselves.

I can tell from their snickering behind me that they do *not* like *Avenged* and they are *not* fans of her work.

"We love Connie's writing about *Avenged*," the girl says with a smarmy smile. "We were asking her if she'd read some for us."

"We saw her writing it all night," Freckles chimes in.

The final guy *reaches for her laptop* and *pulls it off the table*. Connie is on her feet as quickly as I can turn around.

"This is just a blank page," he says disappointedly.

"Sucks," Freckles mutters. He heads back to his seat.

"Well, if she won't read us something new . . . ," the girl starts. She pulls out her phone and plays a video.

I yank the laptop from the boy and set it on the chair behind me. Connie freezes up, one muscle at a time, as her own words from the spring talent show last school year come out of the phone's speaker. Some absolute jerk had found Connie's fan fiction account and read from her work in progress to the whole school without her permission.

She hasn't written anything since.

Connie shuts down even further, grabbing and closing her laptop, sliding back into the vinyl booth, and staring into space. I often think of my sister as the baby she was the first moment I saw her. Tiny, unprotected, naive.

I think of the newborn version of her when I whirl around and smack the phone out of the girl's hand. It goes skidding across the floor and slides underneath the family of three's table. The girl gasps, standing still in shock, and I knock my palms into her shoulders, trying to push her away. Instead, my wrists crack painfully and audibly, and she trips over her own feet trying to get away. She stumbles back onto the ground, hair spread beneath her like a flame.

"Ella, stop," Connie hisses from behind me, but the damage is done.

The redhead looks up at me as I tower over her, anger oozing from my pores.

I've never punched someone, though I've thought about it a lot and dreamed about it even more, especially after the talent show. After I saw how mortified my sister was. My therapist said that's because I have a lot of repressed feelings, but if I talk about them with her, are they really repressed? I don't know; it feels like a gimmick to get me into more therapy sessions.

I don't punch the girl. Of course I don't punch her.

The boy who stuck around helps her up, and without paying, they all scramble to the door. I could chase after them for their money—they either live close or have to wait for a ride anyway if they're Connie's age—but it's not worth it.

"I am *so* sorry," my dad says, having come into the dining room at just the wrong moment, apparently, and addressing the remaining tables in his official Owner of Ashes voice. The man's face is ghost white and appalled. "Your meal will be comped tonight. I'm so sorry for the scene. Ashes does not condone any type of violence." He turns away from the table and glares at me. He's always been really good at showing up when I'm at my worst.

He grabs Connie—who grabs her laptop—and me—barely managing to grab my dignity—by the elbows and drags us back to his office tucked away next to the kitchen.

It smells like French vanilla in here, like usual.

"Why?" he asks, exhausted. He sinks into the chair behind his desk while Connie and I fall onto the worn leather couch in front of it. I take turns rubbing each of my wrists, wishing I had an extra hand to work the tension from my forehead.

"Ask Fists Fitzgerald over there," Connie says, gesturing to me with a look of disgust on her face. "I told her not to—"

"Did you even know those kids? Why were you letting them talk to you like that? What were their names? They're banned from Ashes." I turn to my dad for confirmation. "They're banned. They were—did you even know them, Connie? You just sat there and let them—"

She adopts this sour look on her face that tells me she's about to rant. "No, I didn't know them *by name*. You went to that middle school, too; it's huge. Did *you* know everyone by name?"

Our dad looks between us, his lips a thin line. Then he exhales through his nose and faces my sister. "Connecticut, can you please go wash some dishes?"

She bristles at the use of her full name, and I don't blame her. "Can I leave my laptop in here?"

"Yes."

She slides it across his desk and stomps out of the office, like she thought he'd say no and therefore not having somewhere to put her prized possession would mean not having to do the dishes. The way her mind works sometimes, seriously.

She mutters something about unpaid child labor before the door slams shut.

"You get a hefty allowance," he calls after her. Then he sighs. "Delaware."

Yes, we're literally named Connecticut and Delaware—after our parents' birthplaces. Dad's from Delaware and Mom's from Connecticut. Now we're in Pennsylvania. "Why weren't you watching her?"

I let the tiny buzz of the neon-red Ashes sign behind his desk fill the room, and then I begrudgingly answer. "I was *working*."

I refuse to give him more until he thanks me for standing up for Connie.

He pulls his thick-rimmed glasses off his face to meet my eyes directly. "You really need to make sure you're setting a good example for her. Tomorrow you'll be starting at a new place for both of you, but this is her first time in high school, period."

"I obviously know that."

"You're not acting like it. How would you feel if Connie had pushed that girl?"

"Proud. They were bullying her. Again."

"Ella."

"I think it's a little ridiculous for you to lecture me about setting a good example for her when I just set the *best* example for her."

His exhaustion turns to disdain as he straightens. "And here I was about to let you off the hook."

"Dad—" It comes out more clipped than I expect. I can't explain to him how frustrating it is to be told to watch Connie *all. the. time.* I haven't had a moment to myself since I was three. Why am I being held responsible for her actions? I mean, sure, I kind of pushed that girl to the ground and maybe damaged her property, and Ashes probably has some kind of lawsuit on their hands if this girl doesn't realize she was in the wrong here, but I was defending my sister, which is what he and my mom always encourage me to do. Protect her.

And now I'm feeling bad because I'm blaming *Connie* for something her classmates did to her. Former classmates. At least with the new school, there won't be old problems anymore. It's a fresh start for her and a fresh start for me. I can use it as a trial run for college, test out a new personality or something, because the one I've got now either lands me in trouble or isolates me.

I just keep it all in, though. He's right. If I hadn't let her out of my sight to begin with, I wouldn't be here now.

"What?" he asks.

"Nothing." I drop my head back onto the couch. I swear there's a divot here from the other times I've been in this position. It welcomes me with metaphorical open arms. "What's my punishment? Am I fired?" I shoot up. "Am I going to be arrested?"

His demeanor shifts back into boss mode. "I'm assuming since they ran out on the bill, and were harassing my child, they won't be telling anyone about what happened."

I nod, stomach clenched tight.

"Head to the kitchen for dishes—let Andrew and Taylor go home early. One outburst is enough for tonight; I don't need your mother melting down, too."

In hindsight, it was too optimistic of me to think he'd let Connie and *me* go home early; there's only so much trouble Connie can get into if she's holed up in her room, after all. The internet might be a scary place, but as long as her body stays physically in the house, I can't be held *that* responsible for whatever shenanigans she gets into.

He grabs papers on his desk that he's previously shown no interest in and shuffles them so they fall in line, like he wants me to do. To my parents, I am first and foremost an employee. "You're dismissed."

Two

My punishment does not end when the dishes are done; it carries over to the next day, all the way to the drop-off line of Connie's and my new school.

As far back as I can remember, my mom's been a late sleeper, so it's a bad omen that she wakes up and insists on driving us. She says she wants to see us off for our first day, but what she actually wants is to ply us with her newest dish and wring our brains dry for feedback on it in a place where we can't escape. She wants "youthful" palates to give her "opinions" on a possible brunch option, which just means she wants praise—none of which I can give her, especially not at seven fifteen in the morning when I'm wearing a light-blue polo the color of my antidepressants with the Courtland Academy crest over my heart like I've sworn my fealty to it before ever stepping foot inside.

I don't know what's worse: gulping down monstrous bites of this gluten-free croissant stuffed with veggies and vegan eggs and bacon to get this whole exchange over with or angsting over starting a new school where the only friend I'll have is my little sister.

Not that it will be much different from my previous school year. My social circle wasn't exactly full to bursting.

I'm not some social pariah or anything; I've just struggled in the friend department ever since my depression came to the surface. I've done a lot of work in managing it, and I'm quite functional, if I do say so myself, but part of my therapist's treatment was taking a break from social media because doomscrolling and comparing myself to everyone else's online personas became *a lot* for me, especially so early in my formative years. I took that course of action very seriously and then never returned. I do still see things online, but I'm often lacking context, and that makes it harder for me to relate to people my age. With every missed joke and trend, I'm building a wall between us.

"Croissant's too dry." I get some satisfaction in knowing it pains my mom that I can't eloquently express my thoughts on food. It's food. I took the same health class Connie did, but my understanding of calories is constantly overshadowed by her purple prose aimed at whatever my mom's latest recipe is. I can say that it tastes good or it doesn't, but that's not what my mom's looking for.

"It's flaky," Connie and my mom say at the same time. I hate being in confined spaces with the two of them. It's like they morph into one extra-intolerable person. My dad and I are close, but nothing like this.

"It doesn't go down smoothly," I reiterate, turning toward Connie where she sits in the back seat, still buckled.

"Well, that's because you ate it in two bites," my mom says. "Usually a good indication, but . . ."

"Weird, considering she didn't like it," Connie finishes, her tone teetering into teasing.

Students scramble to claim available parking spots and get into the building before the first bell. There are too many cars, too many people. I thought a benefit of this school was the supposed smaller class sizes, but I think we got duped. Is it really possible that this many people's parents are willing to pay an arm and a leg for their kids to go here, just to be squished into the halls like sardines in a tin? I know the tuition affords the school more things than my public school offered, including chances to award scholarships at the end of senior year, but why not just . . . save that money and know that it's going directly toward your own child instead of thrown into a pool to be given to whoever?

"I liked it, Mom," Connie says. "Wish I had some more to share with my classmates."

Connecticut Parker-Evans: people pleaser. At the age of seven, she begged for a functional child-size kitchen to indulge my mom and has since become so good at baking that she has taken control of our holiday cookie extravaganza, while the most I can contribute is curly bows when I package them. I swear my paper cuts from the personalized cards we mailed with them still haven't healed. Nor have the emotional wounds that about half of them "accidentally" went out with my mom's and sister's signatures scribbled over mine and Dad's. Dad couldn't care less and Mom was too absorbed in rereading the latest *Food Network* article on her rise to fame to really notice. She, and I quote, "makes dietary restrictions for everyone in a good way," according to them.

My mom inches closer to the back entrance of the school, barely a foot away from the bumper of the Subaru in front of us. I can't take this slow pace, the dread that builds up inside me, so I grab my backpack strap and unbuckle my seat belt. I've never had to switch schools before and I'm sure—absolutely *positive*—that the first day will be the worst, and the sooner I start it, the sooner it will end.

"Wait, Ella," my mom says. She eases up on the brake and the car creeps forward again. "The email said—"

"Why can't I just get out now?" Unlike the kids at my old school, the students here don't seem to be congregating outside before class, and it's making me anxious to find my locker and first class.

My mom moves us up a smidge and finally throws the car into park. "Okay, Connie, you can go. Have a wonderful first day. You're a star. I love you."

Instead of being embarrassed or rolling her eyes, Connie smiles brightly and slides out of the back seat. I wait until she clears my door to open it, but my mom latches onto my elbow, stalling me.

"Keep an eye on her—"

"I know."

"Be a good influence for her—"

"I *know*, but if you want that, I probably shouldn't be late.

So . . ." I nod toward the school and watch her fingers release my arm one by one. "Thank you. Love you. Bye."

I hate the small part of me that wants her to want me to linger here. I hate the smaller part of me that can admit I'm terrified of leaving this car.

"Bye, sweetie. I love you. Have a good day." She barely waits for me to close the door before she zooms off and leaves me in completely unfamiliar territory.

I didn't have to transfer to Courtland with Connie. It was my choice—*heavily* influenced (read: guilted into) by my parents— and all the pros outweighed the cons when I jotted down a list on my iPad. Smaller class sizes and more attention from teachers, scholarships, great reputation, more student-funded activities, clean slate, blah blah blah. But the biggest pro, if you ask my parents, was that I can keep an eye on Connie.

Except. I've lost her already.

Most people hurry past me and into the brick building, but some slow when they see me and outright stare. It's made clear from the moment my foot touched down on the sidewalk that I am an invader, a fat girl parading around in *their* uniform with hair I shouldn't have gotten cut this short and knee socks that won't stay up without strangling blood flow to my calves, and I am not welcome here. I'm a cheap cosplayer.

I guess smaller class sizes should have been in the cons, too.

I throw my backpack over my shoulder, take a deep breath, and step inside.

A singsongy voice that is *way* too perky for the hour slams into me like a wall. "Dela-*where* have you been all morning? We're going to be late."

I blink, focusing on the girl in front of me. She is perfect in just about every sense of the word. Her dark brown hair curls away from her round face in luscious waves, and the pale blue of her polo doesn't wash out her tan skin but instead makes it appear richer and smoother than what should be humanly possible. Her skirt is rolled several inches higher than dress code and lies flat over black tights. She finishes the outfit off with black Doc Martens. Again, perfect.

"Oh my god," I breathe, at once happy and nervous. I recognize her somehow, even though she is so different from when I last saw her. "Estefania?"

"*No*, no no no," she corrects quickly, stepping forward and pulling me into an awkward hug. "Stevie. It's Stevie now. Este just reminded me of my grandmother. It was literally her name first."

Estefania Hernández. We were friends in middle school and freshman year, just two girls in the same group of almost-friends, but not, like, *best friends*. When she didn't show up for sophomore year at Cedar Heights High School, I just assumed she moved away—farther away than this—and then, well, I had an embarrassing lack of close friends to focus on and never thought of her again. I had no clue she went here. She's a sight for sore, worried eyes.

"Welcome to Courtland Academy! As a means of fluffing up my college apps, I volunteered to be a welcome guide. When I saw your name, I knew I had to have you."

"Oh, you don't have to—"

"I get out of my classes five minutes early to meet you at

yours for the whole first week; don't you dare take this from me." She pulls her phone from a pocket in her skirt that I'm pretty sure I don't have in mine. I wonder if they're only in the straight sizes or if she added them herself. "Gives me more time for content."

She leans into me and aims the front-facing camera at us. "Say 'Harvaaaard.'"

She snaps a shot as I'm cringing away.

"You want to go to Harvard?" The Este—Stevie—who I remember was motivated by nothing and no one. She barely raised her hand for attendance and only removed her head from her hoodie when every single one of her teachers had begged through frustrated sighs. I almost want to laugh.

"God no, but I found out that the word creates the perfect smile." She flicks to her Instagram page, where row after row of perfect selfies provide evidence of this. "You should follow me. I'm on TikTok, too—@StevieSays. It's basically a nicer *Gossip Girl* knock-off where everyone *knows* I'm Gossip Girl, but still. I'm making a play for 5K by the end of the year. It's been a slow grow since the content is so specific to my audience."

As she rambles and I sort of listen, she links her arm through mine and drags me farther inside, waving and greeting random students. I was under the assumption that all schools smelled stale and thick, but this one is cleaner, crisper, and the floors aren't permanently scuffed, maybe because we're required to wear certain shoes with this uniform.

"Did you happen to see my sister come through? Did her guide . . . guide her?"

It's a useless question. It's clear Stevie doesn't see much happening when she has her phone out. She's only navigating the hallways right now by sheer muscle memory and probably something like echolocation.

"Isn't it disgusting that your sister goes here, too? The last time I saw her was at your thirteenth birthday party and she was basically in diapers. I feel ancient."

"She was in elementary school—"

"Basically sucking on the mommy milkers still." She slides her phone back in her pocket—I'll have to ask her about that—and stops next to a locker. Mine. "I didn't notice her, but her guide is Sasha, a sophomore and *very* fashionable, uses big words. She'll be fine."

I stop myself from worrying about what kind of trouble Connie can get into only long enough to focus on my lock combination. Last year, I had the entire school day to escape from it all. I literally couldn't get lectured for not looking out for Connie when she was physically at another school. Even my parents had to admit that was asking too much of me.

Didn't stop me from feeling guilty that she was apparently being harassed by her classmates, though.

But that's why I'm here now.

I work the dial but the mechanism doesn't give; I swirl it again.

"Let me help," Stevie says, pushing me aside with her hip. "The locks are the oldest thing in the school besides the meatballs in the cafeteria. Sometimes they need a little love."

She slams a fist into the upper right corner and shoves the lock; the door bounces open, nearly taking me out in the process.

I have no books to carry—Courtland Academy prides itself on being a nearly paperless school—so I'll be getting a brand-new MacBook Air in homeroom instead of any textbooks, and all assignments will be given through the Courtland Portal and completed online. I'd be lying if I said I wasn't excited to be getting a nicer computer than the used and abused Chromebooks I rented from my old school. The price of the MacBook is built into the outrageous tuition, so it's not exactly a deal, but assuming no disasters strike and leave me scrambling for a replacement, I'll be going into college with a basically new computer. I leave my backpack hanging sadly on the hook in my locker and go with Stevie to her locker, admiring all the different ways the students are wearing the uniform—untucked shirts, rolled sleeves, slouchy cardigans, knee-high socks, and more rolled skirts. I was expecting to see stricter rule following, especially on the first day, but now that I know these possibilities are, well, possible, maybe I'll take a chance on feeling slightly more comfortable tomorrow. The school store apparently doesn't keep permanent stock of sizes over XL, so when my parents remembered last-minute that we had to buy uniforms, this is what I got. Too-small shirt, too-small skirt. They fit, but it could be easy for anyone to make a case that I'm breaking dress code. At least, I thought that until I saw everyone else.

"I've already been here this morning," she says, opening the door to show off a gold-framed mirror, pictures of mostly just her and several little dogs, and a copy of her class schedule. Before I have a chance to check if we have anything together, she shuts the door, locker tour over.

"Don't worry about your sister, okay?" Stevie unconsciously imitates my posture with her own binder, using it as a shield to protect her chest. "She's going to love it here. The budget is stupidly extra and the classes are easy."

Someone comes over the announcement system—a nasally person who probably can't hear how garbled their speech is from wherever they're delivering this announcement—and says that we should all proceed to our homerooms for a special welcome assembly.

Apparently, Stevie turned a new leaf and cares about punctuality now. She used to live in detention from her tardies, but now being on time means scoping out the best seats and people to sit with, or so she tells me.

"When Courtland finally started letting girls in, my parents jumped at the chance, you know? It's why I disappeared before sophomore year. Started all new accounts under Stevie, broke up with the toxic friends—not you; I couldn't find you online—and decided I'd be different here." She gives me a small smile. "It's kind of hard to be the slacker weirdo one year and then the bubbly makeup girlie the next without getting made fun of or called fake."

"Why *was* there such a change?" At her sharp look, I continue quickly, "Not that there is anything wrong with this."

"I just wasn't confident, and everyone had known me since, like, kindergarten, so I felt like I couldn't be anything else." She shrugs like it's not a big deal, but it is. I completely understand what she means. "If I'm honest, I actually *did* hesitate to be your guide. But only because you knew the old me and then I worried you wouldn't even remember the old me, or that you'd say something—"

"No, I would never," I interject.

"Exactly," she says with a smile. "Exactly. I realized I was worrying for nothing. You were always so nice, and maybe this is a fresh start for you, too."

"Yeah," I say lightly. Stevie doesn't know what it means to me that she's here, and I would definitely not have taken that for granted to, what? Comment that she's changed? Decide that after one second of seeing her, I could sum her up and judge her?

"This is you." She leaves me at my homeroom, which is right next to hers, and then abandons me much like my mother and sister earlier, but with the promise that she'll return.

Before entering the classroom, I take another deep breath. A girl's lungs could get used to this premium, unstinky air. All along the hallway, other seniors are slamming lockers shut, joining friends on their way to their homerooms, and having a perfectly fine start to their final year here.

Each grade has their own lunch periods and hallways for lockers and classes, efficiently keeping everyone separated. It's something the school prides itself on, giving this morsel of information front-and-center placement on the website. This will make things difficult in the Keeping an Eye on Connie department, but might also help signal when something is wrong. Like now. Connie makes a beeline down the hall and I swear I can *see* the drama following her. The worst part is that, deep in my gut, I know I won't be able to stop it.

She finds a break in the steady stream of teenage bodies and rushes toward me.

"Hey," she says, breathless, her eyes wide. She shoves a piece of paper into my hands. "The library offers *free* printing, and it's so fast. I got my first two chapters printed before the announcement, and I'm hoping seeing it on paper will jump-start my writing again."

Connie overheated our home printer attempting to print out her first completed fic—a total of one hundred and twelve *thousand* words—and it hasn't worked ever since. There's just something about printers. When one dies, it's not worth trying to resurrect it.

"Where's your guide?" I ask.

Her face falls. "She went to class—"

"She's supposed to take you to your homeroom so you don't get lost."

I can feel my shields going up faster than Connie's fanfic could print. I'll probably be late, but I could maybe manage to get her to where she needs to be on time. I glance down at what she handed me. It's my schedule, warm from the printer.

"Wow, thanks, Mom," I mutter sarcastically, just so she doesn't get too smug that I actually do appreciate it. I was going to download my schedule to my laptop, but this will be so much easier to access between classes.

"It's okay. I can make it on my own."

"Really?" I ask in disbelief. "Do you know where you're going? Because the bell is about to ring."

"The school emailed a map—I printed that for you, too."

She flips open her binder and pulls out another piece of paper, which she offers to me. She's already marked it with a leaky pink highlighter. I have no doubt she did the same for her own map. "It's how I found you."

I grab her arm with a sigh, intent on dragging her kicking and screaming to her homeroom if I have to, but she pulls away.

"Stop," she hisses. "You're so embarrassing."

I'm embarrassing?

"You're so much," she continues. "I'll be fine."

She turns away and takes a plunge into the ebbing and flowing river of students. Barely two steps away, she trips on her loose shoelace, like a cartoon character, except I couldn't make this up.

Her binder flies open and her papers spill out across the floor. If people don't walk over them, they just step around. So much for that *community* the school website promised. She's lucky she hasn't been trampled at this point because the hall is filled mostly with guys three times her size. It seems Stevie isn't the only one who cares about being on time, even for something as pointless as homeroom.

I rush over and help pick her up. "You okay?"

"Oh god, my chapters!" She ignores me, trying to gather the papers even if it means losing a finger to someone's ugly Sperrys. She tucks each paper to her chest with care. I stoop to help, no one else bothering, until a head of blond curls dips into my sight.

"These yours?" a white guy with an eerily symmetrical face asks.

"My sister's." I take the papers he offered and mimic Connie, keeping the words safe against my uniform. I'm not embarrassed that she writes fan fiction. Annoyed sometimes, sure. Especially now. But not embarrassed. It's her *enthusiasm* for everything that embarrasses me. I'm only being discreet because this work is private and it getting into the mainstream is what caused our school transfers in the first place. People finding out she's FridgedButNotForgotten20 on day one is not an option. "Thanks."

He's like a huge rock in a stream; everyone moves around us as we collect the rest of her chapter. His hand lands on the last sheet of paper and he stops.

"What *is* this?" he asks, standing. His eyes dance over the page quickly and my heart sinks. I try to grab the paper from him, but he turns away, still scanning the lines.

"'Their lives had always been intertwined, like their fingers, like their legs after *sex*. It was always meant to be like this—'"

Again, I attempt to snatch the paper from him, but he's too quick. Connie stands off to the side, horror—*no*, trauma—on her face. The crowd dwindles down as people head into their homerooms, but a few stick around to hear what this guy recites of my sister's most personal work.

"'It was always meant to be them. Nothing could have prepared either for this magical feeling, this moment of destiny.'"

Laughter starts around us and I can't help but think it's because they *think* they're supposed to laugh. There isn't anything funny about Connie's words. They're sweet, if a little naive. I'd say as much if I weren't so taken aback.

The guy clears his throat, reading a little to himself before opening his mouth like he's about to start up again. The silence gives my brain the second it needs to unfreeze.

"That's not yours." I snatch the paper from his hands, accidentally ripping it in half.

"You said it wasn't yours either," he says a little coldly.

He tries to snag my half, but I dodge him.

Stevie's homeroom teacher comes to the hallway from her classroom. She's a fortysomething white woman who appears exhausted with the school year already. "What's going on out here? Get to your homerooms."

"Sorry," the guy says, putting on a lighter, friendlier tone. "I would, but someone dropped their papers." He raises his half of Connie's page as evidence.

"Okay, just hurry up," she says before returning to her classroom.

He snorts to himself—and maybe to the crowd still listening. "Where's your sister? Can I hire her to write my sexts? My girlfriend would eat this stupid shit up."

I snatch the last bit of paper from his hands, save for the piece clenched in his fist.

"What's your problem?" My voice doesn't waver.

"You girls," he says offhandedly, dismissing me with a wave of his hand. "Always trying to make drama out of nothing. It was literally dropped right in front of me. What else was I supposed to do?"

I glance around at the crowd and mumble, "*Not* read it?"

He grins, and if he weren't so obviously evil to the core, I might think it's nice. It's perfect, showing the same amount of teeth on each side, and a good amount of lip on the top and bottom. Cruelly, there's even a dimple tucked into each cheek.

"What?" he says with a laugh. "You don't want attention all of a sudden?" He balls the scrap of paper in his fist and lightly tosses it at my chest. It bounces off and hits the floor quietly. "Could have fooled me."

My mouth drops open. "I'm going to report you to the principal."

"The student council president is in charge of student relations."

"Then I'll report you to them."

His grin grows, and then without so much as another word, he disappears into the crowd of assholes who assembled to rubberneck.

Connie lurches forward, grabbing what's left of her page from my hand, and darts away. She wasn't fast enough for me to miss the tears in her eyes; I can only hope others didn't catch them.

The teacher returns to the doorway and barks, "Homeroom. Now."

After my homeroom teacher, an old man with wiry hairs coming out of his nostrils, takes attendance, he escorts us to the auditorium for our first, and hopefully last, school assembly. Though Courtland's student population is half of CHHS, the auditorium here is double the size, and every seat is full. The stage takes up maybe a third of the square footage in the room and the ceiling has to be fifty feet high. All this unusable space gives the appearance of grandness, but it's not exactly practical in a high school. Who needs perfect acoustics for off-key performances of *Brigadoon*? I glance up, just to check if there is balcony seating. There is not.

The teachers are adamant about us sitting grouped by homerooms and, therefore, grades, so I don't have a chance to find Stevie or Connie and end up sitting next to a guy a few inches shorter than me who smells like he showered with cologne this morning. With every inhale I can feel a migraine building behind my eyes.

By the time my classmates take their places, I'm left in the aisle seat. The assembly starts up with a ridiculous Courtland Academy chant that only half the student population participates in. The half that is apparently as caffeinated as Stevie. This is followed by Mr. Logan, our unextraordinary middle-aged principal with a close-cropped brown beard that matches his thinning hair, droning on about the school rules, the dress code (that no one seems to follow), and the importance of excelling. He never specifies at what, just that we need to always be excelling. If I had my way, I'd be excelling at a nap right now.

Near the end of his speech, he welcomes what appear to be three clones onto the stage and outright lies to all of us by introducing them as different people. The matching uniforms definitely don't help the matter. But wait, I *do* recognize one of them.

"And it's with great pleasure that I announce your student council for this year: senior Dean Hammond as secretary/

treasurer, senior Todd Carlisle as vice president, and senior Thomas Hayworth as Courtland Academy president." The jerk who read Connie's work steps forward last and delivers a shit-eating grin to the audience, his piercing blue eyes dimming in the spotlight.

President? Granted, I don't know how much sway a student council president actually has—I don't even know who any of my student council reps at CHHS were, which is a good sign of how powerless they were—but with all this pomp and circumstance, it seems like it might be a lot here.

And he said he handles student complaints just this morning.

No.

My hand shoots into the air before I can think twice. The principal cuts off his words at the sight of it.

"Uh, yes?" he asks timidly into the microphone attached to the podium.

"Hi. I don't remember there being an election. I mean, class hasn't even started." I let my hand drop and lean into the aisle so he can better see and hear me. Unfortunately, that means I have a ton of eyes directed at me now, not just his.

This school year is certainly starting off worse than I expected.

He laughs a little. "Yes, the election was held last year, per our school student council bylaws, so we can have student government in place as of day one."

He's ready to dismiss me. I can see it in how his eyes shine, how he turns ever so slightly away from me and opens his mouth again.

No, sir. I will *not* be ignored. As long as I remain polite, he can't dismiss me. He *shouldn't*, at least. I raise my hand again.

He blinks. "Yes?"

"Don't you think that since the student body or its needs may have changed over the summer, new elections should be held?" It's entirely possible that Connie and I are the only new students aside from the freshman class and I'm making a big stink about this, like, *me me me*, but if there's one thing I'm good at in this world, it's considering how things affect Connie.

The clones onstage shift from foot to foot, less comfortable in the limelight than they were before. I almost feel bad for Thomas 2 and Thomas 3. It's not like I'm intentionally setting out to destroy something they may have worked for and earned. Just *Thomas*.

"It's not exactly fair to your student council representatives to have to go through another election again, Miss . . . ?"

"Parker-Evans." I decide just to stand at this point. I smooth down the back of my skirt to make sure I'm not giving anyone a show. "It doesn't seem fair to have a new student population under the reign of representatives they didn't vote for. The freshmen, transfers, etcetera."

I am an android programmed for one mission—protect Connie—and I will self-destruct before I let someone stop me from being successful. I won't let Thomas get away with this type of behavior toward her, me, or anyone.

"Yes, well, the bylaws—"

My anger bursts out of me at yet another dismissal. "If you're not going to do another election, the least they can do is wear name tags so we can tell them apart, right?"

An abrupt and loud laugh echoes through the hushed auditorium. I look across the aisle and find a white guy clutching his chest like I'm the most endearing thing he's ever seen. His skin is tanned from the summer, and his dark messy hair falls past his ears. I would have thought that kind of hair on a boy would be against the school rules. Maybe if I had paid attention to them when Mr. Logan was rattling them off earlier, I would know for sure.

Other students try to hide their grins as they glance between him and the principal, then to me. I don't know if he's laughing at me, what I said, or at the reactions of the people onstage, but I'm not entirely sure I like it. It makes butterflies multiply in my stomach. It would be easier to take the brunt of the spotlight tenfold than the heaviness of his stare.

"Something to add?" I ask him with a raised eyebrow. I turn to the stage again when he holds his hands up in defense. "I knew this school had funding, but I didn't realize cloning human beings was possible yet."

"Miss Evans," Mr. Logan says, indicating clearly that he thinks my first name is Parker.

The rest of his statement is cut off by the guy. "Let her talk," he says, his hands cupped around his mouth. More giggles and whispers cut through the tense crowd.

Mr. Logan clears his throat. "That's enough," he says to the boy. To me, he says, "Why don't you have a seat?"

"I don't know," I say, flitting my eyes to the boys behind him, "it doesn't appear there's any room at the table."

There are maybe one or two people—from the sounds of it, girls—who understand my words. I glance around the darkened auditorium and realize for the first time, with the entire student body sitting present, that there are way more boys than girls and visibly gender nonconforming students. And even worse than that, I could probably count the students of color on my fingers.

And look, I'm a straight white girl, so I have little room to talk about diversity and inclusion in the student council of this classist private school. I get that.

But someone had to say it, and my big mouth was already open.

My homeroom teacher slowly turns around from the seat in front of me; his glare freezes me in place. He points to the exit at the back of the auditorium, and that's how I end up with detention on my first day. It's a great indication of what the rest of the year will be like. Of what Connie's *four* years will be like. But the first day has to be the worst, right?

Three

At lunch, Stevie shows me the video—edited during a bathroom break, apparently—that she took of my . . . discussion . . . with Mr. Logan. It already has two thousand views on TikTok and I have no clue if that's a high or low number. Stevie says this video is a break from her normal format, so she's not surprised the count is lower, but pleasantly surprised with how high it *is*. There are people in the comments cheering me on, but also some making comments about my appearance and the supposed whiny nature of my voice. Stevie is quick to delete and block each and every one of them. A curious number have mentioned the "supportive king" who yelled for the principal to let me speak.

So, by the time I fight through the crowd of my classmates all filtering toward the exits and enter the detention room three hours later, I can only assume I am a celebrity, more famous than my mother, and the only reason I don't get a standing ovation from the people already in the room is because they're too cool to be online, like me.

Throughout the day, other students gave me looks, sometimes in what seemed like quiet support but . . . mostly not, mostly annoyance, and walking into detention is more of the same. A small group stares as I enter, expressions ranging from impressed to curious to unwelcoming. I want to flash them or bare my teeth, something to give them a reason for all the staring. I wasn't that out of line to suggest we redo the elections. *Maybe* I was out of line about the name tags—it's not their fault they wear the same uniform or share the same race, but . . .

I take a seat near the back of the room while five heads swivel toward me, as if I might attack if they don't keep me in their sights. Detention starts at three o'clock and with one minute to go, the door opens a final time to reveal *that guy*. The hot guy. The internet's supportive king.

"How nice of you to join us, Patrick," the detention teacher drones. He has his feet propped up on the desk and his computer in his lap.

Patrick takes a look around the room and stops when his gaze falls on me. He makes his way back, stopping momentarily when the only other girl in the room, a brunette with her hair in a fishtail braid, angles toward him with a dreamy smile.

"Hey," he says to her in a low voice. She practically melts into a puddle of hormones when half his mouth quirks into a smile.

But then he drops into the seat next to me.

"Everyone happy with their seat selection?" the teacher asks in a monotone voice. "Great, you're expected to stay there for the next half an hour."

"Wait, Mr. Carpenter." Patrick scoots his desk inch by inch closer to mine. He couldn't go slower if he tried, the metal feet screeching against the floor each time he thrusts in my direction.

My face heats.

He stops when he's about a foot away, clearly in the middle of the aisle. "Now I'm good."

Mr. Carpenter exhales through his nose. "Glad to hear it. Your happiness and comfort are my main priorities here in this place of punishment."

A few of the other students break out homework, one frees headphones and a phone from his bag, and I have to admit I can't read the room. Is this just essentially a study hall for thirty minutes? The one time I got detention in my entire history of public school education, it was heavily implied we were to stare into space and think about what awful things we'd done. In true Ella Parker-Evans fashion, I did not do something awful; I was just late to class three times in a single semester thanks to traffic on my way from the middle school to the high school.

It takes a second for me to realize that Patrick's watching me. I guess I shouldn't be shocked.

He breaks into a warm smile when my eyes slide his way. "I remember you," he says quietly.

"Well, it hasn't even been a day, so," I whisper back. I can't stare at him long because he's too good-looking. It's almost weird how pretty he is and what it does to my body. It was hard to find guys at CHHS attractive because I had gone to school with them for almost twelve years and knew what asshole behavior lurked behind their dimples and sparkly eyes. And how frequently they neglected their hygiene routines.

"Tonight will be twenty-four hours." He bites his lip in what is clearly supposed to be a flirtatious way and—well, I guess it *is* flirtatious because now I'm looking at his lips and thinking about them. What they might feel like. The butterflies in my stomach stand no chance against the hurricane of hormones he's unleashing.

I fold my hands on the desk and exhale a small, shaky breath. He's either bad at counting or a creep. "And what does that mean?"

"I saw you last night, at Ashes."

Embarrassment and realization wash over me in equal parts. I didn't think my face could get any hotter. "Oh. You were there?"

"I was with my parents. I've been trying to get them to go to Ashes for a while now because I wanted to try something off the secret menu, but my dad was really dragging his feet—he thinks it's a waste of money and time to go to a place that's all gluten-free and vegan when no one in our family needs all that just to eat."

"Keep it down, Patrick," Mr. Carpenter says without looking up from his work.

"Sorry, Mr. C." Patrick quickly pushes his desk the final stretch until it bumps into mine. Naturally, we've caught the interest of our cellmates. "You really let those people have it. My dad swore we're never going back after how you treated customers, and the meal was delicious and *free*."

I swallow down the guilt. His dad sounds like a bad time anyway. "They were making fun of my sister."

"Shit. I'm sorry," he says with a frown. "So, do you just, like, eviscerate everyone who crosses you?"

"I don't think I eviscerated anyone."

"That's not how it looks on Stevie Says."

I exhale a small laugh, and tamp down embarrassment at the idea of him watching me make a fool of myself not only once but at least twice. "I'm the one in detention; it's pretty clear he eviscerated me."

"I think you should petition the school," he says, nodding to himself. "Mr. Logan is an asshat and you're right: We need to hold reelections. It's not fair."

It's when he falls silent that I realize I'm rapt with attention, staring into his eyes so intensely that he's probably creeped out. It's just kind of nice to see someone else as righteously pissed as me. I blink and look away, his face etched on the insides of my eyelids.

"What . . ." I try to think it through. "What would even be the point, though?" The damage is done. Connie was already embarrassed. I'll just spend the next year looking out for her like I planned and then—what? I go off to college and she's here with a bunch of leftover ballbags? A redo election, with a student council that can actually make a difference, might change everything. It would definitely put Thomas in his place, and I *really* want that.

"By the look on your face, it seems like you know what the point would be." He slouches back in his seat, but he's still so close that his elbow brushes my arm. It should be illegal to wear this uniform so well. This school is actually air-conditioned, unlike CHHS, which could barely afford to open the windows after funding went to the football stadium, so he opted for a button-down shirt, the sleeves rolled, and a tie loose around his neck. He slides his phone from his pocket and angles it toward me once he pulls something up.

It's the video Stevie posted, up to five thousand views thanks to the mysterious TikTok algorithm Stevie droned on about at lunch. She seems to know so much that they should give her a job.

"About a thousand of these views are me, so don't let it go to your head," he says, his words so close to my face I feel them brush against my skin. He winks. "It's nice to see girls empowering themselves."

I side-eye him and he breaks into a grin. "I'm only kidding, a little," he says. "Look, what I'm getting at is that you stood up for yourself and your classmates. Those dudes only got their student council titles because no one else ran against them. If you got another election approved, you could run—"

"Me? No." I lean away from him, putting enough space between us for me to catch my breath and clear my head. "I don't want to be president; I just don't think that guy should be."

"Thom-ass?"

"Yeah. Ass indeed," I mumble.

"You've only been here a day and you already know the best-kept secret of this school—it's run by chumps who game the system. I think that's a sign that you should be in leadership. You actually *care*."

"Why don't *you* run? Why don't *you* petition?" He's clearly charismatic. He'd win easily; all he would have to do is bite his lip in a few girls' directions, fist-bump some guys, and *boom*.

He taps his fingers against his desk, considering my words. "If it's not you, it's basically pointless. The same people—the same *kind* of people—will end up in power. And the best thing to start some kind of movement is a little bit of change. Besides, politics aren't my thing. I don't look good in a suit."

"I doubt that."

He grins. "Do you?"

"I didn't mean—you're basically putting words in my mouth."

He pauses for a second, his face growing serious. "Is it too early in our inevitable best friendship for me to admit it's not the only thing I want to—"

"Oh my god." Even though my desk is exactly where it's supposed to be, I scoot out of line just to get away from him. I can't feel my face at this point. I am a very blond-haired, very red-faced girl with over twenty minutes left of detention and a monstrously flirty boy next to me. I won't survive.

"I'm sorry. That went too far." He holds up a hand. "I was kidding."

"Just like you were kidding about finding female empowerment . . . *nice*?"

"Yes, similarly." He tilts his head to the side, eyes focused far away, but all I can focus on is what a weird thing that is to say. "Or, wait, no. I *do* think that's nice. Hot, even."

I face forward and will my cheeks to calm down. I've had guys flirt with me before. I've had them flirt with me jokingly, as well. This isn't new; it's just the feeling of excitement, of amusement that comes along with it that's new. Normally, I'm annoyed or frustrated. I've never wanted to give myself a moment to soak it in. It's never been something I was sure I'd replay later and analyze or laugh about. I'm not *bothered*; I just don't know how to react in a quick enough manner. I'm not sure how to play this game, but I want to.

"I really am sorry. I misread your personality." He doesn't try to scoot closer again. He doesn't call me a prude or tell me to take a joke. He just . . . apologizes. Wow, that is refreshing, if not just the bare minimum.

"No, you didn't. It's okay." I slide my eyes to him. "But before you make any more jokes about putting things in my mouth, I have to warn you, I *bite*."

He huffs out a laugh. "Consider me warned."

"Do you always make those comments to people you don't know?"

"No, just to the people I want to get to know." He shrugs. "I think it's fair to come at people with my personality on full blast so they know what they might be getting into."

"Makes sense, kind of." I wet my lips. "I'll petition the school, maybe. But I'm *not* running."

He holds his phone up again, the video of me "eviscerating" Mr. Logan on mute and looping, adding to Stevie's views. "You have to. Everyone will be expecting you to. You put yourself out there, and now you're the voice."

"That's not fair."

"Life's not fair."

I wave my hand at the others in the room, thankful their backs are turned. "These people don't seem very interested in voting for me anyway. I've gotten snide looks all day for just suggesting that we hold a new election. What's so great about this guy that everyone's so offended—does he have some tragic backstory that I don't know about?"

He pockets his phone. "Not unless you count the time he bleach-fried his hair. He had to buzz it all off."

I sit in silence, thinking it over, and he must recognize that because he doesn't say a word, just runs a hand through his own hair. It's silky and dark, and a fresh, clean smell wafts from it.

"I don't know—" I start.

"We need a president who's willing to deck someone when they're wrong—"

"I don't—"

"—willing to stand up for things," he continues, "and I already know that's you." He looks my face over, probably reading the uncertainty as easily as his own name. I don't want to be president—I just want to graduate—but it would be a way to make things good for Connie this year, maybe set things on a path of change after I'm gone. If I'm not directly setting an example for her, maybe I can for the next president when I've left the school. Plus, Thomas is so smarmy. If I could ruin this for him, it would be worth it—even if I suck at the job, even if it's an awful time for me.

"Look, I'm not overly proud or anything, but if I call for a new election and run, and then no one votes for me, I will probably die of literal embarrassment."

"I'd vote for you."

"You don't even know my name to recognize it on the ballot."

"Parker."

"No."

He scrunches up his face. "Parker Evans?"

"That's my last name. It's hyphenated."

"Oh, you're *fancy*, huh?" he says in an impressed voice. But then his whole body stiffens, and his eyes grow large. "Unless you're the child of a messy divorce and, in that case, I'm sorry—"

"They're happily unmarried together," I say by means of explanation.

The panic leaves his face and he holds out his hand. "Okay, good. I'm Patrick—I'm trying to make 'Trick' happen, so I'd appreciate the help on that—and I'd vote for you, whatever your name is. I think at least all the girls would vote for you automatically."

I stare at his hand, the rough calluses on his fingers, and then meet his eyes. "Okay, first of all: that's a sexist assumption. Second: the girls don't even make up half the school from what I've seen, so your theory doesn't hold."

"I see that now, and I'm sorry, but I do think you could win the school over." He shakes his hand a little to remind me that he's offering it. "I've found you very charming thus far, Parker-Evans. I won't be the only one."

I'm just shaking his hand, not making a deal with the devil. Not promising anything to anyone. So why does it feel so final? Why does it feel like I'm agreeing to run for student council president? I *hate* public speaking. I detest the responsibility that I already have. I shouldn't do this.

Except, I should for Connie.

I take his hand. "Nice to officially meet you. Vote for Ella."

"I plan on it," he says with a smirk, standing up and pushing his desk back into line. He throws his backpack over his shoulder and heads to the door despite there being fifteen more minutes of detention. I watch him go with my mouth sagged open.

"Are . . . we free to go?" I ask Mr. Carpenter, halfway out of my seat.

He catches the tail end of Patrick's exit and then meets my eyes with his own dull blue ones. "No, you still have more time. Patrick never had detention to start with."

Four

Stevie shoves her phone in my face, her navy nails topped with a layer of glitter—a hashtag brand partnership, according to my research last night—shining in the morning sun. Taking a video of me.

"You're really doing this, huh?" she asks.

"Well, it might have been easier for me to fade into anonymity after my outburst had you not recorded it and put it out there for everyone to see, multiple times." I push her phone away, forcing it to record the ground.

When she showed me the video already posted online yesterday, my first thought was that she hadn't asked my permission. By posting that, she was exposing me to a bunch of random people who all have their own opinions about what I said, the situation, how I'm dressed, my physical appearance, my age—I could go on forever. As I listened to her talk about her content and followers, I realized that it probably just never crossed her mind because everyone is *so* online that of course she wouldn't ask. To bring it up after the fact felt overly sensitive, and even though now would be a great time to say something, our re-friendship is so new, and I know so little about what it's like to actually be on social media, that I clamp my lips shut tight.

This whole phone-glued-to-her-hand thing is an interesting habit she's picked up since we last saw each other. Always ready to capture a moment, no matter what it might be. Anything could be something that goes viral, after all. Stevie, back when she was Este, was kind of like me—barely online and struggling with how to connect with others, but especially how to connect with ourselves—and I'm not sure how I feel about this change. It's hard enough to live today without every part of my existence being documented for others to judge, but to live in a world where it's happening against my will is another thing entirely.

This morning, Stevie was kind enough to bring Connie and me to school early so Connie could use the library for a quick writing session—somehow undeterred by everything that happened yesterday, her writer's block a thing of the past. I used the extra time to open a petition for another election with the young administrative staff member already wearing coffee stains down her shirt. Interest piqued, she handed over one single sheet of paper secured to an old clipboard.

It's currently shaking in my hands.

I only have three signatures so far: Stevie, a shy boy from my English class, and myself. I would have five, but Connie insisted she didn't know me as soon as our school-approved shoes landed on Courtland Academy property—she didn't even thank Stevie for the ride, she was in such a hurry to get away from the attention I'm apparently attracting to *her*—and Stevie's girlfriend, Lila, who I met at lunch yesterday, has a dentist appointment so she hasn't arrived yet. Needless to say, Connie shared her displeasure with me all last night. I can't tell if she's more embarrassed or mad, but this is for her own good. It's for everyone's own good. She'll see that one day.

Unless I don't get enough signatures. That's possibly even worse than running and losing to Thom-ass.

What's that phrase? Speak of the devil?

"Hi, Thomas. Would you like to sign my petition?" I ask in my sweetest voice. I am just a silly girl with lofty dreams. *Who, little old me? I could never be a threat.*

Thomas and two other guys, who might be the VP and secretary/treasurer but I honestly couldn't pick them out of a lineup, walk to the entrance of the school, their uniforms immaculate and wrinkle-free. Thomas swipes his golden curls back and throws an amused glance over his shoulder at his two ever-present shadows. I can't help but think of Patrick's remark that he bleached his hair once. It looks so natural now, but I guess that's what money and do-it-yourself regret get you. I wonder if the curls are real or he wakes up at five o'clock to perfect them.

"Why would I do that?" he asks.

"Because you're not afraid of competition." I offer the clipboard. "Are you?"

He smirks down at the mostly empty paper. "I don't see any competition."

I steel myself. "Then it wouldn't hurt to sign, right?"

He takes the clipboard and attached pen, signing quickly. "You really don't know what you're asking for with this. My brother was the president last year. And I'm going to be the president this year—redoing the election won't change that. You won't change this school."

He offers the petition to his friends, who sign with some choked laughter, and then before I even have a chance to process how weirdly easy it was, they're headed inside.

Nepotism be damned. I will not let him have this.

I swipe at the little bit of sweat forming under my nose and flip the clipboard right-side up. Stevie hovers behind me.

"Immature shitheads," she mutters over my shoulder.

Below our names are three more:

Ben Dover
Mike Litorus
Hugh Jass

The fact that they could even come up with three different names amazes me. I scratch them out, a little more vigorously than I need to because I'm picturing each of their faces (or face) under the pen, and hike my backpack higher on my shoulder. If I were going to do this with fake signatures, I would have done them myself.

"Were you recording that?" I ask Stevie stiffly.

She swirls her plastic cup of iced coffee and takes a sip, delaying her answer because she's 100 percent trying to find a way to say yes that won't embarrass me. "I can delete it."

"Don't. Post it. Let everyone know that the current—the *former*—student council president has basically endorsed me." I need all the help I can get. "Spin it."

The first bell is going to ring in ten minutes, and students are filing inside, most of them taking obvious steps to avoid me like I'm out here with a petition asking them to eliminate sugar from the vending machines. I only need twenty-five legitimate signatures to put this into effect—twenty-two really—and I plan on getting them all today. There should be some solidarity here; I'm helping them out, too—especially the girls. Thomas offers nothing but a reign of terror—or, apparently, everything staying exactly the same. I could have been swayed to run against Thomas just based on his attitude yesterday, but in my one day as a Courtland Academy student, I found a list of things I already want to change about this place.

Because the school was originally all boys, it was built with one small staff bathroom and one boys' bathroom in each hall. But now, with other genders attending the school, half the bathrooms have been poorly converted into girls' bathrooms, with urinals taking up most of the space and unstocked sanitary product dispensers haphazardly hanging off the wall, and one staff bathroom has become an all-gender bathroom. But if you have an emergency and you're in the wrong hallway, Godspeed. It's basically a metaphor for the school itself: cramming in a new student population but not making the effort to accommodate them. When I asked Stevie, after the assembly and a few curiously packed classes, about why the boys outnumber the rest of us, she let me in on a secret: yes, the academy is now admitting girls, but it didn't halve the boys admissions rate, because that wouldn't be fair to them. There are still just as many of them as before, which means the classes aren't as small as advertised, the budget is not as great as they bragged because it's spread much thinner, and even the glorious, mysterious senior privileges they boasted about on the website are *gone* due to budget restructuring. The school is a sham and I'm really glad I have the biggest gossip on my side to shed some light on it.

So I started my list of complaints. We—meaning me and whoever is actually in charge of the budget—obviously need to restructure *again* because the cafeteria food is . . . atrocious, and there isn't much variety or many options for those with restrictions. The hallways get packed between classes, and if you weren't already acquainted with every classmate, you will be by the time you're done swimming upstream like a bunch of salmon together. Stevie said she would forward her own list of complaints she has about the school. Apparently, she started a note in her phone on day one after she was told to sign in and out for bathroom breaks on a classroom iPad, but wasn't given any kind of sanitizing wipes or sanitizer before or after using it. In her words, "If I *just* washed my hands, why would I come back and touch the dirty thing again?" It's like every semi-good idea was thought out halfway before being executed.

"We should call it a day," she says now after swiping at her phone. She catches my offended gaze and puts her hands up. "I mean, morning. Let's reconvene at lunch where we can get a bunch of Lila's friends to sign for you—there are just enough sporty girls to make up approximately one sad field hockey team, but they are all very eager to fuck up the patriarchy." She smiles wistfully. "And the people who don't agree with them are at the very least *afraid* of them."

Well, add to my growing list of changes the need for more girls' sports options, or making the teams coed.

It feels like cheating by using Lila's intimidation to get pity signatures, but it might end up being the only way. Standing out here waiting for people to keep dodging my petition is not worth the punishment I may get for being late, so I mentally start packing up.

"Sure. You're right." I'm bending down to stuff the clipboard into my backpack when I hear slamming. In the vestibule behind us, two white guys with their school cardigans slung over their shoulders like yacht dads kick and smack the vending machine. I'm ready to ignore them, but then Patrick shows up from inside the school and says something to them that I can't hear. I'm inside before I realize I made the decision to move, Stevie hot on my heels.

". . . just have to—" Patrick gives the side of the machine a swift punch and two sodas roll out.

"Holy shit," the taller of the two guys says with a dopey smile. "I only paid for one."

"That's why they call me Trick. I have a trick for everything," Patrick says with a smile that someone might think is equally dopey and someone else might think is . . . charming.

I resist rolling my eyes at his comment, though. The taller guy hands off the second soda to his friend and when they turn around, I pounce.

"Hi, did you want to sign my petition to hold a redo election for student council?"

The shorter guy snorts. "Why would we do that? We like Thom."

"We voted for Thom the first time."

"Did you have another option?" I ask. "What's so great about Thom? He seems like a bully to me."

"Hey," Patrick says, calling everyone's attention to the vending machine where he's casually leaning. His hair looks windswept, but I can attest to the fact that there was absolutely no breeze this morning to have caused that. "Sign the petition. You can still vote for Thom after, and it might even feel better voting for him knowing that you had another option, but still chose him. I bet he'd respect that."

The taller guy exchanges a look with the shorter one. They have identical noses. Maybe brothers. Then they size me up.

"Thomas signed the petition," Stevie says suddenly. I blink very hard at her, to remind her silently that he did not sign with his real name and therefore does not show up on the list. "But then we all agreed that we'd do this without his help, to make it . . . fair."

"Yep," I add quickly. "We crossed his and—the other two—off the list." I'm really going to have to learn their names, aren't I?

"Yeah, fine," the one guy says, rubbing his cheek so hard I think some freckles might come off.

"You have a point, Patrick," the other one says, as if Stevie and I aren't even here.

"Trick," Patrick says delicately. Stevie shoots him a bemused look as I fish out my clipboard. "I don't think we've met," he says to her, coming over and holding out a hand.

She narrows her eyes at him. "We have. Several times." She takes his hand, though. "Stevie. Ella's campaign manager and social media coordinator."

I hand my clipboard to the guys. "Since when?"

"Since there may be a campaign to manage and social media to coordinate." She shrugs. "I'm *spinning* it."

The warning bell sounds muffled in the vestibule. On the other side of the glass doors, students start scrambling to first period, zipping backpacks and shutting lockers.

"Ahhh, I have to go," Stevie says more to me than anyone else, jolting for the door. "I have to get to class early enough that people can fight to sit around me." She blows me a kiss, which Patrick pretends to intercept and clench to his heart, and then she's gone. The guys finish signing and follow her to the main hallway without a word in my direction.

A few students filter past us, rushing to class from the parking lot, but Patrick heads back to the soda machine and feeds his student ID into the card reader. He selects a Pepsi and when he turns around, I'm not quick enough to hide my disgust.

"What?" he asks.

"It's not even eight a.m."

"I had a late night last night. I'm exhausted."

"I'm not going to ask why, if that's what you're trying to bait me into."

"I'm not going to *tell you* why, if that's what you were hoping

I'd do." He cracks open his soda and takes a swig, wiping his mouth with the back of his hand. "But okay, you twisted my arm. It's a dirty reason." He holds out his hand. "But enough about me. Can I sign your petition or what, Parker-Evans?"

An unfamiliar tingle shoots down my spine. I like it. It makes my heart race. "I thought you'd never ask."

"Speaking of things we thought I'd never ask," he says offhandedly as he takes the pen and signs, "why the hell didn't you tell me you're Ashley Parker's *daughter*?"

I nearly drop the clipboard as he's writing. "What? Who cares?"

"*Who cares?* I care! Yesterday, I said I wanted to order off the secret menu at Ashes. Which is owned by your mother, Ashley Parker, in case you didn't know, *Parker*-Evans." He hands me the clipboard and then scrubs both hands through my hair like he's looking for my brain underneath, making a mess of the curls I actually took the time to style today. "Hello? Ringing any bells? Anyone home, Ella Parker-Evans? *Parker*, like *Ash Parker. The chef*."

I swat his hands away and he pulls them back; I miss the contact almost instantly. "Stop. You're so weird."

"Seriously. Doesn't that seem like the opportune time to say something?"

"Why would I say anything? She just makes food. How did you even know?"

"I put two and two together—the first two being that you work at Ashes and the second two being that one of your last names is Parker—and then I went home and googled you to make sure."

My heart stutters in a completely flattered way that I would never tell anyone about. "That's creepy."

He scoffs dramatically. "I went to detention just to see you and you think a cursory Google search is creepy? I barely found anything, anyway. I bet you google tons of people."

I cross my arms. "I didn't google *you*."

Yet. I was a little busy with Stevie. There is a *lot* of her online.

"So you didn't see all my adorable headshots from my stint on *Sesame Street*?"

I assume he's joking, so I don't question him. "It's not something I just tell people, okay? It's not like you introduced yourself to me and told me what your parents do for a living."

"It's a little different when I literally mention, *to you*, the restaurant she owns."

I roll my eyes. "She's a chef. It's never impressed anyone, and I don't care to impress people."

"It impresses the hell out of me. I'm kind of a fangirl. Hence why I know about the secret menu and begged my family to dine at a place my father thinks is more of a hassle than anything. I want to work in food one day."

He fixes the rolled ends of his sleeves, which drags my attention to his fingers. "If she were my mom, I'd shout that from the fucking rooftop. She's been featured on Food Network, a guest judge on *Nailed It!* She made dinner for President Obama's birthday!"

"I know. I was there." It was actually the first and only time I was impressed by my mother's talent with food. I wasn't allowed to take a phone in, but a photographer was able to capture us together. Maybe I should show Stevie. It could make a good student council poster. "Again, how do you know my mom's life story?"

"The internet." He cocks an eyebrow. "Did you meet him?"

"I *hugged* him." I glance around the empty hall. "Shit. Did the bell ring?"

He takes another gulp of his soda. "Yeah, like two minutes ago, but don't think that means I'm letting the whole Ash Parker thing go—"

I take off at a run to my first class, hoping my teacher will be lenient. If yesterday was any indication, I should probably just be running straight for detention.

Five

With Stevie's help, Lila's strong-arming, and Patrick's charm, I secure enough signatures to walk into the administration office tomorrow morning and start the beginning of the end for Thomas. But a night sits between me and that satisfaction. A night in which I have to babysit my old-enough-to-watch-herself sister. Not that I had plans or anything, but it would be nice if my parents pretended like it was at least a possibility.

"I'm having drinks with Nicolette," my mom says around five o'clock, taking the steps two at a time in her three-inch heels. Her manager, Nicolette, has been guiding her career for the last ten years—ever since a manager was a thing my mother needed to be the kind of chef she's become. Nicolette was strongly against my mother using her prime cheffing years for mentoring new blood, but she got over it when my mom's patience was rewarded in tons of shout-outs and press for "giving back" to the culinary community. "I'll be home around eight, or one."

Connie stands at the bottom of the steps, a dreamy grin on her face. "You look nice."

"So do you," Mom says, brushing her finger off Connie's nose. "How are the school uniforms working out for you guys?"

"Saves a lot of time getting ready in the morning," Connie answers, doing a little twirl in her skirt. The last two days, I've taken my uniform off the minute I got home, but she's comfortable to parade around in hers all night, like it's a costume and she's an actor getting paid by the minute.

"It's itchy," I say with a shrug. "The color doesn't suit me."

Mom reaches the bottom of the stairs and adjusts her shoe. "That's not true. You both look lovely in blue."

I don't recall saying anything about Connie.

It's not until she's standing in front of me that I realize Mom is wearing my dress from homecoming last year. On me, it was a tight navy-blue number that left little to the imagination, but on her—well, I can't find a polite way to say her boobs are spilling out of it, whereas mine still managed to be concealed like the bags under her eyes.

"Is that my dress?"

"Yeah, doesn't it look great on me?" She turns slowly, not for effect, but because if she went any faster, she'd twist an ankle in those shoes.

"You look *hot*," Connie says encouragingly, following Mom to the front door, where she grabs her black purse and keys. "Can't believe Dad lets you go out like that."

"What he doesn't know won't hurt him," Mom says in a stage whisper, winking.

"I hate everything about this conversation," I say, wishing to scrub the last minute from my brain so I didn't have to remember their sexist joke.

"Ella, don't be such a sourpuss; we're kidding," Mom says, opening the door. "I left my credit card on the table. Order some dinner—nothing over forty dollars, please. See you tomorrow!" She places a kiss atop Connie's head and then pinches my cheek.

Once she shuts the door, I ask my sister, "What do you want for dinner?"

She throws herself onto the couch and grabs her laptop. "I don't know," she says. "I have to finish this before I can do anything."

"Well, I have homework to do, so if we could settle this first, I'd appreciate it." I cross my arms, watching her type away. "And what happened to your writer's block? Can I read?"

Just a few days ago, she had sworn she couldn't type a word worthy of anything but the delete button. I'm glad to see that's not entirely true anymore. Way back when she started writing, I was Connie's first beta reader. I kind of miss the banter she'd write between her characters.

"It's just for class, nothing truly inspired," she says, shooing me away. "Order whatever."

Aaaand . . . that's the last straw. I'm over being dismissed. It took *all day* to get only twenty-five signatures in a school of over three hundred. I faced more rejection today than anyone should in their entire lifetime.

"You know what?" I grab the laptop from her and hold it out of reach. "I'm feeling like we should go pick up some food. Get out of the house. Away from the computers."

"Give that back!" Connie stands and dances around, her fingertips nearly grazing her laptop with every maneuver. "Ella, come on! It's *homework*. We can just get something delivered!"

"The grocery store doesn't deliver here. Let's go pick something up to make."

"I don't want to. Just leave me here."

"Mom and Dad are probably gonna be home around the same time—past your bedtime, little baby—so that means I'm in charge and, if I'm in charge, I can't leave you to your own devices or you might, I don't know, disappear off the face of the earth. Who knows with you."

Her body deflates at my words. "I need to write while the words are flowing."

"Fine. Take the computer in the car, but we're going." If I have to be in the house all night with her, I'm going to need sustenance, and money at the grocery store gets you a lot more than at a pizzeria.

She grumbles, "You're just going to make me make the food anyway."

Giant is surprisingly dead for a Tuesday night. I would expect the adult crowd to be getting off work and picking up rotisserie chickens or something to make easy meals at home, but it's just a few lone shoppers who now include Connie and me, because I refused to let her stay in the car. There are weirdos everywhere who wouldn't hesitate to trick my innocent little sister into helping them load their groceries just so they could kidnap her. Not on my watch.

But, in her defense, Connie probably wouldn't do that if it meant breaking her concentration while writing. We nearly got into a fistfight after I put the car in park, trying to get her to come inside with me.

"I want mashed potatoes," she says now, most of her weight against the shopping cart as we meander through the aisles for inspiration.

"Sure, we can make some at home."

"I want the lumpy kind. The real stuff."

"Are *you* going to make them?" I ask with a raised eyebrow.

"I guess I'll have to if I want them done right, but *you're* the one who wanted to make dinner instead of order it," she says.

We lock eyes for a brief second and then I say, "But you could make Grandma's recipe," and she bursts into flustered laughter.

"I could *not*. Not even Mom can manage them."

I smile to myself as I guide the front of the cart around a man aimlessly wandering the aisle, phone in hand. "Maybe Grandma's secret ingredient really was love."

Connie snorts. "I'm pretty sure it was an unknown amount of garlic that none have been able to replicate. And maybe a type of cheese. I don't know; she refused to ever write it down."

We pass the deli and move into the ready-to-go meals section by the beer café, and I freeze.

"What the hell?" Connie hisses, as if she hadn't just run the cart into both of *my* heels.

I nod toward the line at the beer counter. It's three people deep, and the last person in line is none other than Thomas Hayworth.

"Let's go somewhere else." Connie starts turning the empty cart around, but I don't budge. "Ella."

"You can go if you want. Go find something for us to eat tonight," I say, unable to take my eyes off his perfect posture. "Don't go anywhere with anyone and don't leave the store."

"Yes, Officer," she says sarcastically. "Don't embarrass me again."

"I didn't embarrass you. He was the one who—"

"He wouldn't have even known it was me if it wasn't for you. You made it into a bigger deal than it needed to be."

I turn around to properly have this argument, if that's what she wants, but she's already retreated into a new aisle.

Thomas spots me when I'm a few feet away and a smirk lights up his face. I wish I could be as happy to see him.

"No, you're not invited to my party," he says without greeting me.

"Party?" I ask with a blink. "On a Tuesday night? Is it, like, a campaign fundraiser because I'm reopening the elections tomorrow morning?"

"That won't do anything," he says, smiling past me, like if he doesn't see me, then he won't hear me either.

"You know, I didn't realize you were a super senior or maybe I would have just let you have the presidency," I say, patting him on the shoulder. A burst of pride ricochets through me when his lips fall from their smug position. He shrugs my hand off. "You need that win more than me."

"I *did* win, and I'm not a super senior."

"How are you buying an over-twenty-one beverage, then?"

I nod at the case of beer in his hands. Pabst Blue Ribbon. I know next to nothing about beer—mostly that it smells gross— but Dad always says the people he was most likely to kick out of the bar he worked at in college were the people who had one too many PBRs (which is at least one PBR).

He glances around, but it doesn't look like anyone heard me.

"I am twenty-one."

"In human years?" I ask, holding back a laugh.

Again, he shifts his weight and makes sure no one has heard. "Yes. According to my ID."

"Which was issued by the state of Pennsylvania or the state of delusion?"

The guy at the front of the line leaves, his receipt clutched in his free hand. Thomas spins back to me. "Listen. Don't blow up my spot."

"*Giant* is your spot?" I bite my lip at the absurdity. "Please tell me your ID says Ben Dover on it. That way, I can count your signature from earlier."

His glare frosts over. "You probably had to count it anyway, to have enough."

"I had enough signatures without your immature and fraudulent names—thank you very much. It looks like the student body isn't as stubborn as you think it is. They want change." *Or at least fewer than thirty of the students do.*

The woman in front of Thomas finishes buying boxed wine and he steps forward to greet the tired cashier with a smile that he turns on like a light, and the worst part is that it looks genuine from this angle.

"Hi," he says, running a hand through his hair after putting down his case of beer.

The cashier scans the case and asks for ID from Thomas.

"It's a little scratched up—I have to get a new one but I keep forgetting."

The cashier attempts to scan his ID but the machine makes an angry beeping noise. Then he really looks at Thomas's identification. I'd love to know what he sees.

"He can't get a new one until he actually turns twenty-one," I say casually, adding a shrug at the end.

"She's joking," Thomas says with a nervous laugh. "She's—"

I'm walking away.

The cashier says something . . . and then laughs. When I peek over my shoulder before turning down the nearest aisle, the cashier is handing over the beer. *Handing over the beer?* He still got his way. He got that shitty beer with his probably laughable fake ID and he charmed the cashier and I don't stand a chance against this guy if I can call him out on his bullshit and still lose.

I find Connie in the ice cream aisle.

I don't even have it in me to tell her ice cream isn't a meal. It is tonight.

"How'd that go?" she asks, hanging on the open freezer door as she contemplates the two best ice creams: Oreo or Reese's Peanut Butter Cup. Neither of them is dairy-free and, therefore, it's a small act of rebellion in our household. We are not technically vegan or gluten- and nut-free, though my mother and Ashes are. "Are you glad you did it?" she continues in a monotone voice.

"I don't stand a chance of winning against him." I pull both tubs out and drop them into the cart. Connie doesn't look this gift horse in the mouth and continues slowly down the aisle with an impressed glance at me. "He can charm the pants off a pantsless person. Somehow." I jerk a thumb over my shoulder. "I flat-out told the dude working the beer counter that Thomas wasn't old enough to buy it and then he said something that made the cashier laugh and now he's walking out with beer. He won."

"What kind?" she asks, eyes set forward.

"What?"

"The beer."

"PBR—"

"I mean, did he *really* win, then?"

I wrap my hand through the handle of another freezer door and open it, staring inside without really seeing my options. I can't shake the image of his smile.

"You shouldn't have challenged him," Connie says quietly. "It was fine. You didn't need to do that. It wasn't your problem."

When I glance at her, she's a little caved in on herself, shoulders hunched and face angled down. We haven't spoken about what he did to her—only my part in the whole mess. We haven't even spoken about what happened to her last year, the whole reason she had to change schools. Again, it's fine that she writes fan fiction. It's fine that she reads it. I don't judge her or anyone for it, but I just—I can't get past her not seeing how obviously she was being manipulated. I could have prevented it if I had been there.

"You don't think I can win?" I ask.

"It's a little late to ask my opinion."

"Better late than never." I close the freezer door and wait for her answer.

She straightens and faces me. "I don't think he's going to play fair. He has a title to protect."

I step aside to let a family pass.

"I don't have to play fair either, then." I don't have a lot to offer my classmates, but I'm not above bribing them to show even an ounce of interest in what I have to say, what I want to stand for at this school.

She tilts her head to the side, thinking. "You need someone to help you."

"I have—"

"Don't say me."

"I wasn't going to." I scoff. "I was going to say . . . Stevie."

"No, not Stevie."

"Why not?"

"I mean, yeah, sure, use her." Connie pulls the sleeves of her cardigan down and rubs her hands to ward away the grocery store chill. "I just mean, like—I don't know. You need someone that everyone knows. A guy, because you have to appeal to all the other guys."

My jaw drops, but she ignores my indignation. I can appeal to my classmates by being right and providing solutions to problems.

"Right now," she continues, "you're just threatening the boys' way of life. Upsetting the balance."

"Balance is a generous term considering they're literally the majority."

"You know what I mean."

I think of Patrick helping me secure signatures. He actually cares about this outcome—hell, I'm only really running because he convinced me to—and he has sway with the students I don't know yet, but he wouldn't run for the presidency himself. Stevie feels more intent on viewing this whole thing than actively partaking in it. And I don't want to get Connie involved. As much as I know my sister is right, I'm probably on my own here.

Six

The next morning, a front-desk worker announces the redo election over the intercom. Mr. Logan personally accepted my petition and formal bid for presidency before school, with annoyance, reluctance, and more than a little disgust after he froze on the spot and demanded to know if I was the waitress at Ashes he saw assault another girl—but it *was* accepted. Maybe I had to lie right to his face and say that it was *not* me he was remembering, but the election. is. open.

I have roughly a month to campaign until the actual election, and hopefully that gives me enough time to win over this stubborn school.

At lunch, Patrick is nowhere to be found—not to celebrate and definitely not to hear the problems I'm already facing.

Underneath the lunch table, I pull out my phone to text him, and realize . . . I don't have his phone number. Stevie, who's talking Lila's ear off about her new weekly TikTok Live series she's starting tonight, catches my stare and stops mid-sentence. "Yes, Madam President?"

"Campaign Manager," I address her with faux seriousness. "Do you know Patrick's number?" Stevie somehow knows everything, so it's worth a shot. But then she and Lila take turns listing every Patrick known to man just to mess with me. They even include a teacher who was fired last year.

I cut them off. "The Patrick from yesterday, Stevie. The one, you know—" I roll my eyes, hating that she's making me work for this—a clear indication that she *does* have his number and, therefore, I must play along. "The one 'trying to make Trick happen.'"

She dismisses me with a wave. "You know, he'd give it to you in a heartbeat, and I mean that in every way imaginable."

"How exactly *do* you have his phone number?" I'm a little offended that I didn't have it before her. According to Patrick, they just met yesterday. Patrick and I at least have detention bonding us.

"We have chemistry together."

"Does he know you're a lesbian and that's the *only* chemistry you'll have together?" Lila asks, her chin in her hand. Nothing about Lila's delicate freckles, soft curves, or baby bangs would indicate she regularly bulldozes other girls with a field hockey stick in hand, but the slight note of danger in her voice is enough to give even *me* goose bumps, and I wouldn't dare flirt with Stevie.

Stevie boops her on the nose. "He does, and you're cute when you're jealous."

"I'm merely looking out for that poor boy's heart. He wouldn't be the first you unknowingly led astray."

"I lead them nowhere. It's their own fault they assume straight to be the default."

"Sorry—back to me," I say, distracted. If I don't ask for his help now, I may never. "Patrick. Can I get his number? I need to talk to him about the election and I don't know where he is."

"Say no more," Stevie says. It takes a moment for her Contacts app to open—she says it's because her storage is almost full so her phone is running slow right now—but when it does, she discreetly sends me his information.

I fire off a text asking if he's at school today. The lunches are separated by grade, so, if he's a senior like I assumed from my copious amounts of research last night when I should have been working on homework, he should be in the cafeteria right now.

He answers exceptionally fast. Band room, first floor. Tell the lunch monitor you're going to the bathroom.

Something like nerves kick around in my stomach as I throw out my garbage and tell Stevie and Lila where I'm going. Stevie winks at me and Lila gently shoves her shoulder, telling her it's "just business."

Patrick didn't include directions, but I find the band room relatively quickly thanks to the map Connie printed for me. The room is a stuffy, disorganized, overgrown closet filled with instruments, crooked music stands, and seats. Inside, by himself, Patrick strums an acoustic guitar on his lap. His hair slides over his face as he finishes playing a soft, slow melody. When he spots me, that melody turns into a funky *bow-chicka-bow-wow* type thing.

"Parker-Evans," he says with a grin. He leans the guitar between his legs. "Good going with the election."

"Thanks. Imagine my disappointment when my number

one fan didn't show up to the cafeteria at his designated lunch time."

"I have permission from the band director to use the room during lunch some days. The cafeteria can be a little loud."

"Are you in the band?" I ask, taking the free seat next to him. I cross my legs and don't miss how his eyes dart to my exposed thighs. I could have worn khakis today, but I did not.

"Technically—because it looks good on my transcripts—but not really. There aren't many pieces that require a guitar."

"Seems like a waste of talent," I comment as he runs his fingers slowly down a string.

"*Aw shucks*," he says jokingly, but his cheeks redden. "When I first pitched the idea of playing the guitar, my parents weren't very supportive—that's a running theme with them—because they worried about the noise at home—hence the acoustic—and then my dad would go on about how a music career is a highly unlikely way to pay the bills. I was thirteen. I was just trying to find something I liked; I didn't realize I was marrying my future career or something. Maybe I wanted to play the field." He raises an eyebrow at me suggestively. "But he didn't like me liking the guitar, so I got into basket weaving. And caricatures. Bird-watching. I'm terrible at all of it, but at least I am solidly mediocre with some strings." He rests his guitar across the seats on his other side. "I'm actually kind of the best at making food. I mean, the best out of all the things I've tried. I am not great by any means—"

"Patrick." I think of his fangirl moment over my mom and want to cut another one short. I'm on a mission here.

"My friends call me Trick."

"I seriously doubt that."

"Well, they *should*."

"Maybe I'll start."

"If?"

"If . . ." This is the moment, the opportune time to just ask him, officially, for his help. "So, this might sound wild, but I have a proposition for you."

"I'm sorry, but I don't sleep with people for money."

"I—*shut up*."

"I do it for free." He pulls his guitar back onto his lap and plays a few chords.

"*Patrick*." I'm torn between laughing and pulling my hair out—or his.

"*Trick*," he says pointedly, rubbing his pointer finger over a fret. "What's your proposition? I promise I'll let you talk." He glances behind me. "Because we only have a few minutes left of lunch and you sought me out and—"

"And you're wasting my time." I place my hand over his, muffling the next chord he absentmindedly starts playing. I take a deep breath. "I don't stand a chance of winning this election on my own."

He turns slightly in my direction, eyes patient and steady on mine. Waiting for me to talk, as promised.

"I saw the way those guys listened to you yesterday. They weren't going to even sign my petition, but they gave you the time of day—and then those people at lunch. They just lined right up to sign when you snapped your fingers."

"I think you're exaggerating."

"I'm not." I flatten my palms on my skirt, letting it absorb some sweat. "Thomas Hayworth is going to win again unless I have you in my corner."

"I already said I'd vote for you. And I'll convince other people to do the same."

"I appreciate that, but I need a larger commitment, I think. I need you to teach me what these people like, what they want to hear, how to get them to listen to me."

There's a pause where he tries to formulate a response. His eyebrows do a little dance that I don't think he's aware is happening.

"I think they'll see through it all," he says simply.

My shoulders deflate, and I realize now how high and tense I was holding them. "What do you mean?"

"They don't want to be lied to—it's partially why so many of them like Thomas. He says what he's thinking."

"Like when he said my fourteen-year-old sister should write his sexts?" I mumble angrily.

He cringes. "Yes, similarly . . . but he's genuine. You know, for him."

"He's genuinely the worst!" I frown. "I can be genuine!"

"Not if I'm standing behind you and whispering the magic words in your ear." He starts packing away his guitar in a hard black case he had propped behind his chair. I'm worried I've lost him even the little bit that I had him already. "Plus, you're already coming in here wanting to change things on day one; people distrust you based on that. Add in lying and manipulating, and—"

"I wouldn't lie, and I definitely don't plan on manipulating anyone. I want to show them that they *want* change, and I just need you to help me speak their language." My eyes follow his movements. "I'm not asking you to run for anything—I get that you're not interested, but like you said, something's got to change around here. Like, I feel confident-*ish* that I could win over some people, but the majority of students would vote for Thomas on principle—especially because the majority of the students are boys who are used to following Thomas, and his brother before him. I think if people thought, like, you, a cool guy they respect, respected me . . ."

He blinks. "Well, that's a sexist assumption right there. Now who's making the sexist assumptions? I already respect you and I'm a guy."

I sigh, frustrated that my plan—or lack of a plan—collapses so easily on itself, because he's right. If I don't want this school to be sexist, I can't be either. Surely, there are other boys in this school who would hear me out, not just Patrick.

"Is there some kind of compromise here?" I ask. "Maybe something I could offer you that would make it worth your time to help me? Even if they think I'm a try-hard, I'll do much better with you in my corner."

The lunch dismissal bell rings, jolting me out of my seat in surprise. He takes his guitar case and stows it away in a large locker at the back of the room. We have three minutes to get to our classes and this is going so horribly that I might just flee and say it's so I don't get another tardy.

"Okay," he says with a sigh, turning around to face me.

"Okay what? You'll help me?"

"I'll help you, but I'm not half-assing it."

I blink. "Meaning?"

He bites his lip and searches my face for a moment. "Some people around here think we're dating."

I cough out a laugh. I hope it doesn't sound as nervous and flustered as I am. Yes, I've seen the comments growing on Stevie's TikTok by the hour, but I had hoped he hadn't. There are few things as awkward and presumptuous as dating rumors starting when you have a single interaction with someone of a different gender.

". . . yeah?"

"I won't look like a puppet master if I'm your boyfriend," he says, shrugging like this didn't just blow my mind.

I suck in a breath like I'm preparing to say something, but I'm actually stalling for time, getting some oxygen to my head at the thought of us—us doing—him— "For starters, you're not the puppet master; *I* am. You're the puppet . . . assistant."

He smiles. "Okay, sure."

"And second, you think everyone is going to call bullshit when I have you helping me, but *not* if we, what? Start a relationship?" I cross my arms tight over my chest and correct myself, because it sounds too much, too real, too dizzying the other way. "A *fake* relationship? What happened to not lying to and manipulating people?"

"It's just an idea." He says it like it really is just an idea and not some friendship-altering thing he threw out there all willy-nilly. His words are so light they could blow away in a breeze.

Meanwhile, I struggle to form even a coherent thought. We

start fake dating. He initiates me into Courtland culture, introduces me to people, gets them to respect me and hear me out, all while he teaches me anything I need to know. And then no one is suspicious of us spending time together and working the campaign circuit because . . . boyfriend. It's not a terrible idea—even though the reasoning behind it is terrible—and it basically accomplishes what I came here to ask of him.

"But what do you get out of it?" I think of the interesting results my sleuthing brought up last night. "I'd say it would show the student population that you're datable, but your Instagram shows that's not a problem for you."

He huffs out a laugh in response and opens the band room door for me.

I step up next to him. "Yeah. I googled you."

His laugh fades when he sees my serious expression.

"Why didn't you tell me you're the dickhead principal's son?" I ask.

He freezes, panic taking over his features. It's how I must look in front of a crowd. Spotlight causing me to sweat. Red blotches forming on my cheeks. A slight tremble in my bottom lip. I refuse to be embarrassed for admitting I did what he did first, and I refuse to *not* address the elephant he tried to stuff in the closet.

"I had to figure out your last name first, but it was pretty easy when I searched 'Patrick' and 'Courtland Academy.' The first thing that came up was about your dad's achievement: ten years as principal. That was a nice photo of your family."

The photo was taken at some school event this summer.

Patrick wore a suit—and he wore it well, as predicted—while his father went full tuxedo and his mom wore a simple black cocktail dress. They are a beautiful family, but Patrick wasn't smiling in any of the pictures. For a hot moment I had felt angry and betrayed that he hadn't told me. We had been *talking* about his dad and he said nothing. But then I saw all the frowning photos and put it behind me. I wouldn't want to talk about him either.

"It would make him mad," he says finally. "To date you, and help you with the student council."

"Well, you said it yourself. Your dad is an asshole. So far, it doesn't seem like you care if he's mad."

"I said asshat. He's an asshat." He grins and slowly runs a hand through his thick hair. "That's kind of a bonus, sure. I was hoping, though, that . . ."

"Yes?"

"If I help you out, your mom . . ."

Oh. Duh. My stomach sinks.

"I'm trying to convince my parents to help me go to culinary school next year. They don't really want to sink more cash or time into a passion of mine after everything before, though. I think maybe if your mom, I don't know, gave me the seal of approval, it would work wonders. Maybe I could do the apprenticeship she offers."

Before my mom vowed this past weekend to never do an apprenticeship again, her program churned out several prominent chefs, and it had become a sought-after placement for before or after culinary school. Just last year, Iggy found a home in NYC and Carmella moved to Rome. My mom is working with Andrew and Taylor right now—both spots filled, never to be filled again. I couldn't offer him the apprenticeship even if the positions were vacant, but I can offer him a good word, and pissing off his dad. It'll have to be enough for now. I *need* his help.

I thrust my hand out. "I can put in a strong recommendation, but she obviously gets the final say."

He relaxes like an enormous weight has been lifted. Kind of like me any time my Connie shift is over and I can go be by myself to decompress. "Even without you trying my food?"

"It's probably for the best that I don't waste our time. I'm not good with talking about tastes and things. That's my sister. I can tell my mom you're a good friend."

A tingle flies down my back when he grasps onto my hand. "Yes, but I think you mean boyfriend?"

He tugs me closer. A huff of breath leaves my lungs on instinct. Just a foot away is the perfect distance to see how impossibly smooth his skin is, how his shiny hair artfully falls across his forehead, and how his lips curve up naturally at the corners like his smirk is a birthmark. His looks so much kinder than Thomas's.

The bell rings. I'm late to class, again, but instead of worrying if two tardies and a detention in the first three days of school will ruin my chances of becoming student council president, I'm worrying if Patrick can smell the ranch dressing on me from the salad I devoured before coming to meet him. My pulse is practically galloping, but I can't seem to move my body.

"Text me after school so we can discuss this more?" he asks.

"Okay."

His eyes roam all over my face before falling to my lips. When he leans in closer and, at the last second, veers to the side, placing a gentle, tickling kiss at the corner of my mouth, I can't help but release a gasp. He breaks away before I can pull that breath back in and I panic, turning on my heel and taking the long way to class. I nearly run into a bank of lockers in my escape.

He was going to kiss me.

No.

No, of course not. If he was going to kiss me, he would have kissed me. But that wasn't the moment for a kiss. We just made the equivalent of a business arrangement. That's not how you finalize a deal. It was just a friendly-fake-boyfriend thing, something I should probably get used to.

Now if my hot cheeks and racing heart could get the memo . . .

Seven

Stevie can't seem to pick her jaw up off the table when I tell her what I've gotten myself into.

"I have to be honest," she says delicately. "Even for you, this is a little wild." She sips her soda and waits for my response.

"What does that mean?" I stir what's left of my extra-thick milkshake with a spoon. "Even for me?"

She barely *knows* me—or do I just barely know her? This Stevie seems to know all.

"It means sure, yeah, make a scene at an assembly for the feminist movement, but asking that cute boy to be your fake boyfriend—"

"Keep it down." I glance around us, but no one that I recognize from our school is at the All-Hours Diner despite the proximity to the campus. I'm trying to keep this scheme under wraps, so I begged Connie to hang out with her guide-turned-instant-best-friend Sasha after school so there was one less person in the know. Patrick—who will be meeting us here in a few minutes—Stevie, and I will take this to our graves. Which means Lila will, too, but that's okay. "And it was *his* idea."

She examines my face, maybe to see if I'm lying to protect my dignity, and *hmm*s.

"I need you to be on board with this," I say. "I'm not winning this election without both of you."

She's clearly flattered, her cheeks pinkening instantly. "Obviously. But why do you have to pretend to date? Can't he just be your friend?"

I start, trying to tread lightly, "I mean, I asked the same, and it's just—it won't work any other way because of how outdated things are, how unbalanced between the guys and girls. Maybe you don't see how they treat the girls because it's been the norm for you since you started here, but they will only trust me if they think I'm Patrick's girlfriend. He's the principal's son. If they respect him, they respect Patrick, and then they'll finally respect me. It's fucked up, but I don't think I'm wrong."

She nibbles on a crispy fry, eyes out the window next to our booth. "I guess I do keep a tight circle of gals and gays. Where do I come in?"

"You're still in charge of all the same stuff: social media, keeping me in touch with the preferred students. I just need you to bring Patrick into the mix." I push away my empty glass. "You know, make it seem believable."

"I think that's up to *you two*. I can't sell something that's not there to sell."

"Sure you can. I saw you post an ad for a product you said you hated this morning on Instagram. It got a ton of likes."

"Thanks, babe." She smiles, tilting her head toward her shoulder like I'm endearing. "Coming from you, that means a lot. I know you're allergic to the internet basically."

The chime above the diner door rings and Patrick walks in, his eyes scanning the room as he searches us out. He's changed from his school uniform, at least the top half, and wears a plain white T-shirt that fits him snugly. I wave to get his attention and hate how fast my cheeks burn. I've always been an easy blusher, but from the heat I'm feeling now, I swear I need to call the fire department. It wouldn't even be so bad if he hadn't kissed me. I've been replaying it all afternoon and I'm so annoyed with myself. Who gets this bent out of shape over the type of kiss your grandma gives you? He didn't even make contact with my mouth.

He stands next to our booth and I can tell he's deciding where he should sit by the way his eyes flit between us. Stevie doesn't make any room, so I guess that means he's going to sit by me, his *girlfriend*, which makes sense but seems so ridiculous. I scoot over and he slides in, his thighs immediately warming mine when they touch. He doesn't pull away.

"Uh, hey?" Patrick . . . asks. This is the first time I've seen him off his flirty game. I want to memorize the way he worries his lip, the slight crease between his brows. Up until now, I've been uncomfortable with Stevie always recording things or taking photos, but I wish for once she were doing it right now. I'd like to see this again and again.

He looks between Stevie and me once more, and then leans in to give me another grandma peck. He hits strictly cheek this time, but it doesn't stop the butterflies from holding a celebratory parade inside my chest. His lips are so soft.

"Your cheek is hot," he says quietly, pulling away.

I clear my throat. "Stevie knows."

"But don't let that stop you," she says, gesturing to us. "Have at it."

"Oh." Patrick delivers a sheepish grin toward the tabletop and sits up straight. "I wasn't sure, so I just—"

"I appreciate you keeping the lie alive," I say with a nod.

"Anything for my girlfriend." He flags down the waitress with a lazy smile and orders a cheeseburger and fries. "Anything more for you guys?"

Stevie and I beg off, and when the waitress leaves, he angles toward us. "So, what did I miss?"

"I filled Stevie in on the plan and I asked her to help us seem legit."

"Oh good. I could use help with that." He places his arm on the top of the booth behind me. His fingers accidentally brush against my shoulder and my spine goes ramrod stiff.

"Why? You've been in relationships before." Stevie slurps her soda until the straw rattles against ice. "Unlike Ella."

I would have liked him to be completely new to this, like me—I'd feel so much less awkward—but he keeps a pretty long and detailed kiss trail on his socials that's hard to deny. There are at least ten girls currently living on his feed with their lips locked to his, forever preserved.

"I've never been in a fake one for political strategy, though," he says tensely.

"So glad we all get to experience this first together," Stevie says, pushing her empty glass to the edge of the table. "We need to start online." She pulls out her phone. "Let's do a wellness check on your socials. Patrick is active on Instagram and TikTok. A few thousand followers combined. Very good. Great engagement. These will be our main tools to sell this lie." Patrick nods, and Stevie turns to me. "Now *you*, you are a ghost. Even when you were active, you posted sporadically and . . . honestly, the content lacked a lot. More honestly, it was trash. I love you, but what is this shit?" She flips her phone to show me an Instagram post from seventh grade in which I posted a mirror selfie holding a bottle of Jumex Mango Nectar drink, for some reason, right against my squinting and smiling face, and I captioned it— "*One woman's grocery shopping error is my new obsession. Hashtag thanks, mom; hashtag jumeex* . . . spelled wrong," Stevie reads.

Patrick snorts beside me.

"In my defense," I say, taking the phone and looking closer, "*you* liked it."

"*Fine*," she says, grabbing the phone back. "We all make mistakes and/or get hacked." She continues, "It would be suspicious for you to sign up for all new accounts on every platform, so we're just going to do Instagram since I'll be doing most of the video content anyway. This will be more manageable for you."

"Why *don't* you have any social media?" Patrick asks.

"Or . . . recent social media?" he corrects himself. "Are you a serial killer?"

"A little late to be asking me that, huh?"

"I don't have a time machine, so . . . asking now will do."

"I used to have it, but as Stevie so politely put it, I was trash at it, and when I tried to be better . . ." I shrug. "It wasn't good for my mental health, so I quit it."

"Wait, so are we, like, enabling you?" Patrick asks now, his eyes bouncing from mine to Stevie's. "Making you relapse?"

"No," I laugh. "I lurk. I'm fine. I used to crave it and now I can go days without it, and I just don't post."

"It *does* give serial killer vibes, doesn't it?" Stevie asks Patrick.

"Let's focus," I say. "I'll revamp my Instagram. Anything else?"

"No, we'll start with that and see how it goes. I'll send you things to post and help you with captions." Stevie smiles as someone comes by to collect our dirty dishes. "But that begs the question: Are we pretending you two have been dating, or is this a new thing?"

Patrick and I glance at each other, silent. I didn't think about that.

"Truth always helps to sell a lie," Stevie says, pulling our attention back to her. "It's been a whirlwind romance. Love at first sight"—she delivers one pointed look at Patrick—"and you have a reputation for jumping into relationships, so I think people would buy it."

That would explain the girlfriend crumbs all over his account.

He raises an eyebrow. "Rude."

"Not untrue, though," Stevie says with a smile.

"Sure," I cut in. "If that works for you, Patrick, we'll just say we hit it off when we met."

"We *did*," he reminds me with a smirk.

"Oh, yes, perfect." Stevie lifts her phone up, aiming it at us. We both tense. "No, go back to how you were." We don't move. I don't know how we were. "Could you guys look like you actually like each other, please? Patrick, do the cute smirky thing again, and Ella, look dazed."

I scoff.

I don't dislike Patrick at all, so why is it so hard to get the grimace off my face when we lean in close for a photo?

"No, that's not gonna do at all," Stevie mutters to herself, checking out the photo. "Let's try again, but try not to look so posed and awkward this time. Patrick, how about you tell Ella a story. I'm sure you're full of them."

He frowns, but angles toward me. "Uh, I guess the start of a relationship is the perfect time to tell you about my extra toe." He shrugs. "I wasn't born with it. That's pretty much the whole story."

I burst into laughter, and of course that's when Stevie screams like she's hit the jackpot. "Yes!" She accidentally pulls the attention of a middle-aged man hunched over a meat loaf at the counter. "That's exactly it. Now, convince me you can't help but paw at each other."

I stop laughing and the smile Patrick had given in to disappears.

"Okay, okay. I took it too far, but look how cute this is!" She shows us a few photos and they're actually not that bad. I don't hate how I look in them—I might be one of the few people on earth who thinks she looks better laughing than doing anything else—and Patrick looks . . . like Patrick. There's no other way to say it.

Stevie texts the photos to us, instructing me to post it with the caption **already feels like forever #trickdaddy** (which I hate). She advises Patrick to post a different photo to his Stories without a caption, as is his usual style. I can't help but admire his photo choice. Stevie must have taken it immediately after his toe "story" because I'm at peak laugh, Patrick's eyes fondly on me with a smile curving his mouth. He looks . . . smitten. Maybe we *can* sell this.

I promptly follow Stevie and Patrick, and they return the favor.

"Now, Patrick, before your food comes, we should get a few other photos, maybe in your car or one of the stores around here. That way you two can make up for lost time, have something to post at the drop of a hat—use your phones; I don't have any more space until I back my stuff up tonight." She blinks at us when we don't budge. "Let's do this, like, now?"

"Won't they think we're bailing on the bill?" I ask, sliding from the booth after Patrick.

"I'll stay here. Just take some cute pictures—and videos!— and don't do anything with them yet. We're banking them."

I shuffle outside after Patrick.

He starts laughing before the diner door is even closed.

"She's a lot, huh? I don't know how I missed her at school."

I kick a rock gently. "She's well-meaning." When I look up, Patrick snaps a photo of me. "What are you doing?"

"We're out here for a reason. We're supposed to take photos—"

"I think we're supposed to have photos together, not just a bunch of me for your stalker wall at home."

"No, the photos with direct eye contact go into the spank bank; the ones where you're unaware are for the stalker wall." He touches a hand to his chest, indignant. "I'm not just a *creep*; I'm a collector."

I know he's joking, and yet . . . the blush returns, unwelcome.

He smirks. "That stuff really gets to you, doesn't it?" He takes another photo and smiles at his phone screen. "You're cute with your little blush."

I huff out a "*whatever*" and slide my foot against the loose gravel in the parking lot.

"Will being in my car just the two of us make you combust?" he asks.

"Oh, shut up. Wouldn't you get a little flustered if I was constantly pretending to hit on you?"

He directs us to the left of the diner, where a little art gallery resides behind two immature planted trees. "Who's pretending?"

"Patrick."

"It's Trick Daddy now."

"You're impossible to have a conversation with."

He opens the door and lets me step inside first. The gallery is intended for purchases, but I just spent the little weekly money I had after putting my paycheck into my savings on a double chocolate milkshake, so looking will have to be enough for now. I already spot a piece that I wish I had hanging in my room: it's a watercolor of an arm puncturing the smooth surface of a dark pond, hand outstretched with its palm up to a stray beam of sunlight, and in the corner, in the shadows, another hand reaches toward it like it's offering help.

"What, why? I have conversations with myself all the time and I've never had any issues," he says, the door stuttering to a close behind him. "Are my good looks too distracting?"

"You're just—"

"Yours are distracting, too."

"That's what I'm talking about!" I breathe out a laugh. "You're just never serious."

"I'm serious a lot of the time." He drags his finger down my temple and tucks my hair behind my ear.

I open my mouth to respond—though the only words I can think of are "get the fire extinguisher!"—but a middle-aged white woman with a long flowy dress interrupts us.

"Welcome to the Lemon. Let me know if you have any questions about the art. We ask that you kindly do not touch."

"Thanks," I say as Patrick nods.

The woman wanders away, the fabric billowing behind her in a nonexistent wind. Once she's out of sight, Patrick latches onto my shoulders, maneuvering me to the piece I had been eyeing. He pulls out his phone and takes a few photos. "Loosen up."

"I can't. This is awkward."

"Because I brought up my spank bank?"

I burst into laughter and hear the shutter of his phone three more times. He reaches out and brushes what must be the same stray blond curl off my face before taking one last shot, closer.

"All out of storage?" I hold my phone up and snap a few shots of him. "Oh, wow, very nice."

He starts posing in increasingly ridiculous ways until I'm practically acting as a paparazzo, stalking him through the gallery. We ham it up for photos in front of a nude portrait of a man, because we are mature, and then take a few of our own "artsy" shots in front of a giant floor-to-ceiling canvas of one of the many wooded areas in Pennsylvania. Patrick remarks that it's very *Folklore*-esque, which I note is an interesting reference. Then we take a quick jaunt down the hall to more abstract pieces, and I make a close-up my phone background.

Somewhere deep in the gallery, we sit on a worn velvet couch and scan through the photos on each of our phones.

"Which one is going to be my contact picture?" he asks, leaning over my shoulder.

I shrug. "No one will see that except me."

"That makes it even more important. What's the face you want to see when I call you at one in the morning to tell you I can't sleep because you've been running through my mind?"

I push my shoulder into his chest, putting space between us so he can't literally *feel* the heat radiating from my body. "One of the nude portrait shots. Probably the one where you were cradling that man's penis like a hot dog."

He bites his lip, holding back a laugh, and swipes through his own photos. I take a silent and sneaky photo of him. *That* will be my contact picture, actually. He's now frozen in time as he almost always is: hair tousled, smirking, a sparkle in his laughing eyes.

"What about me, then? What photo?" I ask.

He looks up like he's been pulled from a reverie and shows me his phone screen. It's a photo of me that I wasn't aware he had taken. I'm staring at the artwork I hope will still be here one day when I'm able to return with money in my checking account. I hadn't realized I had reached my own hand out, to see how the light of the store played across my own skin in comparison to the two in the piece.

"You like art, huh?" he asks with a small smile.

"I guess. Doesn't everyone?"

"No," he says simply.

I break eye contact and sigh, not quite used to attention on me. "I'm not sure we did what Stevie wanted."

"Yeah, and my food is probably getting cold." He looks longingly to the exit. "They have the best cheeseburgers on the West Shore."

"That is—that is so wrong." I may not have many feelings or opinions about food, but I can't let this injustice stand.

"No, I'm right. Best cheeseburger on the West Shore is from the All-Hours Diner. East Shore: Burger Yum."

"I can agree with the East Shore. But a *diner* burger for the West?"

"You really are your mother's daughter, huh? Food-critic-level takes on the classics? *Pretentious*. Where is your best burger, then?"

I bristle at the assumption that I'm like my mother. That's all Connie. "I don't want to say."

"Oh no," he laughs. "Where? Tell me. Tell me now."

I roll my eyes. "Let's take a photo and call it a day. I'm sure Stevie has an extensive plan to go through still." I flip my phone to selfie mode and ignore how he exasperatedly deflates next to me.

"Okay. You should put your hair up, though. Like you had it the first time I saw you."

I pause before complying. He remembered how I had my hair. I got it cut a few days before school and it's shorter than I'm used to. Strands instantly fall free, probably giving me the frazzled appearance of working a double at Ashes, but he smiles like it looks good. I guess to him, it must.

Again, my insides alight so hotly that my outsides take note.

He stops me after I take one photo. "Do you have something on under your polo?"

"Just a camisole."

"Okay. New plan to kind of make Stevie happy." He grabs my hand and drags me out of the gallery. I give the art one last loving look before focusing fully on the calluses that interrupt the otherwise soft, smooth skin of his palm.

We stop at his little SUV, a Hyundai.

"Take off your shirt," he says, reaching into his back seat and pulling free a gray T-shirt. It says "SkaLa Land" in Comic Sans and has an illustration of a bunch of instruments on it. "Put this on. It'll make it seem like this picture was taken on a different day."

He's got a good point, but even though I have something on underneath, taking my shirt off in front of him feels like getting naked. But then there's the worry that I'm too big to squeeze into it. The shirt is an XL, something that is surely oversize on his slender frame but will fit me as snugly as my uniform. With an exhale, I swap shirts and try not to watch as he strips off his T-shirt, revealing way more of his skin than I was ready for on a random Wednesday afternoon. He puts on his own school polo and tries to slap a wrinkle out of it.

I resist smelling the new fabric on me. "Who's SkaLa Land?"

He blinks, and then his eyes light up and his smile grows wider. "My band! Well, my old band. It wasn't really a band—"

"Trick."

He grins. Takes a breath. "It was the band I thought I was going to start when I was thirteen. When my parents got me the guitar and lessons. A ska band."

"I can't see why they didn't support you," I say sarcastically.

He playfully bites his tongue. "So maybe I was a little enthusiastic. Prematurely so."

"I like the shirt."

"You can keep it. My parents had to order one hundred, so I have . . . ninety-nine more."

"Thank you."

"You're welcome. They all look the same, but this one is my favorite. Consider yourself lucky." He gives up on his wrinkle.

"I'm ready. Make me look pretty."

He shifts into place behind me and wraps his arms around my waist even though they're out of frame. After a deep, calming breath that I hope goes unnoticed, I take the picture and revel in how our smiling faces look so candid and genuine. I'd believe it if I saw it on my feed.

"Wait. Take another." This time he snuggles into my neck and breathes heavily. It tickles so badly that I jerk away. The photo catches a squeal breaking across my face and Patrick looking at me like he's about to devour me whole. Help. The butterflies.

"That's not family-friendly," he says, zooming into himself on my phone. With his dark lashes, intense stare, and pouty mouth exposing white teeth ready to bite, he looks like a sex-ified Big Bad Wolf.

"Let's try again," he says.

"Don't do that again, though. It tickled." And the feeling of his lips made my heart rate kick up to an unbearable speed. I think I'm halfway to cardiac arrest right now.

"That's the whole point, though."

I burrow into his side, refusing to let him have the power position and tickle me again. He's warm and lean, but comfortable. He wraps an arm around my shoulder and then angles in front of the sun, the glow hitting our faces just right. That's the money shot.

I have never been this close to a guy. Embarrassingly, I am so happy to have proof it happened.

When we go back inside, Stevie *does* have an extensive plan for us to sell our relationship, but unfortunately, Patrick has absolutely nothing left of his meal aside from a few burnt fries. He orders more food and we get down to business. I'm starting to think that this won't be so hard to fake.

Eight

Stevie and I part ways with Patrick a little after five and intend to pick up Connie and reconvene student council talk at my house, but then my mom texts me desperate pleas for coffee, so we swing by a coffee shop and then make the Ashes owners' booth our campaign headquarters for the night. The booth is always reserved—for my parents, or my family—out of a mushy romantic gesture my parents made to each other about never being too busy for a meal with the other. They don't notice we've dumped poster materials all over the table, but they do manage to give Connie and me a "hi" and "I love you" apiece before scurrying back into their respective places for the Wednesday dinner service. We're packed, which isn't unusual, but I do see a surprising number of my mom's new tofu taquitos on tables. I've never liked the taste of tofu myself, but tonight it's tasting like money.

I was thinking I'd broach the subject of Patrick's apprenticeship tonight, but by the way she's flitting back and forth from the pantry to the stove, the sounds of pans being dropped, and way, *way* too much sizzling, I think I'll have to hold off. Not a good time.

So, for the past half hour, Stevie's been guzzling down virgin everythings, nodding appreciatively but unhelpfully at anything I say, and Connie's ignoring us so intently that her nose is practically attached to her computer screen. We've gotten precisely zero campaign posters designed, and it's mostly my fault—since Stevie's sugar high has made her very amenable and ready to help.

I delete what I had been doodling on my iPad with a groan. I'm usually really efficient at designing things—flyers and menus for Ashes, and covers for Connie's fanfics, mostly—but when it comes down to making something for me, I'm useless. Nothing I do is as beautiful as any of the pieces in the art gallery Patrick pulled me into earlier today. And I know that a campaign poster doesn't need to be beautiful, but it needs to be *me* and it needs to be easy on the eyes at the very least. This is my second introduction to the student body, so these posters need to be eye-catching and convincing. I won't get a chance to sit down one-on-one with every student; for some of my classmates, this will be their only impression of me. And right now, their only impression of me is a blank page, unfortunately in more ways than one.

My artist's block and doubt aren't helped by the reaction to my Instagram post. I pause my non-drawing to refresh for new notifications—validation is a hell of a drug, and I see why Stevie likes it so much. I'm getting all these wonderful and shocking displays of friendship, familiarity, and appreciation, just because I'm vaguely *with* Patrick. I posted the more attractive but kind of blurry photo of Patrick making me laugh at the diner, and it's a certified hit. He and Stevie reposted it to their Stories and I've gotten a hundred followers just this afternoon.

As if just looking at our photo summoned him, another of Patrick's texts drops down on my screen. I sit in silence, forgetting everything that came before him sending me are we a grumpy/sunshine relationship?

I bat away the heat in my gut as he double texts a blurry picture of us laughing with when you can't figure out who's the grump.

It's me. It's obviously me. He's just being nice.

"Who's that?" Connie asks, leaning over my shoulder. I lock my phone but it's too late. "You're smiling like a fool."

"Yeah," Stevie interjects with a devilish smile. "He's—"

"A friend from school." I shoot Stevie a pointed look that makes her frown. I'm not entirely sure what I'm telling people yet—important people, I mean. On the outside, yeah, it'll look like Patrick and I are dating now, but on the inside, with the people who matter, I'm torn on whether to lie, and Connie wasn't exactly on board with me running for student council in the first place. I doubt she'll be happy to hear I'm intentionally drawing more attention to myself by doing this.

"But—"

"What are you writing about?" I ask sharply, to cut her off. Fair's fair. If she's in my business, I'll be in hers. "When can I read? Also, what can you tell me about the grumpy/sunshine trope?"

She raises her hands. "Okay. I'll let it go." She goes back to her screen, pauses for a moment, and then slams her finger down on the delete button.

What was that about? Stevie texts.

I don't want to lie to everyone, I respond.

She frowns, typing as vigorously as Connie when inspiration strikes. You should have thought of that before asking Patrick and me to help you lie to everyone then.

She drains her glass—I've lost track of what was in it this time—and sets it down on the table between us with a light *clink*.

"Can you show me the bathroom?" she suddenly asks aloud. Yeah, it's probably easier to have this conversation in person and out loud.

"Yep."

We stand from the table and I give a serious look to Connie— who is staring at her blank page like it holds the secrets to the universe. She misses it completely.

"I just mean," I say to Stevie in a quiet voice as we walk away, "that I don't want to lie to people who it's unnecessary to lie to, or tell people who would disapprove."

Steering with her shoulders, I maneuver her toward the bathroom, cutting through a few tables of people chatting away and sharing appetizers. I don't realize that I'm treating her how I would treat Connie until about halfway across the room.

"I can't tell if you'd make a great politician or a terrible one.

All the sugar from these drinks is eating away what's left of my brain." We squeeze through a set of two tables that are supposed to be connected into one for a dinner party later. "Is this going to be a problem? Are you having second thoughts?"

"No, I'm good. I stand by my decision." I pause outside the alcove housing our two genderless bathrooms.

"I didn't actually have to use it," she says with a blink, looking surprised to have ended up here. "I've seen him texting you. Did you two come up with a plan for tomorrow?"

"A plan for what? We've been working on campaign poster slogans and designs."

"A plan for telling the whole school you're dating."

"I thought that's what the pictures were for? A . . . soft launch?" I don't know what she's expecting. Patrick and me to jump on the loudspeaker and spell it out for everyone, complete with a song and dance? People won't care *that* much.

"Oh, Ella, that's not what a soft launch is." She loops her arm around my elbow and guides me back to the booth.

"Okay. Well. What was the point of the photos, then?"

"The photos are just foreshadowing for a bigger announcement. To get people excited. It's like when Taylor Swift drops an Easter egg."

I raise an eyebrow.

She shrugs. "I'm really liking my creative writing class so far."

"Me too," Connie loudly interjects, proving that even several tables away, with music playing through the restaurant's speakers and people competing to be heard over it, we are still within earshot. "Except for the whole writer's block thing, and not allowing us to hand in fan fiction for homework. I've been turning in trash just to submit something at all."

Stevie cuts in front of me to stop at the edge of the table. "Just change the names so Ms. Peters can't google it."

"I hadn't even thought of that."

"That's what so many authors have done." Stevie glances to my iPad and the notebook and markers she hasn't even touched yet. The work must overwhelm her because she says, "Okay, I really have to pee this time."

Connie raises an eyebrow at her, then directs the questioning glance at me.

"She, uh, got stage fright," I say, sliding into the booth next to her.

I watch Stevie stroll into the bathroom on the left and wince. The doorknob on that one gets loose sometimes so I make a mental note to be on the lookout for the door shaking or any SOS texts.

"Just be real with me. Who is he?" Connie asks, closing her laptop. She turns to me with a smile. "I saw the picture. That's the guy from the assembly, right?"

I guess it's now or never.

"Yeah. He's a friend. He's going to help me with the election."

"And?" Connie asks, her chin in her palm. Expectant. "*But?*"

I suck in a deep breath. I don't want to hide things from Connie. We might not always be on the same metaphorical page, or even in the same book, but we are sisters and we are—or at least we *were* at some point—best friends. "Del" was Connie's first word. Not "da-da" or "ma-ma." Del. Delaware. Yes, I would keep her awake all throughout the night whispering it to her so she would pick it up, but that doesn't change the fact that it happened. She can't take it back. We are *bonded*.

"*And*," I press on, taking the plunge, "he's helping me by . . . pretending to be my boyfriend, *but* you can't tell anyone."

She shrieks so loudly that Taylor peeks out from the kitchen, his already overwhelmed expression going the extra mile and morphing into unadulterated panic. I wave him away with a "sorry."

"You guys are going to fall in love!" Connie says. Without breaking eye contact with me, she pushes her laptop open. "Is that why you asked about grumpy/sunshine? Oh, you're *so* the grumpy one."

"No." I plant my hands on the table, firm. "*No.*"

"Yes. Yes, you are—"

"No, I mean don't get ideas. This isn't one of your fix-it fics. This is real life and it's a business exchange."

I thought I could prevent her from getting attached and putting all her hopes and dreams into our fake relationship by being honest about its fakeness from the start, but I forgot about her love of tropes. Enemies to lovers. Second-chance romances. Only one bed.

Fake dating.

"That's what you think until *bam*! You can't stop thinking about him and you've kissed and it's magic and this is even better than I thought—"

"Connecticut. Calm down. It's *just* to help me with the election. For you."

She leans back. "What do you mean *for me?*"

"I'm trying to put that asshole in his place so no one else thinks they can treat you like he did. Can you imagine how this year would go—how the next *three* years would go for you—if he or someone like him was in charge of the student council? I could make real change, potentially. Make the school as inclusive and great as it pretends it is."

"Ella, don't do this for *me.*"

I roll my eyes. "Everything I do is somehow always for you. I don't exactly have a choice." If I win this thing, my parents will be elated; it doesn't matter if Connie doesn't get it yet. I'll have done the best thing I could for her and they can't complain or resent me for it, and then I'll go to college and hopefully, finally, be free. I won't have anything to worry about if I get things squared away before I leave.

She mimics my eye roll. "Of course you do, and your choice was to run for president and fake-date a very cute boy." She holds up her phone to show me my Instagram post. "He's really cute. You're definitely going to fall in love."

Chuckling, she places her focus back on her computer screen. When she begins typing furiously and mumbling under her breath, I know I've lost her attention completely.

I'm not going to waste my time telling her that Patrick and I are destined to be friends and nothing else, no matter what her totally *fictional* trope dictates and regardless of Patrick's jokes and the way they make me dizzy. I have to keep a clear head to win this election, and I can't do that with hearts in my eyes and butterflies in my stomach.

I know she can't help it, though. Connie's just an annoying

romantic. Her one true pair on *Avenged* broke up a few seasons ago, and she's been trying to find a new one to fill the void in her heart ever since. It's what drove her to writing fan fiction in the first place.

Stevie comes back from the bathroom, saving me from spiraling. "That bathroom door needs fixed. I thought I was fated to die in there."

Nine

It doesn't hit me until the next morning that we never discussed what this fake relationship would entail—what the *rules* would be—and that was an oversight on everyone's part, especially mine, since I have never been in a relationship and have no clue what to actually expect.

It's one thing to watch a relationship on a screen, but to try to emulate it with no practice—and basically on a stage in front of a bunch of people who would enjoy watching you fail—is another. No matter what my speaking at the assembly implied, I get stage fright.

Stevie posted one of her usual gossip roundup videos this morning and sent it to me. We all agreed yesterday that she would discuss dating rumors about Patrick and me, but it was still surprising to hear my name come out of her mouth. A few comments declared they knew it all along.

I walk into school with my heart hammering and feel like everyone's eyes bounce off me as I make my way to my locker.

Like they know I'm attempting to pull one over on them, and they do *not* believe it. But this is what the fake dating was supposed to help avoid, according to Patrick.

When I turn the corner down Senior Hallway A, the first person I see, despite the amount of traffic, is him. He leans against my locker with his sleeves rolled up and his hair perfectly windswept. If I weren't already his fake girlfriend, I might (mentally) make a case for trying to be his real one. After the election, of course.

"Good morning, Ella," he says with a hidden smile. *And just like that, I'm no longer Parker-Evans.*

"Morning, *Trick*."

His eyes dance with new life as he straightens and lets me get into my locker. "You know what I was thinking about this morning?"

I drop my backpack onto the hook inside my locker and raise an eyebrow. "That your nickname isn't going to stick?"

"Not with that attitude." He stuffs his hands into his pockets and leans a smidge closer. "I don't know your favorite flower."

I snort before I can hold it in. "I don't have a favorite flower."

"Favorite food?"

"No." I pull my binder from my backpack.

"What about your favorite song?"

"'Violins.'"

"No, not instrument. Although . . . that's interesting—"

"That's the name of the song." I close my locker quietly.

He scrunches his brows together. He's hovering so close that I could easily press the pad of my finger right between and smooth them out. "Huh. *Very* interesting. I'll have to look that up—"

"*I* realized that we didn't discuss what kind of relationship we're going to have," I interject, my voice shaking only a little.

"Oh. Yeah. So . . ." He glances around the packed hallway, buzzing with a million different conversations. We won't be overheard. "It kind of defeats the purpose if we're the couple who doesn't show any PDA, but I could easily go overboard if we *are* that kind—"

"PDA?" My heart practically gallops out of my chest and down the hall. I knew this was a possibility as I played imaginary fake-dating scenarios in my head last night, but him, in the flesh, saying it right now?

"Public displays of—"

"*I know what PDA means—*"

"Attitude."

I huff. "I just mean—I don't know. Can't we just say we're dating and that's enough? Maybe hold hands?" It's not that I have any issue with Patrick getting my firsts. I, for one, think getting the firsts dealt with in meaningless ways is a better idea than romanticizing them. It's just that . . . I could see myself getting distracted with selling the relationship. Again, Patrick Logan is not bad on the eyes. At all. I can admit that in an objective way. Nine out of ten dentists approve of Patrick Logan, and the tenth has fallen ill from the sweet tooth he gave them. But the whole point to this is the election.

He bites his lip. "I won't go anywhere you're not comfortable going, but I do think there should be *something* that makes it obvious we're together, exclusively and publicly. I've had relationships in the past where I was—" He actually *blushes*. "Let's just say I'm not afraid to show how I feel."

As the hallway begins to empty, a girl walks by and gives Patrick a lingering sly smile. He returns it and something hot surges through me. Annoyance?

"Speaking of . . ." I clear my throat and force myself to stand a little straighter. "Maybe you can tone down *showing how you feel*, since you're supposed to be my boyfriend. Exclusively and publicly."

"What are you talking about?" He takes my bag holding my binder, laptop, and other necessities without asking. "You have English first, right?"

I nod, dumbfounded for a moment that he knows that. "I'm talking about you making bedroom eyes at other girls. And—" I didn't think it would bother me this much, but the receipts of his ex-girlfriends on Instagram are hard to ignore. They are stunning and plentiful. "I don't even know who I should be aware of, like, in terms of hookups and girlfriends. Am I going to get my ass kicked in the bathroom for dating you?"

He laughs softly to himself and then frees one hand to intertwine his fingers through mine. The roughness on his skin sends a shiver down my spine that repeats tenfold after he says, "You'd prefer I only use my bedroom eyes on you?"

"That's not what—"

"The only girl who isn't affected by them?" He smirks. "Even Stevie is smitten with me and she told me day one that she is very, very gay."

I roll my eyes to the ceiling, letting him navigate us to my class. He does so with ease, whereas typically I have to do it with the strength of a linebacker.

Stubbornly, I admit, "If we weren't in a business relationship, I'm sure they would have some effect on me."

"Enough of an effect to take you to my bedroom?" He leads me to the bit of free space between lockers where my classroom door stands open and waiting for students. He smiles at me, but it's short-lived as another beautiful girl, this one with expertly contoured brown skin and bright red fingernails, walks by. The look shared between Patrick and her is more than just bedroom eyes.

Oh. So that's what that feeling was earlier. Not annoyance. Jealousy.

I'll ask Stevie to give me the rundown.

No. No, I will not. I'm cool. This isn't a real relationship.

But then, eyes still locked with hers, he gently pushes me so my back hits the cool wall and cages me in. When he does turn his dark eyes to me, his pouty lips quirk into a half smile. Not his usual smirk, though.

"You gonna answer?" he asks playfully.

"I wouldn't go that far. I'm pretty booked until the end of college. Not a lot of free time." I try to bat my eyelashes, act like the breathy quality to my voice is intentional, part of this game—part of the act I'm putting on for our audience of Team Thom idiots and babes Patrick has had or could have. But the truth is, he just leaves me breathless sometimes. I would definitely take him up on his offer if I felt it was real, and if I had the emotional capacity.

He moves in close enough that I'm sure he can hear my heart beating. I'm worried—"worried" doesn't actually seem like the right word—that he's going to kiss me on the lips this time, but he changes course last-minute and kisses the tip of my nose. "I wouldn't need that much time. Maybe five minutes. You can't spare five minutes for your boyfriend?"

I place a hand on his shoulder to steady myself and then push to put some distance between us. I need fresh air to cleanse my dirty thoughts. All I can see in this haze is Patrick and beds.

"Rules," I say, swallowing. "We need rules. And expectations."

"Class starts in a minute."

"What, I thought you didn't need that much time? Think you can last that long?" I bite my lip to stifle the smile spreading across my face.

He clutches at his chest, glancing around the hallway for an audience. "Can someone call 911, please? There's been a murder."

I pull him closer by his school tie. Maybe we'll be fine at this PDA thing. "Quiet. We don't need to draw attention just yet. Right now we need—"

"Rules and expectations," he says.

I say them as they spring into my head, rushing to get them out. "Obviously neither of us should be flirting or hooking up with other people while this relationship is in place."

"I can manage that. No cheating."

"The true nature of this relationship stays a secret between you and me."

"And Stevie," he adds.

"And her girlfriend." Then I cringe. "And my sister."

"Okay." He hands me my bag. "Anything else?"

"There's the expectations part." I wet my bottom lip. "We can keep holding hands."

"Ah, yeah. I should have asked about that, and . . . kissing you. I'm sorry—"

"It's okay. Kissing me on the cheek is good—I mean, it's fine. Am I okay to assume the same?"

"Oh yeah. I'm more than fine with kissing. Like, all types—if you're good with it, I mean." He shrugs, looking down the emptying hallway, but I think it's more to avoid staring at me. "Like, we don't need to avoid it. I suggested this whole thing. I knew what I was getting into."

My grip on my bag strap tightens as I think about it—think about kissing him. He notices.

"We can also not," he says quickly. "I'm not trying to pressure you into anything. I was joking about the bedroom stuff, and you won't be pressuring me into anything." He checks the hallway again. The little jealous part of me that's already taking this relationship way too seriously is wondering if he's searching for the girl he gave the smoldering stare.

"No, I'm—I'm not pressured," I say, growing more confident with each word. I mean them, but I'm shy to say them. "You're not pressuring me. I also knew what I was getting into." I just hadn't predicted how it would make me feel—excited and terrified, all at once—for Patrick Logan to be more than fine kissing me. "Kissing is good with me."

"We can do whatever you want. You can initiate all contact going forward if you want that. Consider me a willing pair of lips in your shenanigans."

I groan. If it were left to me, I probably would never muster up the courage to do anything. "Let's just agree that kissing is fine, until one of us says it's not, and in the meantime, it should keep people from being suspicious." Not that we aren't entitled to our privacy if we want it, and not that some people don't have relationships without sexual intimacy. But okay. We can join the masses of people swapping spit in between classes or during lunch if it wins me positive vibes among them.

"Public appearances?" he asks.

"Like more than just school?"

"Parties, school events. I don't know. Whatever comes up that would help your election."

"Sure." I hold out my hand for him to shake and he looks at it with a frown.

He turns it so he can kiss my knuckles. I panic, not wanting him to comment on my blush, and flip our hands so that I can repeat the action on his hand. The whole panicking, blushing situation is *not* handled well because I catch sight of the heat in his eyes when I check to see if he laughs.

"That was weird," he says lightly. "You're weird."

"You did it first," I mumble. "Gender norms are for the weak."

He reluctantly steps back as the warning bell rings, but even from arm's length, he keeps his gaze steady on me. He raises his eyebrow. "What about four minutes?"

"Four minutes for what?"

"Sex. I can maybe even make it three depending on the foreplay."

I push him a little roughly, but he barely stumbles. He finally laughs, and it fills my chest with a bubbly feeling.

"Goodbye, Patrick," I say in a singsong voice.

"Bye, Ella." He turns away and then spins back quickly. "Wait."

I step back into the hall to let a few students inside the classroom. "What?"

"I just wanted to say you look really nice today."

I glance down at my uniform, trying to catch sight of a wrinkle or stain I missed when I got dressed this morning, but I see nothing. He . . . must be serious? "I look how I look every day?"

He shuffles backward, a grin growing on his face. "Yeah. You do."

I roll my eyes. "I look like every other girl in the school."

"No. You don't." He bites his lip. "You look like my girl."

"So, who is 'Violins' by?" Patrick asks, dropping his lunch tray on the table and taking the empty seat next to me. His elbow brushes against my bare arm and it's enough to put me on high alert. I should have guessed we'd be sitting together at lunch now.

Lila, who's sitting across the table with Stevie, raises an eyebrow at me but says nothing.

"Uh." I straighten. "Joey Cape and Tony Sly."

He nods, typing something into his phone, which he holds out in plain sight, unafraid of the consequences. "Holy *shit*, this song is old."

"My dad played it as a lullaby for me." I subtly push away my lunch and turn toward him. "It might not actually be any good."

"Doubt that. I'm going to listen after school."

I'm not sure what I'm supposed to say to that. It's really sweet. Does a simple "thanks" cover it? "Awesome"? I struggle to figure out what a girlfriend would say to her boyfriend.

Ugh, I'm really going to ask Connie to write me dialogue options, aren't I?

He pockets his phone and takes a huge bite of his taco, hard shell breaking off onto his shirt and tray below. "My favorite song, not that you asked, is a toss-up between Taylor Swift's 'Exile' and 'Sexy' from the *Mean Girls* Original Broadway Cast Recording."

I choke on my water. "That's—surprisingly varied."

"I contain multitudes." He pats me on the back when I cough again. "Let's circle back from before: favorite food?"

"I can't pick a favorite."

"If my mom was Ash Parker, I would probably feel the same way, so I'll let you pass on answering that for now. Mine is a Cowboy Crunch from Neato Burrito."

I nod. "I've had it."

His eyes light up. "And you're realizing now that it's your favorite, too?"

"Sorry."

He slumps. "We'll figure it out."

I free my sandwich from my lunch bag and start peeling the crust off. "You're not allergic to peanut butter, are you?"

He frowns. "No, why?"

I lick a mixture of marshmallow fluff and peanut butter from my thumb. "I didn't want to send you into anaphylactic shock if I kissed you."

He freezes. "We'll get back to that—because it's very important I point out that you're thinking about kissing me when I'm trying to have a conversation about something different—but we need to focus on you not having a favorite food or meal. It's really going to bug me."

"I'm not just sitting around thinking of kissing you."

He pushes his hair out of his eyes. "Wait, why not?" He turns to Stevie and Lila. "Don't you guys sometimes think about kissing each other?"

"Every time Lila talks about something cute her chinchilla did. I just want to shut her up—like, I get it, everything he does is cute. He's a *chinchilla*."

Lila whips her head to Stevie. "Ex*cuse* me."

"What does that have to do with us?" I ask, wanting to stop an unnecessary fight.

"Well, we're a couple now, too," Patrick says heavily. "It's not out of the norm to ask other couples about things we're experiencing, right?"

I resist rolling my eyes and take a bite of my sandwich. "I just don't care for food like that. I'm not a foodie." I guess I'd rather talk about that than draw more attention to the fact that, yes,

I was thinking about kissing Patrick. So sue me for trying not to *kill* him if it were to happen. My mom would tell me it was karma for insisting on eating peanut butter.

"I literally can't comprehend that, though," he says with exasperation. "Your mother is so talented. Her flavor combinations are inspirational."

"Okay, sure."

"Looks like you're fighting a losing battle, Trick," Stevie says. "She hasn't found The One yet."

That's probably the best way to put it. I don't seek out new foods or flavors. They've always been brought to me and then I've been asked for every thought that popped into my head as soon as it touched my tongue. I've never just been someone trying the food for fun. I've never tasted a dessert without knowing how many failed attempts went into it, how many nights my mother made a mess of our kitchen during her experiments, how many nights of crying herself to sleep went into a few minutes of deliciousness. I've seen my mom go through high highs and lower lows, all over . . . food. The thing that she's lauded for. Food's fine. It does the job. Some of it is objectively and subjectively good, but I don't need to shout about it.

Patrick watches me for a moment, eyes narrowed. "I'll make you something you like. One day."

"Good luck," I say.

Lila turns to Stevie. "About my chinchilla . . ."

"Can I make you something? Seriously." Patrick takes another bite of his taco. "Just one thing?"

"Only if you're ready to be either lied to or given a factual account of every flavor I tasted."

"I can take critique."

"Well, in that spirit, you have taco sauce on your upper lip."

"Are you allergic to it?" He wiggles his eyebrow.

I hand him a napkin, which he takes with a smile.

"Hey, you two," comes an unfriendly and most definitely unwelcome voice. When I look over my shoulder, Thomas stands with a sneer—or maybe he thinks that's a smile—on his angular face. The girl with immaculate nails who captured Patrick's attention earlier stands a little behind him with one of the previous student council reps, whose name could be Todd or Dean.

Great. She's another crony. They're multiplying.

"You became fast friends, huh?" Thomas asks.

The condescension leaks off every word, but Patrick doesn't flinch. He wraps his hand over mine, even though mine had dropped to my lap. Neither of us moves and I hope no one notices the goose bumps that now pebble my thighs. "My girlfriend and I were talking; did you need something, Thom-ass?"

Thomas narrows his eyes in a way that makes it clear he's not sure if Patrick called him Thom-ass or Thomas. Patrick and I share an amused look that makes it clear Thomas didn't mishear.

"We bonded over what a shithead you are," I add, squeezing Patrick's hand.

"What a coincidence. That's how Nadia and I bonded." He gives me a smug look that does nothing to aid my feelings about him.

I blink. "What?"

Behind me, Stevie laughs and it riles Thomas up even more. Before he can say anything, Patrick says, "You two bonded over what a shithead you are? Should we start a club?"

"I'll definitely let you be the president of that, Thomas," I add.

Patrick nods. "Seems only right."

Thomas glares, his mouth a severe, thin line. His eyes dart to Patrick's hand on mine and then turn to slits. "I meant we bonded over what a shithead *you* are, Patrick. Obviously."

"He's not a shithead," I say with confidence. I don't add a joke. I don't say anything else. Fact.

"Sure," Thomas says, nodding, "and you're not just the flavor of the week."

Patrick flies out of his seat without warning and I stumble up to hold him back. Thomas backs away a few steps, but grins when Patrick doesn't move toward him. The guy and the girl, Nadia, look shocked and uncertain what to do. Nadia's hands are clenched into small fists by her sides.

"Whoa. Calm down," Thomas says in a slick voice. "You said it first."

Heat stirs in my stomach at the words. Did Patrick already try to sell our relationship to someone . . . and call me the flavor of the week? If that's how he has to behave to make people believe we're the real deal, I don't know if I can do this. I thought we respected each other. I thought the whole point of this was for people to respect me.

His shoulders are tense under my hands, but he slowly takes

his seat. I stay standing, watching Thomas and his friends retreat to a table across the room. He sits, but continues to watch us while Nadia says something to only him.

"I'm sorry," Patrick says quietly, pushing his tray away.

"It was hot," Stevie says. She shrugs when Lila rolls her eyes. "What?"

"The good news is that I doubt anyone will question you're together at this point," Lila says, nodding at the turned heads of our classmates.

Patrick reaches for my hand again when I finally take my seat. He doesn't say anything, doesn't even look in my direction. Before he can tuck into himself, I intertwine our fingers and lay our hands on the table. Maybe now isn't the best time to ask him about Thomas's statement. I'm probably just in my head.

"It was," I mutter to what's left of my lunch. I pin a half smile onto my face and wait for him to react.

I'm not sure he heard me over the ruckus of the cafeteria until he asks, "What?"

"It *was* hot."

Finally, a smile cracks on his face and the tension rolls out of his body in one big wave. "I said I wouldn't let anyone talk shit."

"Because you knew they would. Because of your relationship history?" I thought he was just protecting my feelings because people would talk shit about *me*.

"Yes, and my non-relationship history."

"Which is?"

He raises an eyebrow. "Not exactly lunch conversation."

"Nearly punching my opponent isn't lunch behavior."

He pulls himself free from my grasp to face me. I do the same and he places his hands delicately on my knees. The goose bumps return.

"You're not the flavor of the week," he murmurs.

I narrow my eyes. "Did someone say I am?"

"Just Thomas."

"We don't care what he thinks."

He shakes his head. "No. We don't. But I just want to make sure you know."

"Well, I do know that. I'm your fake girlfriend. You don't have to, like, assure me of your intentions with me." Though it feels very nice to be assured, especially when it involves him absentmindedly drawing little circles on the exposed skin of my thighs. "I just need to be on the same page as you. If we're pitching this as a fling or something—"

"No, we're not."

"He said you said it first."

He sounds strangled when he says, "I didn't. I didn't say that about you."

"Okay." I believe him, because he sounds agonized at the thought of me thinking he would talk about me like that.

He sucks in a breath. "Someone's worth doesn't come from their partner or how long they're together or what they do together."

I glance at Thomas over my shoulder. He's still staring. I meet his gaze head-on and harden mine.

Patrick laughs gently, his breath hitting my cheek. I turn to him with a question in my eyes.

"Don't be protective," he says. "That's my job."

The honesty I manage to see in his expression, in the frown lines around his mouth, makes me place a hand along his jaw. I swipe my thumb over his bottom lip.

"It's both of our jobs." To think he has been mistreated because of something so stupid makes me want to scream.

He turns into my palm and kisses it, alighting a scorching fire in my stomach.

It shouldn't, but this loyalty he's already showing me makes me feel better about my maybe-lie concerning a currently unachievable apprenticeship with my mom. I can give him something tangible in the meantime as I put together something real.

With Thomas and whoever else watching, I lean in and kiss Patrick. On the lips. My very first kiss.

He's caught off guard but takes only a moment to lean in, winding his hands through my hair and pulling me closer, until his thighs hug around mine, the fabric of his pants rough against my skin. Every inch of contact feels like a buzzing plea for more, like he's been patiently waiting and I've finally given in, but his lips brush mine so gently, carefully. My breath catches when I pull back and I see him sitting there, hot darkness welling in his eyes.

"We'll make them regret crossing us," I promise.

Ten

Friday goes by in an awkward fashion as Patrick and I quietly continue to figure out our fake relationship, and then the weekend is spent finally making posters. On Saturday afternoon, Stevie bursts through my front door with materials in hand and Lila on her tail to beg me to just make something, *anything*, to put on the walls so that it doesn't look like I made a fuss of redoing the election and then chickened out of actually running.

After some thought, I realize that I'm putting too much pressure on myself, that something beautiful and realistic isn't really a style useful for my campaign, or possibly even respected by the Courtland Academy students, so I settle on some fluid bursts of colors and eye-catching text screaming VOTE FOR ELLA. After maybe two hours of working, Connie comes out of her drafting cave to lend us a hand in adding glitter and other texture to my posters to make them really stand out, not that we expect Thomas to have anything flashy—or even anything at all. He's so sure he has it in the bag that I wouldn't be surprised to see zero mention of him anywhere along the hallways in the remaining weeks leading up to the election. He still hasn't removed "CA President" from his social profiles—and really, who even adds that in the first place?

Patrick and I text a few times, but mostly we keep to our normal weekend lives, almost like the kiss didn't happen, though we did, rather clinically, discuss in private after that it was the right move to shut down rumors. In the Stevie-Patrick-Ella group chat, though, our relationship is alive and well. Stevie instructs Patrick to post a photo of the two of us to his feed, and he almost listens by posting a photo of only me. He captions it, without Stevie's advice, **madam president** ♥.

The calm I had achieved over the weekend was apparently the type to come before a storm because, on Monday morning, my homeroom teacher instructs me to report to the auditorium ahead of a student council debate during first period. In front of the whole school. Without warning.

I try to relax on the walk there by telling myself that I've already spoken in front of the whole school, that I'm already literally putting myself out there on posters and befriending new people every day. I picture myself walking onto the stage, the stupid theater lights shining bright as I stop behind one of two podiums, confident and prepared. But I'm neither. I didn't know about this debate at all—in fact, it never crossed my mind—which feels like an oversight on both Stevie's and Patrick's parts. If I had proper foresight, I might have worn my cardigan to hide the ocean tide of sweat at my armpits.

This is it. This is my biggest act of sisterly love and duty thus far. I will fight for this win and put into place new rules that are kinder, greener, and for the benefit of all the students, especially Connie.

I push open an auditorium door and find Thomas, Thomas 2 (Todd), and Thomas 3 (Dean) congregating on one side of the stage, arms crossed while in conversation, and two people I vaguely recognize sitting in the front row, a few empty seats away from each other—close enough to be friendly but far away enough not to be awkward. Tana Smith, a girl in my prob/stat class who gave me a stealthy but supportive thumbs-up the day the election was announced, pushes her waist-length box braids over one shoulder and leans in to say something to Kat Simms, the only (out) nonbinary person I've met at this school. They wear rainbow suspenders attached to their uniform pants. I wonder if either or both of them are running for president; I hadn't heard a peep about other opponents or candidates outside of Thomas's camp.

I approach cautiously, my heart hammering. I'm not the type to initiate conversations or friendships typically, and there's a chance they both laugh in my face when I ask if I can join them. But instead, they smile and tell me to take a seat.

"Are you both going for president, too?" I ask after clearing my throat of the fear clenched there.

"God no," Tana says with a warm laugh. "That's too much pressure. But VP . . . it still puts 'president' on my transcripts, you know? I'd be cool with that."

I nod and twist toward Kat. "You?" I ask hesitantly.

"No competition here," Kat says, raising their hands in

defense. "My mom got some parent newsletter that mentioned the election and she insisted I go for something—she's still in that phase of acceptance where she thinks I'm the spokesperson for everyone and should act that way." They glance at the huddle of boys. Despite Kat being white with short blondish hair, I wouldn't confuse them for one of the clones, and it's not just because of their suspenders. Kat's features seem to sharpen to a point starting at their winged eyeliner down to their chin, drawn like a sketch rather than a softened finished piece. The boys boast baby faces and the immaturity to match.

"She'll be crushed if I don't win secretary/treasurer, but I'll be fine," Kat continued. "I will feel sorry if either of you win, though. Working with the hive mind there won't be fun."

I wish this meant less to me, so I could have the same nonchalance about the outcome.

"Not winning is *not* an option for me," I mumble.

"He's a dick, right?" Tana whispers, her brown eyes bouncing from mine to over my head—to Thomas.

"Yes!" I hiss back. I shrink down in my seat between Tana and Kat. "He made my little sister cry on the first day, so I refuse to back down. I'm taking this precious presidency from him even if I die trying."

"That's the spirit," she says with a broad gleaming smile. "I hope it's you, for all our sakes. Thomas's brother was just as stuck-up as Thomas, but Thomas thinks he has something to prove, so he's worse."

The back door to the auditorium opens and all three of us turn to eye the newcomer, size up the competition, but it's

Patrick. He speed-walks down the aisle and stops in front of me only long enough to grab my hand, say hello to Kat and Tana, and then pull me to my feet. He guides us up the stairs on the side of the stage and back behind the heavy dark curtain.

"What are you doing here?" I ask, caught off guard, but not entirely hating it. "I'm so glad you're here."

"I came to wish you good luck and figured it would look better if I do it in person instead of over text—no one really knows when we're texting so it doesn't count."

I blink. I hadn't thought of that; suddenly, his lack of text messages this weekend makes me feel a little . . . sad. "I don't even have my phone on me. They're not allowed, you know."

"I'm me," he says with a smirk.

"Nepo baby," I mumble.

"What's Stevie's excuse, then?"

"She's *Stevie*. She's powerful."

He laughs. "You're right. How are you feeling?"

"I'm feeling like this is more like goodbye than good luck. I'm going to die out there unless you've got some tricks up your sleeve." I narrow my eyes at him. "But that's why they call you Trick, right?"

"I am, embarrassingly, not living up to my name today," he says sheepishly, stuffing his hands into his pants pockets.

I hear the doors open again and dull chattering starts up. I peek through the musty curtain as our classmates are herded in, the seniors taking the front rows. Kat and Tana stand up to allow people to take their seats.

Patrick sets his hands on my shoulders and dips to my level.

"You're going to be fine as long as you just show everyone who you are."

"Who am I?" There's no way he could know after a week.

"You're smart, funny, caring, driven. You have everyone's best interests in mind. Don't stoop to Thom's level, no matter what he says."

I stretch out my neck with a sigh. "I hate how the better people are never supposed to throw hands."

"It's about respect. Showing people who you are when you're standing alone—not who you are in comparison to someone else." His hands slide down my shoulders and drop off near my elbows.

"Hey, you're good at this. Do you want to take my place?"

He smiles. "Do you need anything from me?"

"A time machine. A teleprompter with a carefully prepared speech that has been proofread by Stevie. A body double—"

"Haven't got any of that. I was thinking water?"

I shake out my arms, which have decided to go frighteningly numb at the worst time. "No. I'll just have to pee the entire time I'm up there then."

"You've got this. I promise."

"You can't promise that." I grab his forearm and lean in, hoping it'll look cute if anyone can see it from the audience. "Did your dad tell you what the questions would be?"

"No—"

"Why didn't I get any warning about this? I had no time to prepare, and I'm terrible at public speaking. I would have failed my speech class sophomore year if I hadn't been allowed to record my speeches ahead of time instead of reciting them in class."

I glance at the stage and notice there aren't any podiums like I had imagined earlier. I guess that would be a little too perfect, wouldn't it? Courtland Academy would never give me something to literally lean on. Patrick looks with me, and his hair catches the light from the stage. At least I'll be able to spot him in the crowd and have something to metaphorically lean on.

"What will the questions be like? What should I focus on?"

"Uh, no clue. We've never had more than one person run before, not the whole time I've been here. This is all new territory."

I find the nearest wall and slide down, not even caring that my skirt bunches up higher than I'd usually allow it. When I hit the ground, Patrick crouches in front of me, worry lines between his eyebrows.

"That wasn't supposed to make things worse; I'm sorry."

"No, it's fine," I say tightly. "I should know that. It's good information to have."

"On the bright side, you're taking this from Thomas before he ever really gets to have it, and I bet that makes him *so* mad. His brother had it for three years and he'll have it for none."

"Just—" I swallow. "Adding more pressure."

"Shit." He wrings his hands. "Well—no one here knows what a debate *should* be like at least. We're all in this for the first time together. There are no expectations of what's good or what's—"

"Horrendously bad, ill-prepared, and poorly worded."

He scrunches his face up, holding back a smile. "You're proving yourself wrong here. That was surprisingly eloquent for off the top of your head."

"You shouldn't be back here, Patrick."

Principal Logan stands a few feet away with Thomas, both sneering in our direction. Thomas has on every single piece of the school uniform that it's possible to wear at once: tie, vest, button-down, blazer, khakis, dress shoes. He even has an American flag pin on his blazer that shines in the low backstage lighting when he crosses his arms, a microphone already in hand. Principal Logan holds two other microphones and some notecards.

"Just wishing my girlfriend good luck," Patrick says, standing and taking me with him. He only releases one of my hands, holding on tightly to the other. "Not that she'll need it."

Thomas scoffs but remains silent. Maybe because his role model is present.

"Take your seat," Principal Logan says to Patrick, no hint of fatherly love in his expression. A chill runs down my spine. My dad has been harsh with me before, but never has he come off as unloving as Patrick's right now. "You shouldn't have left your homeroom."

"Got it, boss." Patrick turns to me and plants a kiss on my mouth that I wish others weren't around to see—though I guess that would defeat the purpose. His lips leave me woozy and weak in the knees. I only realize I've clutched onto his forearm when he reluctantly breaks away. I hope he's front and center in the crowd somehow—somewhere I can see him and ground myself through this nerve-racking debate.

"Ms. Parker-Evans," Principal Logan says gruffly, handing me a microphone. It nearly falls from my sweat-slicked palm. "The presidential candidates will be going first. Turn this on only when it's your time to speak. Stay behind the white line to avoid feedback." He addresses both of us now, one hand on the curtain and the other grasping his notecards and microphone in a viselike grip. "There will be three questions and then we'll open to student questions. This will last fifteen minutes. Do I need to clarify anything?"

"Do we both get to answer all of the questions?" Fifteen minutes doesn't seem like a lot of time when two of us need to answer three questions each. I adjust my grip on the microphone.

"Yes. Short, succinct answers, please. We didn't account for a debate when planning the school hours this year, so we need to be as brief as we can." He stares down his nose at me for a long second, and then turns on his heel and pushes aside the curtain.

"Do we go after him—" I start to ask, but then Thomas takes the lead onto the stage without a word and I'm left following him like a little baby duck that has stupidly imprinted onto the only human she's seen.

The curtains open, revealing the murmuring mass of students now filling most of the seats in the room. My stomach roils, and I suddenly forget every single thing I know and dislike about this school.

After a quick introduction in which Principal Logan *accidentally* refers to Thomas as Courtland Academy student council president—as if that mouthful could be accidental; it's so much someone could choke on it—he asks the first question.

"What do you think the main issue facing Courtland Academy is right now and how do you plan on addressing it?"

Fear freezes me so suddenly I'm thankful Thomas just starts talking and takes the pressure off, even if it was rude of him to not even pretend to grapple with who should speak first. With the lights beating down on me, it's hard to see the crowd at all, but I know they're there. I can hear the rustling, the whispering, can feel their stares. It's a haunted darkness. I hope they can't see the sweat beading on my forehead.

"The main issue facing Courtland Academy right now is a lack of funding for after-school clubs and sports that help our wonderful students show potential universities all that they offer. My plan to fix that is to sit down with the school board and go over the budget to see where we can reallocate those funds from."

People applaud his answer. I've only been here for a week and I can tell that funding is not an issue this school is facing. Courtland Academy has a vending machine around every corner, a student store, iPads in every classroom, and brand-new uniforms on every student and athlete. The school has the money, thanks to outrageous tuition costs, but it's utilizing it in poor ways.

"Ms. Parker-Evans?" Principal Logan drawls.

I lift the microphone to speak for the first time, and what comes out is a gross little croak. Scattered laughter rings out through the auditorium and I only gain a little bit of confidence when I hear Stevie hiss, "Shut up!"

I squint into the crowd to try to find her, but my eyes land on Connie instead. She's in an aisle seat near the back, but her double thumbs-up is enough to stop me from fleeing the scene.

What could I change about Courtland to make it better for Connie? That's the real question here.

"Uh, the biggest issue I've witnessed in my short time here is the separation." I drop the microphone to my side so I can clear my throat. Thomas rolls his eyes when I continue. "I mean, I could say it's a diversity issue at its heart, but I don't want to scare everyone with the D-word. Everything here is separated. The students, the grades, the lockers, the classes and actual class*rooms*, the lunch schedule." I gain some momentum and loosen up. "When the original student council was announced, it was three white senior guys. No variety, no inclusivity, no *new perspective*. Shouldn't the goal of each student council be about making the school better than it was before? Opening it up to more possibilities?" I move the microphone to my other hand and try to discreetly wipe sweat from my palm on my skirt. "This school isn't only seniors, and it's not only boys anymore. There should be representation of all the grades and genders and interests, not only in student council, but in electives, school clubs, at lunch. There's no reason to keep everyone separated—that alone causes issues with the lunch times and makes it so the cafeteria staff is working most of the day and, I'm sure, prepping and cleaning all morning and night. It's not efficient—but that's a tangent for another day."

Principal Logan blinks at me, his cheeks a little red. "And how would you *fix* that, Ms. Parker-Evans? Please, be succinct."

A few snickers litter the room.

"We'd merge things. Mingle. Imagine the class discussions that could create," I say. "There's no reason for there to be, for example, a creative writing class designated for each grade when it could be made up of students in every grade."

Mr. Logan rolls his eyes and then proceeds to steamroll through the second and third questions—"How would you handle a dispute among classmates?" and "What is the main goal of your presidency?"—to which I answer pretty well, in my opinion. I'm sure Thomas would say the same for himself. I'm hoping the audience has caught on to how his answers are different from mine. We prioritize different things. He focuses on keeping things the same—which is dangerous at a place like this, in a time like this—and I want change. He says a dispute among classmates should be handled through punishment, and I say it should be handled through mediation. His goal is to make Courtland Academy "the best in the district through academics and sports," while mine is to unite the school in a healthy and happy way. It'd make it easier to keep an eye on Connie, but then after I'm gone, she'd have a support system in place. Guidance. Mentors. A safe place.

I sound like the hippie-dippie my parents raised, and even though I stand by my answers, I can tell I haven't won over the crowd by the way they respond to Thomas. I try to tell myself that the boys cheering him on are just louder than everyone else.

By the time we're done with Principal Logan's questions, I realize this wasn't really a debate at all. It was a way for Principal Logan to show off his prize candidate and also highlight how my ideas will disrupt the school's way of doing things.

With five minutes left before we let the vice presidential candidates take the stage, we open the floor for student questions.

A white guy with his hands shoved into his pants pockets comes up to the microphone placed out for students and gives Thomas a bro nod. "There's a lot of congestion in the halls between classes. How will you fix that?"

I allow Thomas to go first—again, not that he even hesitated a moment to see if I wanted to answer. "Easy. We eliminate the forty-minute study hall periods after lunch and dedicate that time to longer lunch periods for better digestion and more time between classes so fewer people are tardy and get more time learning." He ends with a cheesy grin that shines too brightly.

I lift the microphone while the crowd claps. "Actually, I think eliminating the study periods is a bad idea. A lot of students rely on that to catch up or get ahead on homework so they have time for other things." At least, they did at my old school—I'm not sure if anyone here knows what an after-school job is. "We could make it shorter and allocate that time to moving between classes, but we can also see better traffic flow if we mix the classes and locker assignments. If everyone in one hallway isn't trying to go to one place, we'll have better chances of people getting to class on time and no need to mess with the current class lengths, which have been set for a reason."

Scattered applause. I try not to let it ruffle my imaginary feathers. My mom's Have It Three Ways Cake wasn't a hit at first either. It just took the one right person to yell praises about it and the rest was history.

Patrick approaches the microphone next. Relief floods through me, putting tiny fires out beneath my skin—the opposite reaction I've typically had when seeing him. He'll go easy on me. He'll set me up for a perfect answer to start a standing ovation, *and* everyone will see us interacting.

He asks, "There are a lot of dietary restrictions that aren't being addressed here. Do you have plans to incorporate gluten-free and vegan lunch options?"

Of course that's his question. It's almost like the spirit of my mother possessed him.

I don't let Thomas go first this time. "Yes. And nut alternatives for those who may be allergic. It's important that as our school is diversifying and changing, it's evolving with us—whether that means in terms of diet, accessibility, or gender inclusivity." I bite back a smile, feeling the most comfortable I have on this stage since, mentally, I am addressing Patrick and only Patrick. I even managed to hold in a laugh at the thought of *me* giving up *peanut butter.* "As for lunch options, there are ways to create meals that are vegan and nut- and gluten-free and delicious for everyone to enjoy. That way, we can cut costs by wasting less food and even cut down on the amount of preparation the cafeteria staff needs to do. We'll have, say, two options each day that everyone can eat instead of a handful that only some can."

Patrick smiles and leaves the microphone, not even waiting for Thomas's answer.

But his answer comes. And it sucks.

"I haven't heard anyone complaining about the lunch options before. We have incredible food here and there are enough ways to get a full meal without changing it. We could put that time, energy, and money into other things."

Someone—Lila, it sounds like—boos him. A few others take up her call, and then Principal Logan shushes everyone, but not before someone yells, "Why do we still have meat loaf on the menu in 2024?"

The next, and last, student question comes from an Asian boy I don't recognize. He runs a hand through his hair. "Can we get the senior privileges back? At least for the guys; I mean, it's not our fault that the school admitted the girls and couldn't afford them anymore. Shouldn't the budget be balanced by now?"

Thomas leaps to answer, straightening his jacket. "Of course. That'll be one of the first things on my agenda. It was before and it's still a priority of mine now. And I'll make sure it's for *every* senior."

He raises his eyebrows at me, begging me to top that.

"Well—" I cut myself off. I don't even know what the senior privileges were, and I think Thomas can read that clearly on my face. *Shit*, how did Stevie not prep me on that?

"*For those who don't know*," Thomas says heavily, loving that he's schooling me in front of everyone, "senior privileges included things like discounts on the school store and local restaurants, reserved parking, passes to leave the campus for lunch, and free admittance to every sporting event." He smiles at me so sugary sweet that I want to throw up. "The senior class became too large to continue them."

"Knowing that," I say forcefully, "it doesn't seem like the issue has fixed itself. The entire student body is larger than it's ever been, which means it's more expensive than it's ever been. How would you bring the privileges back if it's an issue of over-population and budget?"

Thomas blinks at me, stunned that I volleyed the question back. His mouth opens and closes like a fish, and I choose to step over the time I had given him. Principal Logan wants a brisk debate and I think I have an answer.

"I'd like to work out a system so that every student can earn privileges, not just the seniors—" I can't even finish my thought before the angry murmurs rise up from the audience. I try twice to begin my thought process again, but it's too late. I've lost them. How dare I suggest that privileges at this already privileged school be earned? How dare I suggest that the lowly freshmen, sophomores, and juniors be able to work toward the same privileges?

The presidents' section ends abruptly a moment later, after Principal Logan has quieted everyone—my answer still incomplete. If this was my only chance to win over the students—win over the *seniors*—I definitely failed.

Eleven

Around seven o'clock on Friday night, Patrick *calls* me.

We've texted—a lot, especially after the debate, when I required so many pep talks to get me through the rest of the week—held hands, kissed, and yet, when his contact picture fills my phone screen, pausing Stevie's latest TikTok in the background . . . I nearly yelp like a startled dog. Calling is so much more intimate than a text message.

I answer and can't even manage a "Hello?" before he launches into his own words.

"How's your chemical imbalance?"

I blink. "Excuse me?"

"You know, your depression."

When his usual charm and antics weren't pulling me out of the dumps by Wednesday, he got scarily serious and asked what was up with me. Historically, stress makes my depression worse, but I admitted to him that outside of my mental illness, this whole campaign felt perilous. We then spent an entire lunch period coming up with ways I could feel more in control and less overwhelmed. It was surprisingly sweet, even though it involved me demanding a schedule of upcoming student council events from his dad so I couldn't be caught off guard again—to which Principal Logan told me he needs a week to "resurrect it from the grave it's been in since 2013." That's apparently the last time he bothered to create an official one. I assume it's because he's been picking his people's champion, and all the students have just gone with it; no need for the dramatics when there's always just one candidate. But once I got the ball rolling, each new thing was a little easier. Patrick introduced me to some Courtland Academy "influential" people like Carter Chang, the guy worried about senior privileges, and talking to them one-on-one wasn't that bad. I wasn't quite as hated as the chorus of dissension had made me feel on Monday morning.

"I'm okay," I say slowly, my gut twisting with new anxiety. I *thought* I was okay. "Why are you asking after my mental well-being right now? About to drop a bombshell on me?"

His little chuckle sends a shiver down my spine. "Kind of. I'm outside with Stevie and Lila. We're going to a party and we want you to join us."

My heart lurches into my throat. "Why? Where? I'm not ready."

"Peter Liu's house. He has a pool and Jacuzzi—but you don't need to do anything with that information if you don't want to." He mumbles away from the phone, "Stop giving me that look, Stevie; I didn't mean anything by it!"

"Who is Peter Liu?" I peek through the closed curtain and

spot Patrick's SUV idling in the driveway.

"My best friend, some days, like today. Stop looking outside and get ready."

I jerk back, letting the curtain fall, and pound up the stairs. "What kind of party is this? How am I supposed to dress?"

"Um—hey!" It sounds like two people are scrabbling over the phone.

"Ella, dress cute, okay?" Stevie says, clearly having control of the conversation now. "Trick says this is a campaign thing, not a social thing."

"It can be both," Lila says in the background. "She'd want to be cute for either anyway."

"Do you need me to come in and dress you?" Stevie asks.

"No." I gnaw my lip, thinking it over. "I can't just leave Connie here, though. My parents are at the restaurant."

"She's old enough to take care of herself," Stevie says.

"Bring her!" Lila and Patrick yell.

"I'm not bringing her. I'll be out in a minute." I knock on Connie's door.

"Come in."

I crack the door open a bit and lean on the doorframe. Her room hasn't changed much in the last few years, unlike mine when I started high school. I purged all the things I felt were kiddish and tried to go for a minimalist look, which was only doomed to fail by my bad habit of never cleaning or organizing and also holding on to things way past their usefulness. Hers has been warm and cozy since she was little, though, and I think people would be surprised by its casual sophistication.

Mixed textures, pops of color.

"I'm going to a party," I say levelly.

"How basic of you," she mumbles to her screen while typing. But then she stops, fingers frozen above the keyboard. "Wait. You? Party?" She blinks and then her eyes light up. She shuts her laptop with a *snap*. "Is Patrick going? I'm coming."

"You weren't invited." The last thing I need is Connie distracting me. How can I show my classmates that I'm super chill and cool if I have to put a leash on my sister and drag her behind me everywhere?

Ugh, but leaving her here could be worse.

"If you don't want me telling Mom and Dad, I am." She pulls black shortalls and a patterned crop top from her closet. "Black Keds or strappy sandals? What are *you* wearing? Let me help."

And like the rest of my life involving Connie, the decision is made without my input.

Peter Liu's house is massive in a super intimidating way. It's surprisingly Victorian for this area of Pennsylvania and gives off the air that the Liu family is 100 percent a coven of witches. I'm expecting a bolt of lightning to strike somewhere in the background just to illuminate how sharp the turret is and how forbidden this place should be for a bunch of teenagers hoping to get sloshed.

"Why have I never met Peter if he's your best friend?" I ask Patrick as he pulls into a parking spot along the road. I'd be lying if I said his parallel parking skills weren't impressive.

Stevie, Lila, and Connie squish out of the back seat, ignoring my question—but it's a good one. I shouldn't focus on the girlfriends of Christmas past, but on the ghost friends of the present. I haven't met *any* of them.

"He's a year ahead of us, goes to Lock Haven." He unbuckles his seat belt. "He's home for the weekend and wanted to hang out. I suggested the party instead."

"This was your idea?" I lean out the window and instruct Connie to stay with Stevie, giving them both death glares until they roll their eyes at me and proceed inside. Lila encouraged Connie to text Sasha to join her so she's not the only underclassman. From what I've seen and heard of Sasha, I like her. I can trust her. She hasn't led Connie into any bad situations or stick-and-poke tattoos.

"I thought it would give you a good opportunity to get to know your classmates outside of school." He shrugs with one shoulder. "Let them get to know *you*."

"So, the debate really *was* awful?" All week he assured me that I was fine, but this is not the move of a fake boyfriend who thinks his fake girlfriend did fine in her student council presidential debate.

He laughs, putting his hand on my shoulder and squeezing. "No, of course not. You were awesome, but these idiots don't know what's good for them."

"Is Thom coming?" I need a heads-up if I'm going to be sparring with him in one way or another.

"Well, he was invited, but I don't know if he'll show. He had some Future Douchebags of America dinner to attend."

"Future?"

We share a cheesy, secretive grin, our noses nearly brushing.

Outside the car, Patrick weaves his fingers through mine, pulling my knuckles to his lips in a delicate brush even though there's only one or two people outside vaping on the porch.

"You look really good," he says quietly.

Cue the cheek flames.

I haven't been to a party since before high school started, so I wasn't sure how to dress, and Connie's was the only outside opinion I allowed, because if I had Stevie come in, then Lila would have, and then Patrick, and how embarrassing is it to have your fake boyfriend know how hard you struggled to look not even a tenth as hot and casual as him?

"Thanks. You too."

Connie urged me to not overthink it, so I opted to wear an oversize black band shirt of my dad's with a tight, short, black skirt underneath. I had tucked in the shirt, then pulled it out, then tucked it in halfway before deciding to just let it hang loose—the perpetual concern of a fat girl. Do I make sure people can see that there is some kind of curve and definition to my body or do I say fuck them, fuck society, I want to wear a baggy shirt? It's not like people can't see that I'm fat anyway. Every once in a while, like when I'm walking or raising my arms, the skirt becomes visible under the shirt and the peekaboo effect gives me a strange new confidence. It's not sexy, but it makes me *feel* sexy in a way. I threw my hair into failing but cute space buns and then finished the look with black Doc Martens Stevie insisted I buy last weekend. This probably wasn't the best way to break them in. My feet already hurt even though I followed Stevie's step-by-step guide to protecting my heels.

Patrick opens the front door for me and when I walk through, a tall, bulky guy wearing a Jason Voorhees mask jumps in front of me screaming.

He cuts himself—and my shout—off when Patrick steps inside after me.

"Trick!" He pulls Patrick into a hug so tight that Patrick's back audibly cracks. "I missed you. I was starting to think you had me throw this party just to keep me on my toes."

"Yeah, sorry I'm late. I didn't want to come anymore."

"Everybody, out!" the guy yells to the crowd. A few people around him look confused, but mostly he's ignored. I guess it's a good thing he's joking; if this were an actual emergency, there would be a lot of casualties.

"This is Ella," Patrick says, pulling me to his side. "My girl-friend."

I blink, open-mouthed, at the guy. ". . . hi."

"Oh shit," he says through a muffled laugh. He pulls the mask off, revealing tanned skin, full, blotchy cheeks, and shaggy black hair clinging to his neck from sweat. He wears a navy beanie despite the warmth gathering in the house. Smiling, he says, "I'm Peter! Nice to meet you, girlfriend."

He shakes my hand gently, and the act is ridiculous. "Trick has said a lot about you. Running for president, right? First stop Courtland Academy, last stop leader of the first Mars colony."

"My aspirations for leadership definitely stop after student council president. It's more of a petty project than passion."

I have no clue if Peter is in on the secret, but because we're in a crowded room, I don't let my act drop for even a second.

"Yeah, well, he also says you're good at art—like design and stuff. That's a pretty necessary skill these days. About half my friends at school do graphic design work. It's, like, mandatory."

I frown. "No, I'm not—I mean, I just do it sometimes."

Heat bubbles in my gut. Patrick has *actually* talked about me? I want to ask if he also mentioned my mom, but it wasn't the first thing—or even the second thing—out of Peter's mouth so I'm hopeful he hasn't. I'm not sure why it would bother me if he did.

"So," I start, unable to help myself, "what's with the mask? It's September."

Peter gestures grandly to his house, full of kids, and I notice . . . some of them have similar masks propped up on their heads to make it easier to drink and talk. "It's Friday the thirteenth!"

"Courtland loves a good theme," Patrick says.

"And an easy one," Peter adds.

"Noted," I say, nodding.

"Hey, any chance you've seen three beautiful girls come through here?" Patrick asks. "One with an invisible crown on her head and a phone glued to her hand, one with short brown hair and freckles who could kill you with a look, and the last with curly blond hair and stars in her eyes? They would have been together."

It takes a second for my brain to move past my instant jealousy and realize he's talking about my friends and sister. Where *is* Connie? And also . . . how would Patrick describe *me*?

"Um, no," Peter says sheepishly, pulling his beanie off his head and slicking back his hair. "I was upstairs, getting reacquainted with Manny." He wiggles his eyebrows.

"Old habits die hard," Patrick says.

"Not too hard, apparently," he says with a nod at Patrick's and my connected hands.

"Well, not too hard now, but you weren't there when she first stepped outside and I thought she was only wearing the T-shirt."

I shove him instantly, drawing attention from the crowd around us. Peter loves it.

"Let's go find the others," Patrick says through a laugh.

In the large backyard, Stevie, Lila, and Connie snap photos draped together in front of the sunset. Mostly Stevie is leading Lila and Connie in a photo shoot, but she does take a few—and insist Lila and Connie take a few—of herself by the time we reach them through the crowd. There are a few people actually in the pool and Jacuzzi, but the majority of our classmates are loitering on the lounge chairs, playing beer pong, or discreetly passing joints. The music plays low and tame, not a single noise complaint to be found here. Peter must have a lot of practice with this.

Stevie insists we all take turns with group shots and couple shots because the sunset is "ad-worthy." It's not even awkward this time to press myself into Patrick and have couple pictures taken. When he's not giving me butterflies, he's making me feel so secure—with my body, my place at this party, my choices. I never realized how comfortable someone could make me feel by just making me feel wanted and like my words are valued.

"Oh, look who showed up," Lila mutters while Stevie is busy approving which photos, with or without her in them, we can post. We follow her gaze until it lands on Thomas Hayworth, followed by Todd and Dean.

"Who even invited him?" Stevie asks, tucking her phone into her emerald-green cross-body bag.

"My *boyfriend*," I whisper.

"Like, personally? Are you telling me everyone here was personally invited to this thing?" Connie asks, looking around with a frown. "That just seems inefficient. A mass email would have sufficed."

Patrick smiles at her, charmed, and tousles her hair. She squeals, pretending to be annoyed, but I know she's delighted. And smitten. I'll have to tell Patrick that when it's the three of us he can't be all boyfriendly to me and sweet to her or she'll really get her hopes up.

Instead of standing and glaring like we are, Peter takes the initiative to go up and do that weird bro hug thing with them. I'm half-convinced Patrick will follow when I notice how he's standing next to me, his eyes locked on Nadia. She's so small that I hadn't noticed her behind the boys, but now that I have, she's hard to look away from in her bright red minidress. And there's that jealousy again, right on cue.

"Who are you staring at?" Unease dances in my stomach at how off Patrick looks. Something happens every time he sees her—I disappear, he disappears, things go wrong.

"No one. Just Thomas's girlfriend." Patrick laces his fingers with mine. "Want to get a drink?" He drags me inside to the kitchen without waiting for an answer.

"She's dating him? *She* is dating *him*?" I ask when he lets go of me so he can get a drink from the stainless-steel refrigerator. It seems like the drinks intended for guests are laid out across the huge island in the room, in coolers and half-covered in ice, but I suppose when you're best friends with the host, the rules don't apply.

"Yeah." He takes a swig of his soda, the fancy niche branded kind in bottles, and grimaces. "Wish this were stronger."

"There's beer—" I start, angling toward the open cooler nearest to us.

His frown deepens. "I'm driving all of you home."

I don't know what to say to that. It's more initiative and responsibility than I'm used to someone my age taking with me and Connie. Usually I'm the adult.

"What's the deal with her? Nadia?" I caution to ask, leaning casually against the counter. Maybe it's not so casual. He boxes me in as others grab drinks and we both seem to sigh in contentedness at our positions. Safe.

"She was a friend." He blows some air between his lips. "Now she's not. She's *Thomas's* friend."

"Girlfriend," I correct him. Obviously, they can be both, but why do I feel like I'm missing a secret code? "Are you having regrets inviting him? We can leave. I don't mind." I realize when I glance around the room that we left Connie out there—with Stevie and Lila, but still, without me. "I just need to grab Connie."

"No. Not unless you want to?"

"I am very clearly not a party person," I say through an awkward laugh. "But at the same time, we came here for a reason. So . . . I'll follow your lead."

"Then we'll stay. I really think people will like you when they get to know you one-on-one."

"One-on-one?" My eyes must go wide because his face splits into a small smile.

He gently places his finger on his chest and taps it. "Two-on-one; how about that?"

"That sounds better." I kind of hate how much better it sounds. The only relief I get from the thought is that even after we "break up," I'll still have Patrick. We'll be friends—it's not like *I'll* ditch him for Thomas—and maybe we'll even be best friends. For a fake relationship, it really feels like we're making something real here. "Even though it was your silly choice to invite them, I will tell them all to leave. If you want. I'll do that for you."

"Oh really?" he says, a spark in his eyes and that familiar smirk crawling its way onto his mouth.

"No, but I'll tell Peter to tell them," I mumble.

He laughs. "*So* kind, but no."

Eyes on the floor, he steps closer to me so that less than a foot of space separates us and it feels like everyone else is fading away. I can't even make out the rhythm of the music playing throughout the house on expensive speakers because all I hear is the beat of my heart . . . which rapidly picks up speed now that Patrick places his hands on my hips. My T-shirt rides up a little.

Focus. *Focus.*

I blink my head clear, and I spot them over his shoulder, entering the kitchen.

"I should tell you that they're right behind us," I say in a low voice.

"I could smell the scent of suck-up and betrayal," he mumbles. He glances over his shoulder at the same time Thomas opens the refrigerator.

"What do you want?" Thomas grunts at Nadia.

"Water," she says awkwardly, clearly trying to avoid the lump that is Patrick hunching over me. It's almost like he's *trying* to block me from them. I thought the point of being here was to show me off.

"Hi, Ella," Nadia says softly, taking the water from Thomas but locking eyes with Patrick.

"Uh, hi."

"Hey." Patrick clears his throat and turns around to face them. "I don't think you two have met yet? This is my girlfriend, Ella. Ella, this is Nadia, Thomas's girlfriend," he adds unnecessarily.

Nadia gives me a warm smile, her chestnut curls bouncing around her sweet round face, but Thomas stares back with his usual sneer. It's so overpowering that I nearly don't notice he's wearing normal clothes and not his usual Corrupt Businessman full suit. It's a plain white T-shirt under a gray hoodie, but it's still only moderately unstuffy.

"Nice to officially meet you," Nadia says. She nervously brushes her palms against her dress. "You did a great job at the debate the other day."

I slide past Patrick and step slightly in front of him, becoming as much of a safety blanket for him as he is for me. He wraps his arm around my front and rubs his thumb in circles on my clavicle, keeping me tucked closely to his chest.

"You don't have to lie." My tone comes out a little more bitter than I wanted it to.

"Oh," Nadia says, sounding a little surprised. Her dark eyes grow wide when she looks between Thomas and me. She is definitely seeing the gremlin Thomas describes when she looks at me now. "No, it's not a lie. I actually think you might have my vote." She smiles, nevertheless persevering through my meanness, and cracks open her water bottle. She squeezes it too tightly and the smallest amount of water splashes out and over her hands.

I *hate* how this makes me like her, like when Connie rolls out of bed Sunday mornings with dried drool somehow on her forehead. She feels like the kind of genuine Patrick is trying to make me.

"She's just being nice. It's her fatal flaw—like Courtney Delvey's acne." Thomas throws his arm around Nadia's shoulders and pulls her into his side. "She's obviously going to vote for me. You know, I'm actually surprised you showed up here after what happened at the debate." His voice turns lilting, almost sounding too relaxed. *Forced* relaxed. "You didn't exactly win over the crowd with that last one."

"I get it," I say. "Senior privileges are important."

"You were nervous, right?" Thomas leans in a little closer to be heard. "Maybe we can have a redo right here. Less pressure, no rules."

I raise an eyebrow. "You want to have a debate?"

"I was thinking we could gather up some people and host a game of school trivia."

Of *course* he was thinking that. Because I only know what's readily available on the website and he treats Courtland Academy like the key to acing the SATs.

"Wow, you know how to party." I can only muster up sarcasm at this point. He's not worthy of anything else. "You want a redo debate but not a redo election?"

His demeanor changes from confident to annoyed as quickly as he stands straight. He narrows his eyes. "I'm trying to help *you*."

"And why would you do that?"

"I need a few more volunteer hours," he says in a condescending voice. "Charity looks good on college applications."

This motherfuc—

Behind him, Connie walks into the kitchen with her phone in front of her face. I don't see Stevie or Lila with her, but before I can snag her, Sasha shows up and they throw themselves into a tight embrace. I really have no choice but to participate in this game now that she's initiated the buddy system with Sasha. In the past, Connie has always been an easy out in awkward situations, but I know for a fact no one would buy it this time if I suddenly needed to babysit her or leave with her.

"You know what? Sure, why not?" I glance at Patrick, who shrugs. "Let's do it."

"Great," Thomas says with a menacing smile. "Care to make it more interesting?"

"How so?" Patrick asks before I can open my mouth and stupidly say *obviously*. I'm not rich, but I can afford a wager. I have money saved up from my endless summer shifts.

"Strip school trivia." Thomas places a kiss on Nadia's head for no reason. "For every question wrong, we lose an article of clothing."

Patrick balks. "*No way.*"

I place a hand on his chest to calm him, my own heart racing. I definitely don't want to do that, but I can't back down now. "No." I don't know what else to say; it's the only thought that comes to mind. No, what? No, it's okay? No, I won't do that?

"He knows more about the school and has on more clothes than you," Patrick says slowly and quietly, just so I can hear him. "I won't let you do it. This night was supposed to win people to your cause, not have you end up naked on the internet."

Peter comes inside, followed by Stevie and Lila. We're drawing a crowd even though we aren't speaking loudly. Sensing the tension, Peter pauses the music on his phone, and the song on the speakers stops abruptly.

"You're not my boss," I say evenly to Patrick. I lower my voice. "You're my boyfriend." Despite my lungs practically disintegrating inside me, I heave in a solid breath and exhale. "I have to do it. If I chicken out, everyone will judge me for it. The douchebros will say I'm not feminist because I didn't want to get naked and shake my boobs around—"

"Is that something feminists do?"

"Frequently. Keep up."

"How about—" he starts. He faces Thomas. "For every question she gets wrong, *I'll* take off one article of clothing." He runs his eyes up and down Thomas's body. "Unless you've got a thong under your boxers, I'm thinking we have the same amount of clothing on."

Thomas opens his mouth, probably to argue or unnecessarily defend his manliness, but Nadia places her hand on his arm. She says, "If you say no, that's a little creepy, like you have other intentions with her."

Patrick quickly points at Nadia. "Yes, similarly."

Thomas narrows his eyes at her. "You're just jumping at the opportunity to see him naked again."

Well, that certainly wasn't said quietly enough. Adrenaline kicks through my body. So Nadia has seen Patrick naked. I can assume, pretty safely now, that she is one of his hookups he mentioned before. *Friend*, he had said. But there is more than one type of friend out there, and apparently she's the kind that doesn't end up on Patrick's Instagram to be memorialized forever.

Nadia rolls her eyes. "I'm just stopping you from making a girl undress who didn't jump for joy at the thought of stripping in front of a crowd. Patrick is consenting, and he's eighteen."

Thomas sputters out a "fine" and we gather in the living room, the two of us standing in front of a bunch of people who crowd across every inch of Peter's couches, chairs, coffee table, and carpet. Peter pulls the school's website up on his phone and stands between us, far enough behind that we can't see his screen. Peter lends Patrick his beanie, putting him at the same number of clothes as Thomas. We're given blank note-cards from Peter's study stash and Sharpies to write our answers.

"Draw," Peter says in a dramatic voice, "to the best of your abilities, the school crest."

"Shit," I say loudly, causing a few people in the room to laugh. Stevie is, of course, filming this. At least, as she quickly promised, "up until the point where it could be debated as child porn." I can't remember the crest to save my life even though it's on every single piece of my uniform, but because Thomas is scribbling away, I do my best to draw something that is enjoyable if not correct. I don't need to be right, per se; I just need to be lovable.

Peter tells us to stop after a minute and Thomas shows a crude but undoubtedly accurate school crest. His linework is terrible.

I flip my notecard around and laughter bubbles into the room, surprising me. They're laughing with me, not at me. I drew what is unmistakably Grogu from *The Mandalorian* using the Force to hold up a beer bottle.

"Wow. I wish I could give you the point, Ella, but that is *not* the school crest." Peter sighs, dropping his hand onto Patrick's shoulder. "Lose the beanie."

"I'm not worried," Patrick says with a shrug. "Ella's got this."

He pulls his shirt off instead, showing everyone his lean torso and just how much confidence he's placing in me. How am I supposed to concentrate when *that* is standing right next to me? My eyes dart to Nadia, who is pointedly staring at Thomas, and then to the crowd. Connie's face draws me in and I take a deep breath, steadying myself.

"I had to give the fans a little taste," I say to the room with fake conceit.

A few people catcall—one of whom is Stevie—and Patrick winks at me. Thomas doesn't look so pleased, considering he got that point.

"Next," Peter says, scrolling on his phone. "What is the phone number to call when reporting a student's absence?"

Shit, again. The only phone number I can think of is that song my dad hums while doing the dishes.

"I'm sorry, but 867-5309 is not correct," Peter says with a frown when I flip my notecard around. "It doesn't even have an area code."

Thomas, of course, has the number memorized even though he's never once needed to call it—so he says. Patrick works his jaw for a moment before trying to smile at me and the crowd. More people have showed up. More phones are out. Thomas and Patrick are both technically adults, but this is getting weird.

"Still confident. I believe in you. You'll get him next time," Patrick says, unbuttoning his pants. I can't watch. I know he's doing it in front of the whole room, that it's part of the game, but it feels too intimate to see him that way, especially when he keeps his eyes locked on mine. He's my fake boyfriend and this level of undress is too real.

"You been working out without me?" Peter asks him off-handedly, checking out his body with mild curiosity.

"No, I've been too lovesick." He throws a smile in my direction.

The room is packed, but I see Tana squeeze through the crowd to join Stevie and Lila with a small greeting.

"Which teacher oversees the outdatedly named Gay Straight Alliance?"

I actually know this one. Stevie even fist-pumps with her free hand. She wouldn't shut up about Mrs. Powell-Jones the other day when she signed me up for the club. No surprise here, but Thomas doesn't know this answer. I think he tried to be funny by writing "Mr. Gay?" on his card, but no one laughed.

"Mr. Gay teaches calc, homophobe," Peter says with an eye roll.

"How was I supposed to know?" Thomas asks in offense. Lowering his voice, he adds, "His name isn't Mr. Calculus."

Stevie and Lila simultaneously start a boo that gets taken up by the room.

Peter hushes the crowd and asks, "Why does Senior Hallway B have the nickname 'the Void'?"

I jot down: *the electrical incident of 2013.*

Stevie clued me into the incident on my first day of school when the flickering lights made me nauseous as she navigated me to class. Apparently back in 2013, a desperate teacher tried to plug in a popcorn maker, record player, and Apple TV all at the same time for an end-of-school treat and tripped the breaker. Ever since then, the lights blink and hum to their own beat.

Sadly, Thomas also writes down the correct answer, but! Patrick keeps what little clothing he has on! This is a win for us both because if he lost anything more, I would definitely not be able to pay attention, even with the whole room staring at me and judging my shameless ogling.

But. Then. The next three questions take a turn for the worse, leaving Patrick standing in front of our classmates in only his gray boxers covered in little cartoon pieces of sushi. I can barely breathe from stress, the overpowering heat in my face, and . . . a feeling I don't want to fully address. Something that needs to stay tucked deep down underneath my motivation to win.

"Are . . . are we going full monty?" Peter asks Thomas and Patrick with panic in his dark eyes at his best friend's lack of clothes.

Thomas, missing only his hoodie, smirks. "I've got no problem with it."

"Of course you don't." I cross my arms over my chest. "I'm just going to concede," I say quietly to Patrick.

"No. No, you're not. I didn't come this far and get this naked for you to back out." He shuffles in place, hands cupped over his crotch. "Can you just *try* on this one? Please? I don't need my junk all over the internet *before* I'm famous for something else."

"I *have* been trying," I hiss at him with wide eyes. "Let's just stop."

"No. Peter will pick an easy one. No backing down. There's only one more question."

"You didn't even want me to do this in the first place."

"Imagine if you had!" he whispers.

I roll my eyes and release a breath through my nose. "Bring it on, Peter."

The crowd waits with bated breath.

"What year was the school founded?" Peter asks with a heavy glance.

"1969!" I scream out.

The group hollers "NICE!" and Patrick lets out a scream, gathering me in his arms and swinging me around the room. I think I kick someone, but truthfully, I don't care. My mind has gone completely blank, my entire system shocked by the areas on my body where his warm skin presses against mine.

A small but mighty chant of "Ella! Ella!" fades away when Peter cranks the music up, ending our game and the buzzing building between my fake boyfriend and me, and Patrick finally puts me down. My heart gallops from adrenaline, but then I realize his nearly naked body is pressed against mine, so I give us some space.

"I don't know why you guys are celebrating," Thomas says, gathering his hoodie from the ground with a mean swipe. "You lost."

I break into a smile. "Did I?" I cup my hand around my ear. "That sounded like *my* name they were chanting."

Thomas stalks off, disappearing into the crowd, and Nadia rushes after him. Not that I need an old flame reigniting for Patrick, but she needs to dump Thomas ASAP. Better to be single than with him.

Patrick finishes pulling up his jeans and buttons them. "So, you were playing, right? You knew what you were doing and you were never going to let me show my bits and pieces to our classmates." He zips.

I laugh nervously. "Oh, yeah. Sure."

"*Ella.*"

"Everyone loves an underdog!"

He squeezes my cheek playfully before joining Peter and some others, accepting their congratulations even though we didn't *actually* win. He loudly responds that I did all the hard work, which makes them laugh. I definitely need to talk to my mom about him. It's not fair that he's doing all *this* for me and I have basically nothing to offer in return. The least she can do is sit down with him, even if it comes to nothing because she's set on never mentoring again. Who knows, maybe he could even charm her into one last apprenticeship. I'm sure he's accomplished more difficult things.

We stay until the end of the party, helping Peter clean up the mess of his house, and I receive countless pats on the back for getting the "class hottie" nearly nude. Tana is one of the few to stick around, and she gives me the play-by-play of every single sour face Thomas pulled whenever the crowd would whoop over Patrick losing a piece of clothing. Several people even promise to vote for me based on this alone. It's a bit of a dirty win, but maybe I don't mind playing dirty. Maybe the only way to take this pig down is getting dirty with Patrick.

Twelve

By study hall on Monday, I'm finally, fully feeling like a presidential candidate, like I'm not just begging for a baby to kiss, but like I'm having to choose *which* of the many babies I've been presented to kiss. My classmates in desks closest to me say they plan on voting for me, that they like how I put Thomas in his place (even though I didn't really), and that they're happy they could see everything go down via Stevie's trivia video—which I know is making the rounds because she texts me with every major milestone in followers and views. I've nearly been caught on my phone about six times today by my teachers. When that flattering discussion dies down, I talk with Kat about their mother's enthusiasm for the secretary/treasurer role and how it will teach them to better manage their own finances one day, but they still plan on using their allowance on energy drinks.

"Ella?" Mr. Roberts, our study hall teacher, calls in a questioning tone. He stares at me over his laptop screen. "You're wanted in the principal's office."

The announcement causes a few conversations, and my heart, to stutter. I haven't done anything wrong—aside from questioning his precious Thomas Hayworth—in a while. I don't know what he could want to talk to me about.

My classmates' eyes stick to me as I grab my things, sign out on the iPad, and leave the room. I can feel their curiosity like a physical presence following me out. I've done my best to avoid tardies lately, and haven't spoken out of turn. I've already served my undeserved detention last week for, wait for it, jaywalking in the parking lot—Principal Logan was downright smug to slap me with that one. So I don't know what this could be about. It's only when I see Stevie, who should relax me, in the hallway that I panic more.

"Are you going to the principal?" she asks me in a quiet voice, our two paths intersecting around the corner from the front offices.

"Yes. Are you?"

"*Yes.*" She latches onto my arm and slows me down. "We need to strategize. What did you do?"

"Why do you assume *I* did something?"

"Because *I* didn't."

"Okay, weeeell," I drawl out, "neither of us know what's happening. Let's just wing it?"

"That's a terrible idea." She waves me forward through the doorway leading to the offices. "After you, *badass.*"

Inside the quiet and clinical annex of desks and offices, the secretary takes our names and guides us to Mr. Logan's office. He sits behind his desk, typing on his laptop with a focus that could give Connie a run for her money. His face is brick red.

"Sit," he barks at us without looking away from his screen.

Stevie and I exchange a heavy, questioning look but do as we're told, planting ourselves in the two chairs across from him. I don't sit too far back in the seat, in case I need to hightail it out of here. He's nearly vibrating with anger, a volcano ready to explode, and I don't intend on being one of his Pompeian victims.

Finally, he finishes off a few slams against his keyboard and looks at us.

I wish he didn't.

"I have been informed of a video today," he says, tone teetering away from his typical condescension and into disgust. "One that is racking up views online and stars my son nearly in the nude. It's being referred to as Courtland Academy school trivia."

Oh.

I nearly black out. My face goes cold and numb, and I try to blink away the darkness crowding in at the corners of my vision. It's not enough that Patrick and Thomas are eighteen, obviously. Stevie had said to me she needed to do some editing and take precautions so that TikTok wouldn't remove the video. But I hadn't thought of how Patrick's *parents* might feel. How the *school* would feel. It's not like its image obsession is news to me.

Stevie and I stay quiet—me, out of panic, but I think she's not saying a word because she doesn't want to admit fault. She's fully waiting for an imaginary lawyer to come help her.

"Anything to say for yourselves?"

Stevie clears her throat. "Both guys were consenting and eighteen."

I finally work up the nerve to help her help us. "And it wasn't like it was in school," I mumble. Not so brave about speaking up now.

"You probably don't know this yet, Ms. Parker-Evans, since you're new and would rather make waves than smart decisions, but Courtland Academy has a code of conduct, which *does* extend outside the school in certain situations."

My mouth dries up. I glance at Stevie. She is supposed to tell me these things. She's not supposed to encourage them. Hell, anyone should have told me this!

"This was brought to my attention because one of the participants in the video says he did not consent to being filmed."

My mind goes to Patrick first . . . but no. Thomas. The sore loser couldn't stand that Stevie was getting views and I was getting clapped on the back and Patrick was getting heart eyes from his girlfriend.

I swallow, trying to force my desiccated mouth to produce saliva. "Thomas?"

"I can't say who."

"Well, I know it wasn't Patrick. It was his idea to take my place after *Thomas* suggested the game with *me*." I wet my lips and lean forward, emboldened. "Your golden boy wanted me to be in Patrick's place!"

Mr. Logan slams his fist on the desk. "You will remove the video. You will delete it from your phone."

Stevie blinks. "It's my highest-viewed video—"

Mr. Logan directs his steely gaze at her. "I do not care. You are eighteen years old, Ms. Hernández. The video is on your account, your phone. If Mr. Hayw—*anyone* were to press charges, they are going to come after you first."

He angles to me now. "As for you, Ms. Parker-Evans, if you think you stand a chance of winning an election like this, at my school, you are sorely and *stupidly* mistaken, though I shouldn't be surprised.

"Detention for both of you today. Remove that video of my son and Mr. Hayworth or you can expect legal actions to be taken."

We sit in stunned, nervous silence for a moment. Then he points to his door and we both scurry out like mice running from a hungry cat.

Out in the hallway, I lean against a locker and slide to the ground, Stevie following. My heart hammers so loudly in my chest that I'm sure the classroom closest to us can hear it.

"I'm *in* the video" is the first thing I can think to say.

"Right? Why are you being reprimanded?"

"Thomas," I say with clenched teeth. "What a *dick*."

"I can't take it down," Stevie says in a low whine. I realize she's clutching her phone to her chest. "It's *still* going. I'm getting new followers practically every second. All the comments are about how this election drama is the best thing I've posted about."

"You have to take it down, Stevie." I pry the phone from her viselike grip. "Did you know about the code of conduct?"

"I mean, everyone is vaguely aware of it," she says off-handedly, grabbing her phone back. "It's common sense not to tarnish the school's reputation or post stuff like this, but it was *Thomas's* idea—it's not fair that he can just take it back because he's unhappy with how it made him look."

"That's how consent works, though," I gently remind her. "He can take it back. I hate him, but . . . he has every right to not want a video of himself online. Even if the only reason he's upset it's online is because it's not me and Patrick embarrassed by it."

She sighs and unlocks her phone. "I'm not taking it down—"

"Stevie."

"Hear me out!" She pulls up her TikTok account. "I'm not taking it down, but I will make it private. I just—I know it sounds trivial to you, but it's my best work and I don't want to see it just disappear. Maybe one day, but not today."

I sigh, too, and let my head thunk against the metal locker door. "Is there anything else I should know?"

"What do you mean?"

"Code of conduct? Rules? Am I going to be caught off guard one day when Thomas tells me that I can only serve detention so many times and still be elected for president? I need to navigate more than just the social aspects of this whole thing."

"I'll forward you the PDF; it's probably still in my junk box somewhere. We can buddy read in detention today." She stands and reaches down to pull me up. "Where do you want to hit him? The ego? The dick? The voting booth?"

"All? Is it too much to ask for all?" I dust off the back of my skirt. "I want to hit him in his smarmy Principal Logan spot the most. I bet that man will rig the election if he can't get me removed from the running."

The bell rings, ending study hall. After agreeing to regroup in detention on what actions we can take to do more than just react and give in to Thomas, I book it to class, but I guess I can't get *another* detention today, right?

Patrick intercepts me halfway there. His soft mouth is curved in a frown. "Hey, I heard that—"

"Yes." I let him maneuver me to the side of the hallway. "Thomas cried wolf and now Stevie and I have detention with a side of legal problems."

He sucks in a breath. "I don't think he can do anything legally—he's playing up to the camera after every question. He *wanted* to be filmed." I shrug, because it might not matter. If he wants to take this further than just school drama, he possibly could. "Why do *you* have detention? You're in the video, too."

"I assume because it's a way of punishing you and me in one go."

"Are you okay?" He reaches up to push a blond curl behind my ear. It doesn't stay there.

I shrug with one shoulder. "I'm more annoyed that I feel like what little victory I had has been taken away."

"That's not true. Just because Stevie takes down the video doesn't mean people suddenly forget it. You're a champ."

"No, I'm literally a loser," I say with a small smile. "But yeah. I wish there were a way to fight back." I tighten the grip on my bag and Patrick works to pry it free from my grasp.

"I could go find him and give him the old one-two, if you want." He places his arm through the strap and lets it hang from his shoulder. "Meaning: one, I tell him he sucks, and two, I tell him no one likes him."

I shake my head, grin plastered on my face. "I appreciate the offer, but wouldn't want you to get hurt."

He winks.

"Instead, let me know if you can think of any way to get him out of the race completely, because it now feels like that's what he and your dad are trying to do to me."

Patrick runs his hand through his hair. "Yeah, if we don't do something, it's just like we're letting him get away with everything."

I straighten. "I'm not *letting* him do anything. I'm actively trying to stop him."

"Yeah, I know. I'm sorry. I didn't mean it like that. I'm in the fight, too." And the way he slumps reminds me of the tension between him, Thomas, and Nadia. Maybe he has more to fight for than just a chance to work with my mom. But he hasn't said anything and it's basically none of my business, so . . .

"I have to get to class." I take my bag from him; he reluctantly releases it.

"Okay, not the one-two, but can I at least punch him? Once? I have class with him next period and I'm sure just walking in and decking him would get him to not only stop harassing you, but also stop him from asking me for the answers to all the worksheets."

My stomach rolls at the thought of seeing him after he pulled this stunt. "You have class with him?"

"Yeah, calculus—*not* with Mr. Gay. With Ms. Lynch."

I can't help the smile that creeps back onto my face.

"He never wants to put in the work," Patrick continues. "He's always joking about me getting him the answers from my dad, or trying to copy my work, and one time last year, he asked if we could be 'study buddies.' I think he just wants to come over to my house and make small talk with my dad. He's so weird."

"Wait. Trick."

He stops babbling with a smile. "Yes?"

I hesitate, on the edge of an idea that I may not be able to come back from . . . but I jump. "When's your next calculus test?"

Maybe I didn't know the rules, but I can certainly play his game.

It's almost four o'clock and Stevie is having a meltdown around the corner from the front office that has called the attention of the remaining staff and Principal Logan. One minute she's crying about a bad test grade and the next it's some distant, sick (fictional) relative. Even though we had all of detention to figure everything out, and ample inspiration from Principal Logan's speech on the code of conduct, we didn't get much of the plan actually planned; Stevie couldn't even make up her mind about what emergency to fake and decided to let her gut lead her dramatics.

Inside Principal Logan's office, Patrick types on the computer, hoping to find the upcoming calculus test answer key. He knows that Mr. Logan has access to a server that houses *all* the answer keys, but admits this is his first time ever trying to navigate it.

Once he does—if he does—I'm going to slip the key into Thomas's locker.

I think.

He has quite literally asked for it.

So what he does with it when he receives it is up to him.

My heart races as I keep watch at the door. I tell myself I'm really doing this, that he deserves it—I saw him tell someone who receives scholarship lunches today that they should get expired food—but it's likely I might chicken out and just shred the damn paper once it's been printed. This might all be too far, too risky, too much for a school election. I'm putting more than just my own fate at this school on the line here.

"Anyone coming?" Patrick asks, eyes on the screen.

"The title of your students-break-into-the-principal's-office porno?" I worry my lip between my teeth.

"That would be funny if not for—"

"I know. I'm nervous." I exhale slowly. "I'll obviously tell you if someone is coming."

"I've almost got it," he says in a calm voice. "Are you sure you want to do this? I still have no issue with punching him."

"That will just get you into trouble and then he'll look like an innocent victim again and go on to win this election and I'll spend every day wishing that I were the one who got to punch him." I peek outside the door, but the front office is still silent. "I'm just going to slip this into his locker. The rest is up to him."

He raises an eyebrow. "He's going to use it. Especially if you claim to have a promising hookup for more."

"Any chance your dad wouldn't punish him?"

He hits one final button with a flourish and the printer behind him kicks on, sputtering out the demise of my opponent. I hesitate to pick it up, so Patrick does.

"I guess we'll find out." He swivels back to the laptop. "What do you want this note to say?"

"'This is just a taste. A man like you has bigger things to stress about. Signed, Team Thom'?"

"Mysterious, but supportive. A guy like him won't question it at all." He types it and sends it to the printer next.

Before leaving the office, we take turns messing with each other's hair like we've just had the make-out of the century. I pinch Patrick's cheeks for good measure, to give them a nice blush; all he has to do is grin for me to be matching him. In the name of this being our cover-up story in case we're caught, he doesn't comment on how easily the red appears on my face.

He shuts the office lights off on our way out, but then I backtrack to flip the overhead light on—the way it was when we snuck in. Patrick folds the papers and slips them into his back pocket, clearly understanding that I'm not mentally or emotionally ready to handle them.

In the past, I've been quick to react on Connie's behalf, but this is a full-fledged plan of attack that I'm executing here. I prefer the former. It doesn't leave me with all this time to second-guess my actions and think of all the ways it could go wrong.

The quickest way to Thomas's locker takes us past Stevie's theatrics and the turned backs of several adults, including Principal Logan. I give her Oscar-worthy performance a quick thumbs-up and then hustle to Thomas's locker. Her fake cries echo in the empty halls.

"What about the security cameras?" I try my best not to search our surroundings and count how many have their eyes on us. That would look suspicious.

"What about them?"

"Won't they catch us putting this in his locker?" I freeze and suck in a breath. "Won't they catch us sneaking into your dad's office?"

Instantly, I feel so naive for thinking some messed-up hair saved me from suspicion. I am way too easily convinced to do things when Patrick's the one saying it'll be okay.

"The Void." He shrugs. "Should be fine."

"What about it?" I scurry forward to catch up with him. He hasn't missed a beat.

"The cameras don't always work because the power unit was installed in the Void. They haven't worked properly in years. My dad says the pretense of cameras is enough to keep people honest, so he doesn't get them fixed."

"What about the digital fingerprint?" I ask. "It'll say the answer key was last opened at the time we were leaving the offices, and if the cameras *do* happen to record us . . ."

He puts a hand on my back and gently pushes me forward. "This isn't my first time in espionage. I opened a whole bunch of documents and cleared the printer log. It'll look like a glitch or something."

We walk in silence for a moment. He's probably silently patting himself on the back and, meanwhile, I'm wondering if I'm going to get arrested for this.

"What sort of espionage are you used to?" I ask.

"Mostly just clearing my search history before letting my mom borrow any of my electronics, but it sounded like I knew what I was doing, right?"

I release a shaky little laugh. He squeezes my shoulder and lets his hand drop.

"Your dad knows the cameras don't work and won't get them fixed?" The question is quieter than I intend it to be. I almost feel bad this time for pointing out that his dad is the worst.

He sighs. "Yeah . . . Yes. I know." His eyes shift to mine. "An asshat."

"Is that why you're going this far to help me?" I readjust my bag over my shoulder, watching our steps sync up on the recently polished floor. "Like, *above and beyond*?"

"You win the election and I get a dream apprenticeship to prove to my parents that I'm not totally useless."

Guilt hits me instantly. I've made zero progress with the apprenticeship, but completely for lack of trying. I've been so absorbed in our charade and the campaign that I'm not thinking about anyone else.

"That wasn't the deal," I say through a forced laugh. I did not tell him to risk everything for me. I'm certainly not doing equal work on my side.

He links his arm through mine, and it feels entirely too normal, too good.

"All you have to do is help," I continue, "not secure my

victory. This could really come back and hurt both of us."

"You think it's worth it."

"How is it worth it to you, though?"

Please don't say the apprenticeship—but what else would *he say?*

He tilts his head to the side and cuts his eyes to me. "I get to occasionally kiss a beautiful girl."

I huff a laugh. *Of course.*

He pokes his finger into my cheek. "And make her blush by telling her things she should already know."

"I'm serious."

"I am, too. I just—I don't know. My dad pisses me off." He glances at me for just a moment, his eyes flitting away before I can properly read the emotion there. "I can't share things I'm excited about with him because he just thinks I'm trying to scam him into wasting money on something I'll give up. And he won't even consider helping to pay for culinary school because he thinks it's another one of those things."

"Well, not everyone has that luxury to begin with. There are scholarships and student loans—"

"Yeah, I know," he says gently. We turn down Senior Hallway A. "It's just that he'll support me in a loving, fatherly way and pay for half my schooling if I go into something practical. Something like dentistry or—"

"Accounting." I stop next to Thomas's locker, not looking at it like it knows what I plan and is judging me for it. "I think that's what I'm doing."

He scrunches his face up. "Accounting? What, why?"

"Like you said. It's practical. It's steady. Stable."

"That's boring. You're not a boring person."

"Some people find numbers fascinating!"

"Yeah, sure, but you're not one of them. The other day, you refused to do the mental math to figure out if you could afford another ice cream cone at lunch. You hate math and money. You like art."

I'm hit with the sudden realization that despite us only knowing each other a few weeks, Patrick really *knows* me in a way I haven't allowed others to. He's the friend I've been craving all this time, someone I don't have to care for ahead of myself. Up until now, I've had to do the right thing for Connie, and my parents, and I hadn't considered being selfish and picking something that would be . . . just for me. I've seen my mom and dad struggle with money throughout my life because of the paths they chose, and doing something practical—even though graphic design feels more practical by the day—feels infinitely safer and more beneficial to everyone in my family. Accounting feels sturdy, timeless. Of course Patrick is right, I hate math and money. But it's a factual thing that I can turn off when I clock out. I can still do something else, something creative, in my free time.

Patrick frees the papers from his back pocket and hands them to me. When I take them, they're warm, like a warning, like something with a beating heart and an intent to kill.

Patrick takes a step back. "There's no going back from this once it's done."

"Technically, there is." The second part of the plan is to report him anonymously. I could just not do that.

If I don't, though, then he's just getting a free pass to cheat, because of me.

My phone vibrates in my bag and when I dig it out, there's a message from Connie on the screen.

I saw Stevie's close friends story. Thomas is a shithead, she says. I was there, it was his idea! I'm writing him into my next chapter just so I can kill him off.

I take a moment to picture what the rest of the school year will look like without having to worry about him making some ridiculous rule that results in miserable students—like the one his brother implemented last year that made it against the dress code for students to wear sneakers with their uniforms. Hypothetically, Connie is happy. Kids aren't bumping into each other in the hallways, and if they do, it's because they're friends. Thomas is practically scenery in this fantasy. He sticks with his clones, and occasionally they might try to stir up trouble, but I put a stop to it with a firm, golden fist. When his discussions with the counselor don't go well or result in improved behavior, detention. When that doesn't work, suspension. I imagine I could have him expelled by the end of the year if he really deserved it.

If this doesn't get him taken care of, at least.

The only real goal I'm aiming for is getting him removed from the running. Tit for tat, or whatever. You can't be student council president with cheating on your record—it is very clearly stated in the fine print. I also can't exceed ten detentions, even once I've secured the presidency, so I have to be squeaky freaking clean . . . after this.

I quickly text Connie back that I'm excited to read, and just that small moment of distraction leaves me vulnerable.

Somewhere nearby, footsteps echo throughout the hall.

"Do it now," Patrick whispers frantically, trying to help me jam the papers inside the locker.

Together, we manage just as someone rounds the corner. Patrick slams me against the locker, his lips latching onto mine. We're both so nervous that we don't even move. One long, lingering kiss.

"Wow, is this show for me? It's a bit hetero for my usual taste, but okay."

When I open my eyes, Stevie stands next to us with mascara streaked down her cheeks. She had applied extra before we parted ways.

Patrick breaks away from me, standing tall. "I resent that. That's bisexual erasure and I won't stand for it."

"Oh, come *on*," Stevie groans. "The one time my gaydar didn't work. I almost always assume everyone is gay until proven guilty."

"And how has that been going for you?" I ask.

"I am disappointed a lot," she says without missing a beat. She sighs. "So, did it work? Did you get it?"

"Oh. Yeah." I point at Thomas's locker. "All that's left is the anonymous tip."

"I was thinking about that," she says, starting our walk toward the nearest exit. "Thomas is like the leader of your dad's standom, right?"

Patrick nods. "Yes, as far as he's concerned, my dad invented oxygen."

"So, it's not a stretch to think that maybe your dad would . . . bury this for him?"

"I had that same worry," I admit quietly.

Patrick grimaces. "It's not exactly a one-way street between them. My dad has referred to Thomas as 'upstanding.'"

"No, it's cool." Stevie slips through the door Patrick opens for us. "I was thinking maybe I'd start the rumor around school that *someone* has been caught cheating, and then use a burner account to say who exactly has, allegedly, cheated."

"Okay." I nod to myself. I don't want Stevie to get in more trouble with her online persona, but this seems doable. "Okay, sure."

"That could work." Patrick pulls out his car keys. "If his name is out there for it, it's harder to brush under the rug."

"Exactly." Stevie clasps her hands together. "It'll be okay. This will work and then he'll be out of our hair."

I stop, caught between both of them as they start to separate toward their cars. They're doing so much for this, for me. I'm practically in the back seat. "Am I terrible?" I ask them.

They both whirl around, eyes wide.

"What? No." Stevie rushes toward me.

Patrick places his hands on my shoulders. "Not at all. Yesterday I saw him look at the garbage cans—*including the recycling bin*—and then put his plastic water bottle in a landfill. He's a terrible person, like, at his core."

"He's awful," Stevie says, crossing her arms. "I heard him refer to a sophomore girl as Most Likely to Get a Botched Nose Job."

"That's a new one," Patrick says, dropping his hands.

"You never hear him talking about how guys like him are Most Likely to Bully Them into a Botched Nose Job," Stevie mutters.

"He thinks being president means he'll have total control of the school and I could honestly see my dad letting him. He'd think he deserves it or something," Patrick adds. "A vote for Ella is a vote for change, and that scares them. It's why they're holding back election schedules, giving you detentions, and threatening you with *legal action*. They would rather see you removed than an option at the polls."

I stand there for a moment, taking in both their earnest expressions. This is for the betterment of our entire school, this is for Connie, and the only thing Thomas *deserves* is to get knocked down a peg.

"Okay. We finish this tomorrow."

Thirteen

The next morning, Stevie takes a video while walking from the parking lot to the school and, in it, she starts the rumor. She doesn't give it any more attention than any other topic she addresses in the minute-long TikTok so it doesn't come off as an obvious setup; in fact, she spends more time talking about and applying a new shade of lipstick that she was gifted by a brand. But it takes off once she uses the anonymous account she made to implicate Thomas in the comments. It's all anyone talks about in the halls. I've been jokingly asked my stance on cheating by several classmates. I sit on pins and needles, waiting for an announcement from the office or a tearful admission of guilt from Thomas during lunch, but . . . nothing.

Stevie says maybe we should have posted the video on Instagram Reels so the teachers would see it.

That night, after no movement on the school's side, Stevie, Patrick, and I FaceTime to create another plan of action: Patrick will plant the itchy idea of a senior cheating under Principal

Logan's watch at dinner when his apparently attentive mom will ask him about his day at school. He'll lean into the rumor, really juice it up. The three of us are certain that if Principal Logan hears of cheating, it'll drive him mad. If he doesn't know that it's Thomas at first, he may even be enraged enough to actually pursue the culprit. Then, when he does, *bam!* He finds out it was Thomas and he can't try to shove it under the rug.

It will go so smoothly that it will feel like it was part of the plan all along.

The next day starts with Patrick informing Stevie and me that there will be locker inspections of all Ms. Lynch's students to address the rumors of cheating, but these inspections will not be announced and the students will not be informed. There is a zero-tolerance policy for cheating at Courtland Academy, and that apparently gives the administration the right to invade students' privacy.

I spend all morning holding my breath and jiggling my feet, waiting for word that something was found in Thomas's possession. My hand cramps from trying to massage away a migraine at the stress.

At lunch, Thomas is suddenly and discreetly escorted out of the cafeteria by Principal Logan and Ms. Lynch, and then I know we're successful. Thomas goes with as much dignity as possible, which isn't much considering he keeps saying, "I didn't even *use* the answer key yet."

Way to incriminate himself.

I fight to keep my expression neutral, like someone who's interested in gossip but trying to set a good example for the student body. Stevie tells me to wipe the smirk off my face, so I guess I'm not nailing it.

A few people crowd around our lunch table to ask if I know what happened, if I'm secretly behind it, and I keep up the act of innocence. I nearly feel bad for what I've done, but then I remember that Thomas is trash, he had two days to rid himself of the answer key, and no one forced him to basically admit he was *going* to use it in front of the entire senior class. I guess when you're so used to the world handing you things, you wouldn't question being handed one more thing.

After last period, when everyone is traveling from their lockers to the parking lot, I spot an office aide pulling Thomas's uninspired campaign posters down from the wall. He hadn't put up many, but most of them were recently taped—or glued, I found out—over the top of mine. I stop her with a smile and offer to take care of the rest of them. I make sure they end up in the proper recycling bin as an act of defiance against Thomas. I feel free. With every poster I rip down, a piece of me loosens and floats into the air until I'm weightless.

That's what Stevie and Lila find me doing a few minutes after the halls turn silent. Stevie wraps her arms around me from behind and lifts me a few inches into the air.

"Hello, President Parker-Evans," Lila says with a grin. "Where's the First Man?"

"I'm not sure, actually."

I wish he were here right now to celebrate. I hadn't given it much thought, too thrilled with the outcome, but if I'm the only one running for student council president now, it's not like we need to carry on the charade much longer—just long enough that it doesn't look so obvious that it was all for show. I think I win now—like Thomas did at the end of last year—assuming no one else wants the job. A part of me is disappointed, but the other part of me is so damn relieved. I don't want to lie; I don't want to jab people where it hurts—even if they are deserving of it. This type of sabotage and dark thinking can be behind me. The election, winning, is in front of me.

"He didn't get caught, did he?" Lila asks, and the worry in her voice immediately carries over to me.

"No—I mean, I don't think so." I lock eyes with Stevie; she knows everything. "He didn't, right?"

She shrugs, a grimace on her face. "I haven't seen him."

I pull out my phone to text him but find several messages from him already waiting, some as recent as five minutes ago. So, not in trouble. I respond to his CONGRATS with a picture of the three of us ripping Thomas's poster.

Stevie pulls out her own phone. "We need to memorialize this, publicly."

She starts recording as I tear down another poster.

"Hey, Ella. What are you doing?" she asks in an overly rehearsed voice I've come to know as her TikTok voice.

"Tearing down these posters like I'm tearing down the patriarchy." For good measure, I rip the latest poster in half. I'm too proud and ecstatic to cringe at myself. "So satisfying."

"Is it true you're the only remaining candidate in the race for student council president at Courtland Academy?"

"Well, I'm not saying my opponent was disqualified for

cheating, but—" I pull the last poster off the wall. "I'm not *not* saying that."

"Great use of the English language there," a voice says, interrupting us. "Your teachers would be proud."

Principal Logan stands before us with a steaming cup of coffee in his hand and a sour look on his face. "No, go ahead. Don't let me stop you from celebrating your win *by default*. There's no other way it would have worked out in your favor, but I suppose you'll take what you can get."

Our mouths drop.

I'm about to say at least I'm not a cheater, but. Well. I'm not *not* a cheater.

So, instead, I stand there and stare. At this adult insulting me. At this man with power over me who is choosing to abuse it. I'm glad I've pissed him off this much. I hope Patrick relishes his dad's discomfort at the thought of working with me instead of Thomas. I will make this year hell for him and everyone who gets in my way if that's what I have to do.

"I know it was you," he says quietly, deadly.

I can't move, can't breathe. I say nothing. I do nothing. Stevie's good under pressure and she's used to putting on an act online, but I don't know how she's responding, and I can't even imagine how Lila's face must have crumpled. Her game face usually requires headgear.

"If you hadn't gotten my son involved, I would be doing something about this." He takes a step closer. "You are not sneaky. You are not innocent."

I clear my throat. My voice wavers when I say, "I didn't do

anything. It was Thomas. He admitted to it. We all heard him in the cafeteria."

Sure, I was involved with getting the answer key, but Thomas saw it, planned to use it—he *asked Patrick for answers*. I led that horse to water and he drank the lake dry. Is that really my fault?

"You think you're better than him. You're just a different kind of problem." He continues down the hall. We watch him retreat, my win draining from the three of us with a speed that gives us whiplash.

"I can't believe that just happened," Lila whispers after him. She watches until he turns down the hall and then whips around to us. "What a fucking prick."

"You really ruffled that chicken's feathers, Ella." Stevie's sagging face turns amused. "He's so threatened by you."

"Did you get that on camera?" I ask Stevie, noticing her phone still in her hand.

"Oh my god," she says, laughing. "I forgot I was recording." Undoubtedly something that happens a lot. She taps her screen and then plays back what she got. We crowd around her to hear and his words are clear as day.

"Don't do anything with that. Okay? Not yet." I stuff my last pile of Thomas's posters into the recycling bin and wipe my hands on my skirt. "We'll just keep it in our back pocket until—if—we need it."

"He's a trash bag," Lila says with a frown. "Why wouldn't we use it now?"

"We could get him fired for talking to us like that." Stevie

185

pockets her phone. "If they were making such a stink about the code of conduct when I posted that trivia video, surely the principal mouthing off to a student will tarnish the school's reputation further."

"Yeah, but it also threatens Patrick and me—and you, Stevie. You were involved, too. And he's Patrick's dad, remember?" Trying to get him fired was never part of the plan. Just removing Thomas from the running. "Patrick, who has helped us—me—more than anyone; no offense, Stevie."

She rolls her eyes. "Fine. I'll sit on it."

After that, I promise myself it'll be smooth sailing from here on out. I revert back to giddy the rest of the night, knowing the election coming up is secured. It doesn't even bother me when my mom insists on making Connie her favorite meal for dinner—chocolate chip funnel cake, which is *not* a meal—or when my dad ignores my closed door so he can give me my work schedule for next week. Nothing anyone does will annoy me now that I have victory in my sights.

After dinner, when I'm nursing some water to help my queasy stomach, Patrick FaceTimes me. Just Patrick.

I answer on the third ring, after running upstairs to my bedroom and making sure I don't look as atrocious as I feel. With the election in the bag, this might be a breakup call.

"Miss President," he says as greeting.

"First Dude." I squint at his background. I can't place it. "Where are you?"

"At home. Just finished having dinner with my parents and

we've got my dad *pissed*. It was amazing. He bitched about your 'grassroots campaign' for half the time it took him to eat his tandoori chicken and then my mom was like, that's your son's girlfriend, and made him stop."

A tingle shoots from one arm to my other at his casual reference to me as his girlfriend. Especially since he used present tense.

"I'm glad we could leave a mark." I settle down into my bed, holding my phone at an angle. "So, tell me, is he just a raging misogynist?"

"Guilty until proven innocent." He mirrors me, a gray pillow coming into view. "So, how are you celebrating?"

I think for too long and he cracks up.

"I didn't mean to put you on the spot. You can lie to me about the booze and drugs you have stashed off-camera. I won't judge you."

"Yes. So much booze and drugs. Definitely not celebrating by ironing my uniform so I look suited for the job tomorrow."

"To each their own. Me? A little light masturbation does the trick."

I can't help it; I snort. Loudly.

"How can you just say that?" I ask through laughter. "Don't your parents eavesdrop on you every time you're on the phone?" I'm sure mine would if they weren't already busy doing it to Connie.

"My room is soundproofed." He angles his phone at an amp and electric guitar. "Only took a week of practicing my chords for them to cave. I told them soundproofing was an investment in their sanity."

"Why did they go all in on your guitar playing just to tell you not to pursue it? You're actually good at it."

"They encouraged me to play at first, to help my ADHD, but I wasn't good in the beginning. Naturally. Enthusiastic, yes. But good? No. So then my parents were telling me I should consider something else, and I moved on. I still play, obviously, but I know there's no hope of a real career with it one day, so . . ."

"Shouldn't they have directed you to something less . . . loud?"

He grins, some of his hair falling into his eyes. "There's structure to music, but yeah, it can be loud. There's a routine to learning and practicing, though. It helped a lot. Turned me into a social butterfly instead of, like, a moth that keeps hitting the light over and over. I met a lot of friends through music."

"I can't imagine a time you weren't as put together as you are now."

"I can't believe you think I'm put together." He switches cameras to show me a massive dry-erase board hanging on his bedroom wall. It has a ton of things written like a list that I can't read. He flips the camera back. "My always growing to-do list would disagree."

"The fact that you have a to-do list is great. If I wasn't motivated by revenge and fear, I wouldn't remember to do most things."

"Fear?"

I shrug, but he can't see. "Just, like, Connie stuff."

"So, what's the deal with Connie?" He makes himself more comfortable on his bed, and the way I'm partially snuggled into my own bed makes me feel like we're in the same place. "I've noticed tension."

"I don't know. It's hard to explain to people who don't have younger siblings—you don't have younger siblings, right? You've never mentioned any."

"I do not. My parents had me and reconsidered the dream of the two-point-five kids real fast."

"Their loss. You could have started a family band."

"My dad could use the stick up his ass to play drums."

I snort. "Stop."

"That's cute," Patrick says with a smile. "I like when you snort." He imitates me.

"Stop."

"Fine. Back to Connie."

"I guess I've just grown up being told I had to be this and that for her. I had to babysit her, keep her out of trouble, be a good role model, all that. And then . . ." I inhale softly. "I let her down last year. I let my parents down. She got bullied pretty badly, and so we transferred to Courtland."

"I haven't gotten the vibes that you resent her for it, though."

"No. Of course not. I mean, I try not to. It's not her fault, and I chose to transfer with her. To be with her." I shrug.

"It's not your fault either, though."

"Logically, I know that. I know that there was nothing I could have done—we weren't even at the same school, but I don't like feeling powerless. My parents . . . they gave me a lot of authority over her and then I just couldn't *do* anything."

"I'm sorry I didn't ask sooner."

"It's okay. Why would you?"

He smiles, squinting. "Because we're friends?"

My face heats. "Yeah."

"Oh, come on," he laughs. "Even declarations of platonic friendship make you blush?"

"I'm not blushing. I'm ill. All this talk of feelings is making me sick."

He bites his lip. "Do you think you'll feel better by this weekend?"

"Probably; why?"

He sits up. "My parents are going to be out Saturday night and I was thinking of making you that meal. The best meal you'll ever have. Your future favorite meal that you'll compare to everything you'll ever eat again. And every time you even think about food, you'll think of it. And me."

Warmth settles in my stomach. That's not exactly an invite you'd give to someone you're fake dating and about to fake break up with because your charade has come to a neatly wrapped end. "Oh. Will other people be there?"

His mouth sags open for a moment. "Uh. Just you. And me."

"Oh. I guess that could be a good final hurrah for our relationship, huh?" I sit up straight, too. "We can post about it, a whole romantic meal—you could make a TikTok about preparing it. It would definitely make us look even more legit if we continue dating even though Thomas is out of the picture."

His confusion fades. "Yeah. I meant more like you'd come as my friend, though."

And there it is. Disappointment thuds in my stomach even though I shouldn't be disappointed. This is what I expected all along, what I *planned* for. This is what I can handle until there's a "president" in front of my name. Starting something real, something else, with him right now would be . . . too much. This is for the better.

"Oh. Sure. You more than upheld your end of the bargain." His next question will be if my mom can make it. I can feel it. We are transitioning into the final stages of this deal.

"No," he says, a wrinkle forming between his brows. "This is coming out weird. You're my friend, but you're still my fake girlfriend. Until the election's over. We're still going to shove you in everyone's faces until they like you as much as I do." By the end of his speech, I'm not convinced, but he is; he smiles so brightly I can see the hope in his eyes.

Still, relief makes my shoulders dip.

"Oh, okay. Yes. I'll be there, then." I pause, the anticipation that he'll still ask about my mom stopping me from showing too much excitement. I've tried to remain an unbiased party so far, someone who doesn't know if he's good or bad at cooking so it doesn't matter if I pitch the idea of one last apprenticeship to my mom and she turns it down because I have no genuine stakes in the outcome, but he wants me to try his food as a friend, as his fake girlfriend, and I won't pass this up no matter what position it puts me in. There may not be many more opportunities to say yes to something like this.

"Sweet," he says. "Like you."

I shake my head a little, unable to stop the smile forming on my face. His own grin grows slowly, eyes locked on me.

"I . . . look forward to . . . tasting it," I manage to say without outright laughing at the absurdity. And the . . . accidental innuendo.

He raises an eyebrow. "Is that so?"

"Yes." I instantly touch my exposed cheek, checking for warmth that *finally* has not come to tattle on my feelings. "I'm not even blushing this time!"

"Yeah, I'm proud of you." He looks away, putting on an obvious show of fake bashfulness: biting his lip, fluttering his eyelashes.

"What is it?"

"Oh, it's nothing," he says in a put-out, breezy voice.

"What is it, *Trick*?" I try again.

His cheeks redden. Maybe it's *not* for show. He's blushing, because of me. *I* made *him* blush.

"Don't call me that right now," he says quietly.

"But you want to make Trick happen, *Trick*." I relish how my words cause him to squirm, the screen blurring with his adjustments.

He pulls the camera closer. "It's even worse when you pretend you don't know what you're doing."

I narrow my eyes, trying to hold back a smirk. "What are you talking about?"

"Don't play coy. You're lying on your bed, *snorting* and blushing, and you're going to *taste* my food, and you're calling me Trick. I'm a mere mortal. My mind's going to dirty places right now, and don't pretend yours isn't."

I choke back a stunned laugh because, while Patrick has teased and taunted me about similar things before, it has never felt so . . . real. My blush returns with a vengeance, heat crawling up my neck. I can see it displayed back to me on my phone screen, blotchy and embarrassing.

"*No*, that is not my fault! Only you would list all of those things and convince yourself I'm flirting with you. Maybe you're just a little weirdo. No one else would like that stuff."

"You know I'm a little weirdo!" He laughs into the camera. "You know what you're doing, Ella!"

"I'm just talking with a friend." My eyes flit to the time in the corner of my phone screen. I deflate at the time displayed there. Just when things were maybe starting to get good. . . . "And I have to go, actually. It's getting late and I still have homework to do."

"You're saying all the right words." He narrows his eyes at me and lowers his voice, saying again, "You know what you're doing, Ella."

But does *he* know what he's doing to me? I gather all the confidence in my body and direct it into my words.

"*Good night*," I say in a singsong voice.

"Stop trying to get off the phone—"

I hang up, the screen frozen on both our laughing faces, and take a breath that feels like the first in several minutes. I drink in the fresh air blowing through my open window and let time cool my face. It's unfair he has that type of power over me when he's not even trying, but at least—maybe—I am starting to wield some power of my own over him.

The phone call might be over, the election may be called, but *we're* not over just yet. He's still with me.

Fourteen

About two hours before I'm supposed to head to Patrick's house for dinner, I start to panic. I don't know what to wear, I don't know how to act, and I'm suddenly terrified of being alone with him. What if his food is bad? What if it's *good*? What if I can't hide how much I think I like him?

I reach across my unmade bed and grab my phone, dialing Stevie's number without a second thought. I pace the room until she picks up.

"I'm off duty," she jokes as a greeting.

I stop moving. "I need your help."

"I'm on duty," she says instantly. I can hear how she perks up by just the tone of her voice. "What's up?"

Sure, I could tell Stevie my real dilemma—that I've caught feelings for Patrick like a bad cold and I'm spiraling—or I could frame this in a way where she can't refuse to help me.

"We need more content for socials," I say confidently. She's said it so many times before that I have the jargon memorized.

"We're running low, so we planned a fake date night and need your . . . creative direction."

"Cute, say less. Have you picked out your outfit yet?" she asks. I hear rustling on her end of the line. "Actually, never mind. I'll be at your house in like twenty minutes."

True to her word, Stevie shows up exactly twenty minutes later and walks me through outfit options and practically guides my hand when I do my makeup. We take a few solo photos in different outfits for me to "bank" and post at later dates—because I often "don't like getting dressed up," according to her. Since she almost exclusively sees me in my uniform, I'm not sure where she's getting this information (but it's annoyingly true). As the clock counts down to our departure time, she is fully convinced that she was invited by both Patrick and me, and not just me. That is, until we walk up to Patrick's two-story house and he opens the door, face falling when he sees her standing there.

He quickly recovers, but it's not fast enough. Stevie's brain mimics her phone, always capturing every moment to replay it on command.

"Hey," he says, breathless. He steps aside and lets us in.

"Hi," I say, hanging my bag up on the hooks by the door. He has a foyer. I didn't think those were real around this area. Most houses, you open the door and walk right into the living room.

"Hey," Stevie chimes in awkwardly. "Thanks for the invite," she says pointedly, eyes glued to me. "Would we be able to use your bathroom? Wash our hands?"

Patrick directs us to the half bath a few feet away and heads into the kitchen for finishing touches to what smells like a delicious meal. Stevie pulls me into the small bathroom and slides the door closed, caging me in, eyes wild.

"This is a date," she says.

"No it's not. You're here."

"It was a date before you invited me! Why did you invite me? The look on that poor boy's face . . ." To her credit, she does begin washing her hands in the seashell-shaped sink.

"It felt . . . weird. I don't know! I didn't want to get into my head too much about it and make it weird for him, because it's definitely not supposed to be weird. We're friends. He said so. I figured if you were here, it wouldn't be a wasted night—"

"Wasted night?" she hisses, soap foaming over her hands. "Do you *hear* yourself? The election is basically over. He probably wanted to celebrate with you, his friend, his *fake girlfriend who he probably wants to make his real girlfriend*."

"No. No." I get peer-pressured into washing my own hands, elbow battling for space with Stevie's. "He just wants to show off his cooking skills because part of our deal was that I'd hook him up with an apprenticeship with my mom, which may or may not exist anymore."

She rinses her hands clean. "Ruthless. He wants to show off his cooking skills to show off his cooking skills. To you. Only you."

My hands are still half-soapy when she barely dries hers and turns to the door. "I'm going to tell him that I'm just dropping you off—"

"*No.*" I follow her out the door, my hands dripping on the

real hardwood floors beneath our feet. "Stevie—"

"Everything okay?" Patrick asks, coming out of a room along the hallway. The dining room. I can see the sturdy table behind him, a dish of something steaming in the center.

"Yes," Stevie says with a pep in her step. "I was just dropping Ella off and now I'm on my way—"

"Oh." He furrows his brows and turns halfway to the dining room. "I set a plate."

"He set a plate! You can't go." I wipe my hands on my jeans before more water can fall. Now I have dark blue lint stuck to my fingers. "And you're my ride."

"Patrick has a car," Stevie says.

He looks to me and—is that hope in his eyes? "I do have a car."

"Stevie, you're staying," I say with more authority than I actually have. Who am I to say who can stay in Patrick's house? "We have work to do still."

She sighs quietly. "That does smell really good, Patrick. Is it okay if I stay?"

At least this time he tries to hide his frown. "Of course?"

"Your parents would be pretty mad if a hot thing like Patrick dropped you off at home tonight, wouldn't they?" she asks.

"Yes," I say, before turning to Patrick and adding, "Not that I'm calling you hot."

He bites his bottom lip, confusion sticking to every feature on his face.

"Not that you're *not* hot!" I add.

Stevie rolls her eyes and passes Patrick. "What did you make for dinner, honey?"

He watches me, concern reflected in his downturned mouth. I scurry after her, eager to get out of the spotlight of his eyes. Every glance he's given me has been a loud, obvious question of "What's Stevie doing here?" and I can't be held responsible to answer, because my answer will be that I was afraid of what this could be—and worse, what it probably wasn't, but I built it up in my head to be. I can't have this. I am *so* close to the presidency I can practically smell it.

Or maybe that's dinner.

"Eggplant Parmesan and homemade garlic bread. Mostly vegan."

Despite his clarification, my mouth starts watering as I take in the dish and the scent wafting from it. If I have one single guilty pleasure food, it's melted cheese—and this nondairy cheese is *actually* melted; a feat! When he said he was making me a meal, I assumed he would make something in the microwave, or chicken nuggets from McDonald's put on a fancy plate. I'm not exactly someone you spend hours cooking for.

"Okay, yeah, definitely not leaving," Stevie says, dropping into a seat at the head of the table. It forces Patrick and me to take the seats across from each other, but it's fine. Things are getting more normal by the second.

Until Patrick's foot brushes against mine and it feels like a shock of electricity racing through my limbs. He doesn't apologize, and why should he, but I look up expecting him to, and our eyes lock. . . . He's blushing again.

So much for normal.

Stevie begins serving herself without any inhibition and passes the dish to me. I copy her before offering it to Patrick.

"So," Stevie starts, biting into a slice of bread. "Oh my god. This is amaz— Ella, try the bread. Now."

She does not have to tell me twice. As soon as it hits my tongue, I'm transported into a food daze. That fast. It's warm, buttery, flaky, and the garlic is richer than what's on the store-bought bread.

"Holy shit," I say through a mouthful. I meet Patrick's eyes. "You made this? What part of this?"

He smiles. "All of it?"

"The bread? The garlic butter?" I thought I was bringing Stevie here to keep me from making a fool of myself, but I did not account for going over the deep end into Patrick's cooking and eating like a caveman. There is absolutely no saving me from myself.

Laughing, he says, "Yes, all of it."

"It's—" Stevie does a messy chef's kiss, her fingers coated in garlic butter. "Thank you. Oh my god."

"I'm glad you like it." He glances up from his plate and meets my gaze for a small second. He doesn't smile, but there's a new warmth in his eyes. "I'm glad you both like it."

"I was ready to talk business, but all I want to talk is bread," Stevie says. She reaches for another piece. "It's criminal. I haven't even gotten to the eggplant."

"It's not gluten-free. The bread. I think that was assumed, but I should probably put it out there in case." He looks between us, catching the tail end of both of us stuffing our faces. "Don't think it's a problem, though."

"Not at all," I mumble with my mouth full. "My mom likes

to swear they taste the same—gluten-free bread and bread-bread—but she's a liar. She's just trying to convince herself."

"I don't know," Patrick says, tearing his piece of bread in two. "I've had your mom's gluten-free bread and it was pretty good."

"Stop sucking up," I say offhandedly, wiping my mouth.

He smiles at me, and only me.

Maybe it's not totally hopeless to think that Patrick really wants me, that we can make this fake relationship into something real that doesn't also distract me from my presidency and Connie and my job and my future. Maybe . . .

He clears his throat after a moment, and straightens. "So. Business?"

"Yes." Stevie brushes her hands clean on a cloth napkin. "Now that Thomas is disqualified from the election, Ella is going to win—*but* I don't want it to be a lazy win."

"She still needs a minimum number of votes," Patrick says, cutting into his eggplant with a butter knife and fork. "It's not like we can just stop working now."

Despite knowing this—despite *understanding* this—it still feels a little offensive that he doesn't think I can manage the minimum number of votes to solidify my reign—I mean, my presidency.

"Yeah," Stevie says, nodding. "I think we should keep up what we've been doing—and maybe unofficially tap Tana for VP?"

"What do you mean?" I ask. "She's already in the running."

"Yeah, but we need to make sure people know you're

basically a package. Two peas in a pod. Allies. It brings her supporters to you and vice versa."

"Okay, that shouldn't be a problem." I say it instantly, because I don't even need to think about it. Tana is kind and caring and driven. We've already aligned ourselves "unofficially" by not being the three douchebags who had already won the election—Kat, too.

"I like Tana," Patrick says, twisting his fork so a picturesque pull of cheese wraps around the tines over and over again. My mom will want to work with him for this reason alone. He has mastered vegan cheese. "She listens when people talk."

I nod. "And obviously we're doing the same for Kat."

Stevie nods. "Assuming they don't just drop out of the election. I heard them talking about how their mom watches my TikToks."

"She has good taste, apparently," I say with a smile.

"Yeah. Kat refuses to see that reason. They're mortified."

I finally dig my fork into the massive, cheesy pile of eggplant on my plate. I pause with a forkful in front of me and sheepishly tap Patrick's foot with mine under the table. He looks up and I grin, taking a huge bite.

Wow. I've had eggplant before—not often, because my mom hates it, and I've thought she was justified in hating it—but never like this. What has often been a mushy, tasteless experience is a well-seasoned, perfectly textured bite. The eggplant is not hidden by the cheese or the sauce, but *highlighted* by it. How could Patrick's parents ever deny him this talent?

"Patrick." I blink a few times after I swallow, trying to

collect myself. "Patrick, this is amazing."

Stevie takes her own bite and exclaims something through a full mouth that we can't understand. She puts her thumb up instead.

The awkwardness from earlier is gone by now, and all of Patrick's hesitation is replaced by pride. The blush looks good on him. I could get used to it.

We run down the clock, eating every last bite of the food, talking about the next steps in the election, and taking photos and videos, before Patrick needs to clean up for his parents' arrival. Stevie and I ask to help, but he insists that he's okay to do it on his own—I'm not ready to leave just yet, even if it means I may run into my archnemesis. His salty words after Thomas was removed from the running still ring in my head, but they can't stop me from how I'm feeling about his son.

After carrying our dishes into the kitchen, which is top-notch and as updated as possible—probably a godsend for Patrick—Stevie leaves the room with a quiet thank-you and goodbye, but I linger.

He spots me over his shoulder as he starts methodically putting away spices. "Hey."

"Hey."

"Did you like it?"

"Yes. So much. Did you?"

"The food? Yes, similarly."

"Not the experience, though?" I can't look at him right now. I am ashamed of bringing Stevie to third-wheel, and if he's smart, he'll never let me live it down.

"It was . . . unexpected. But any time with you—and Stevie—is a good time." He closes the cabinet door, sealing away three shelves of spices in clearly marked glass containers. "Mostly with you."

I can't tell if my heart sinks or soars. I am so confused about what I want, what I need—what *he* wants. "Patrick . . ."

"It's okay."

"No."

I have no clue what I'll say or do, but I just know if I don't do or say *something*, I may perish. Stevie was right; this was a date. Just him and me. And it was hands-down the most romantic thing I've experienced, even if I ruined it myself by providing a chaperone.

Before I can think my way out of it, I lean up onto my tiptoes and press a kiss to his lips. My first *real* kiss, one that no one else gets to share in. When I pull away, breathless from my bravery—or stupidity—those lips tip into that smirk I love.

"There's no one around," he says quietly. He peeks over my head at the doorway, where Stevie disappeared. "Just us."

"I know." I kiss him again, pushing my right hand into the hair at the scruff of his neck while the other rests against his chest. He wraps me in his arms and returns my pressure, the soft intensity quickly turning into biting, needy kisses. I can't seem to touch him enough, be touched by him enough. Each of my limbs feels like there's a firework, or seven, exploding and flaring and dancing with life inside it. I am vibrating with how much I want him.

He moves us all the way across the room, until my back gently hits the counter. When I flinch, in surprise more than anything, he pulls back, just a hair.

"Are you okay?" he asks against my lips, forehead pressed to mine. "What are we doing?"

I blink a few times, trying to clear my head of the haze his lips have left me in. "I just wanted to tell you that it was amazing. You're amazing. I wish I hadn't brought Stevie like a security blanket. We could have been doing this the whole time. Between slices of bread, of course."

I can't keep pretending like I don't want him for myself, can't keep pretending that there is some unspoken, unseen clock counting down to when it will be appropriate to let me feel the things I've been feeling toward him, about him. I can have him *and* win the presidency.

"You could have led with that," he says.

"I got distracted."

He huffs out a laugh, his breath dancing against my nose. "I thought maybe you didn't feel the same way. I was going to cry myself to sleep tonight."

Feel the same way.

"No, don't do that."

"I might still. Tears of happiness." He places a gentle kiss on my cheek, partially on my lips. The act taunts me, reminds me of that first kiss that shook me to my core and made me question everything. Heat curls in my stomach now, and, surprising even myself, I pull him closer by the collar of his T-shirt, one of the ninety-nine SkaLa Land shirts. He leans in with an open-mouthed smile and closed eyes, ready.

"Don't act like you didn't see this coming," I say. He opens his eyes. "You've had me wrapped around your finger since you put yourself in detention with me."

"No, it's totally been the opposite—"

"Do you want to spend this time arguing, or do you want to make out? Because I want to make out with you while I still have the chance."

"Make out with me whenever. You'll always have a chance."

"No, I'm pretty sure now that you'll become a famous chef and travel the world and have anyone you want, you'll forget all about your fake high school girlfriend of a month."

"Fake High School Girlfriend would be a good song title." He groans. "If only the music career had taken off first." His expression grows serious, fonder, as I laugh. "I don't want just anyone, though," he says softly. "I want a girl who's met Obama."

"What a coincidence. I've met Obama."

"What a coincidence, indeed." He leans in for another kiss.

Stevie suddenly clears her throat, and we rip apart to see her stepping into the room with a hand over her eyes.

"I think Patrick's parents just pulled up," she says.

I apologize for distracting Patrick from cleaning. He assures me that it's fine, dropping a kiss on the back of my head as he ushers us outside. It's already so comfortable and natural that I nearly don't catalog it for replaying later, as if it's not a big deal when it very much *is*.

"I'll call you," he says.

"Can't wait," Stevie says with a wink.

I mouth "bye" to him as his parents exit their car. We offer stiff introductions that Principal Logan seems keen on hurrying through with his wife, and then get into Stevie's car. At the very least, Patrick's mom seemed nice. I understand where Patrick gets his looks now. She's a stunner.

We sit in Stevie's car for a moment, the night's breeze trickling in through her cracked windows, as she attempts to find her car keys in her bag.

"You better not have recorded—" I start.

"I was supposed to be there for content, though."

"Stevie!"

"I'm *joking*. I obviously didn't take any when you two were making out." She raises an eyebrow. "But I kind of wish I had, so I could shove it in your face that you were not only wrong about tonight, but that you're a little shit who has liked him all this time and still kept him at arm's length. Release that boy from his suffering; he likes you so much and I bet you're still going to be all professional like—" She adopts a monotone voice that is, apparently, supposed to be me. "'We are exchanging services.'"

I sigh.

"*Well? Do you* have feelings?"

I roll my eyes, to distract from my blush. "I'm only human."

Stevie squeals, kicking her feet. "So even though the internship thing can't happen, you're going to keep going through with all of this? *And* pursue a real relationship?"

Oh, shit. The apprenticeship.

Life was so great when I forgot all about it.

But now that I've had his food, and know his skills, I have to fight for him. Even if I know it's futile.

"Stevie, I don't know. I'll have to talk to him, and my mom . . ."

"You should." She turns her keys in the ignition. "Don't start a relationship on lies."

A sharp rap on the window makes us both scream. In the darkness, silhouetted by the porch light, Patrick stands with my bag in his hands. I roll down the window, my heart racing.

"You forgot this." He looks over his shoulder, like he's dreading going back inside. His whole energy has changed now.

"Thanks." I take it through the cracked window and offer a smile. "You're, like, my knight in shining armor." I cringe instantly. "Or, you know, a ska T-shirt. Whatever. You know what I meant. Pretend this never happened."

I try to laugh off my embarrassing fumble, but he just thrusts his thumb over his shoulder. "I have to go clean up."

"Bye, Patrick," Stevie and I say in charmed unison. We sound like two swoony little girls seeing their pop-star crush in person for the first time.

He fades away into his huge house to probably face repercussions caused by my presence—story of our relationship—but I can't help feeling completely unapologetic. I wouldn't take back what we said or did for anything.

Fifteen

Sadly, my ooey-gooey feelings don't last past Saturday night. In a strange turn of events, Patrick and I exchange fewer messages after our date than ever before. I text him, allowing myself to express some of my giddiness while thanking him again for the amazing meal, but not too much because I obviously want to play this whole thing casual and chill.

He doesn't respond.

Naturally, this leads me down the rabbit hole of checking on him online, because that's something people do, and something that I, apparently, do now.

Yes, he could be busy. He might not be online at all, which could mean he doesn't have his phone—I wouldn't put it past his dad to punish him for everything that's happened, and for having two girls over without his permission. But this search leads me to revisiting the girls and guys who live on his Instagram. They are all so beautiful, photogenic, and charming.

Worse, Nadia doesn't appear even once. He said she was a

friend—and it was heavily implied by Thomas's words that they had hooked up—but she's nowhere to be found. The sheer volume of photos with others that Patrick has posted makes me feel Nadia's absence as if it was a presence. She's so glaringly *not* there that it's suspicious, worrisome.

I type her name into the search and click the first account that comes up. Her profile picture is her surrounded on every side by cherry blossoms. The pink petals complement her makeup and deep brown skin—and before I can think any more kind thoughts about her, I flit down her page and find a *year's* worth of photos of her and Patrick.

They go past friendliness. There's homecoming. There's prom. There are weekend getaways with their families. There are group shots with other couples. They kiss. They hug. They hold hands. I scroll, scroll, scroll, and it's just Patrick and Nadia taunting me.

Patrick never told me that Thomas's girlfriend used to be *his* girlfriend. He quite intentionally did *not* tell me.

I wonder if he deleted her photos from his account before or after he asked me to be his fake girlfriend.

I try to keep my thoughts and feelings all organized inside my head and heart. I try to be mature and calm. Patrick has feelings for me now, in the present. He told me so. But when I gave in to the feelings I reciprocated with perhaps a few too many text messages . . . he ghosted me.

But, taking a big breath in as I walk into school, I keep in mind that I also hid something important from him: my mom said, before I ever agreed to this plan with him, that she is absolutely done with apprenticeships. Hopefully, we can both forgive and forget, and move on. There is so much more to come from our partnership, to happen between us, and I refuse to let jealousy and little white lies ruin it all. I can get over it for him.

I approach Patrick's locker, my nerves in my throat, and find it open, his slacks and shoes the only thing visible from behind it. Weirdly enough, he's ditched his worn shoes and replaced them with . . . not exactly boat shoes, but something equally as bulky and ugly.

"Wow," I say on my side of the locker door, "sweet kicks. Where'd you get 'em, Grandpa?"

Patrick's hand slams the locker door and—*oh*. It's all of him.

"You—" I falter at the sight, any bit of what I wanted to talk to him about flying from my brain: uniform on correctly, sans any kind of flair like enamel pins or buttons, tie looking so perfect it must be a clip-on, and, most important and devastating, his hair is cut short. "Have ears," I settle on.

He gives a pained half smile. "Thanks for noticing."

I soften my grimace into a matching half smile. "They're cute."

"I think so, too. Thought I'd show them off."

"Showing them off is indeed what you're doing." I want to ask *why*, though. I don't, and instead I focus on something less personal. "Is your tie actually tied?"

"Who knew you didn't just double-knot it? Not me."

"What brought on the change? Halloween isn't for a month." I nudge him in the side, but he doesn't smile. Something's off.

Maybe he's just self-conscious about the haircut. Maybe he's dressing differently to distract people from it.

He pointedly avoids my eyes. "It just felt right. I've got to get to class."

Not a day has passed since we started dating—fake dating, at least—that he hasn't walked me to my first class, so I can tell something is definitely up. Now that we're whatever we supposedly are now, not that we've defined it yet, shouldn't he for sure be walking me to class? It has to be that he regrets what's happened. We went too far; we blurred too many fine lines. I can tell him it meant nothing if it means we can go back to being normal. Because *this*, this is not it.

Was there ever even a normal between us, though?

"Okay," I say instead. "I have to find Stevie anyway."

He shrugs his backpack onto his shoulder. "Yeah. Bye. I don't want to be late."

Since when? Since things got too real?

"Same." I decide to walk away from him before he can do it to me, confused tears welling up in my eyes.

I text Stevie that I need moral support and she meets me at my own locker. To her credit, she stops whatever text conversation she's having as soon as she sees the distress etched on my face. She even pockets her phone entirely.

"What's going on?" she asks quietly.

I glance around, not wanting anyone to hear about my fake relationship problems, which are very real today. Unless I'm overreacting . . . Stevie will tell me straight.

"He's being weird. He got a makeover and looks like a body

snatcher got to him or something."

"Maybe he's being weird because you're being weird about his new look." She narrows her eyes at me. "Like that time in seventh grade when I dyed my hair red and you froze up because you hated it but didn't want to lie to me."

"It was so patchy and bad." I roll my neck. "*Ugh*. I told him 'you have ears' like a dumbass."

"That's pretty bad."

"Yeah, he's probably just reacting to me being weird. You're right."

"Or maybe he's freaking out over you guys kissing."

"Why would you say that?" I hiss at her, dragging her closer to me. "I've been trying to avoid even thinking it. I'm freaking out. This was all supposed to be fake. For the campaign."

"Oh, please, Ella. This was never fake."

"So then why would you suggest he's freaking out?"

"Because now it's real and there's pressure! And because according to you there are still jobs to do—you have to get him a gig with your mom and he has to make sure his dad doesn't pull some stunt to get you disqualified now that his golden boy is out."

"You're not helping." I cross my arms and swallow hard. "And you never told me about Nadia."

She pauses, eyes reading something in mine. "Patrick didn't?"

"I figured that she was *maybe* a past hookup, but I didn't know they were practically married." I stare at her heavily. "No thanks to you."

"Or your boyfriend," she says with weight. "He didn't tell

you and this whole thing was his idea. It's probably the reason he wanted to fake-date you in the first place—make her jealous."

"No," I say, shaking my head. "No. If he wanted to make her jealous, he had plenty of other options that didn't involve an elaborate fake relationship."

"The other options wouldn't have humiliated his ex-girlfriend's new boyfriend."

"Stevie, stop. I wish you would have said something." I drop my arms and deflate. "I wish either of you would have said something. I feel stupid and used and—*crushed.*" I whisper the last word just as the warning bell rings. But Stevie can read my lips.

"I'm sorry." She rubs a hand down my arm. "I assumed he had told you, and I didn't bring it up myself because . . . I don't know. If he hadn't, it didn't feel like my business to say."

"And it's your business when you post all those videos online about drama at our school?"

She flinches away. "You said you love those videos."

"I'm sorry," I say. "I'm panicking. I'm sorry."

"I do approach those videos from a mostly unbiased position, you know. And I've used them to help you."

"I know. I've seen them."

"You clearly didn't see the one I did on Patrick and Nadia, then. Maybe now that you're in the know, you can give it a watch and get the details you're looking for."

I sigh. "I probably should."

She squeezes my shoulder in goodbye and leaves me spiraling at my locker.

★ ★ ★

I'm on my way to lunch when I pass by a guy with a stack of papers over his arm. I double-take when I process that it's Patrick. I don't know when I'll get used to the haircut.

"Hey," I say, voice shaking. "Got a minute to talk?"

He glances at me over his shoulder and pulls the printouts to his chest. "Not really."

"Okay. What about when you get to the lunchroom?" Unless he's not sitting with me. Did we break up? I was under the impression we would be *starting* to date now.

"Probably not." He steps to the side of the hall to let the last of the senior class file into the cafeteria. It's too easy to be the victim of a stampede in this place. "I'm . . . sorry about this morning," he says, the words nearly coming out of the corner of his mouth. Like he's trying to be quiet. Like he's ashamed of the words. He pushes back his hair, the part of it still long enough to get in his eyes, and sighs.

I start. "I feel like things are awkward between us since we—"

"It's not that." His tone is clipped.

"So, what's going on?"

He sucks in a long breath and releases it before answering. "I overheard you and Stevie talking in the car. About the apprenticeship that's not going to happen."

I immediately step closer. "What? I—"

"Don't lie more." All the joy that usually bounces in his words has worn off. He's tired. He's mad.

At no point when he was ghosting me this weekend did I think he heard our conversation. It seems like a major oversight,

215

but I guess I was distracted with *his* lie to me. "I'm sorry. I did plan on trying to get her to—"

"You didn't have to lie. We could have found some other thing for the deal. But you got my hopes up and you—you just didn't care like I cared. You're selfish. My work toward you getting the presidency was so important to you, up until the point where you had to return the favor."

"I mean . . ." I suck in a breath and let it out. "I mean, if we're going to talk about lying and the deal . . . why the hell didn't you mention Nadia?"

He drops the papers to the ground. They land with a huff next to his feet. I don't even know what they're for—maybe part of his punishment from his dad. He takes a steadying breath, the look in his eyes one of someone pivoting to excuses, lies, distraction.

I continue, "Your ex-girlfriend Nadia. The one dating Thomas. The double whammy of making her jealous and taking his presidency from him? That seems like something you should have mentioned. You were already getting the apprenticeship—*because I was going to win my mom over—and* upsetting your dad. What did I get out of this arrangement, really? I've still had to pull so much weight."

He leans in close, his voice low. "I could have been expelled for what we did with the calculus answer key."

"You didn't have to. You *encouraged* me. That was your choice, Patrick."

"Okay, sure." He reaches down to the stack of papers—*posters*—and shows me what he's hanging up. "Just like this is."

My heart stops at the words on the poster: WHO ARE YOU VOTING FOR? IT'S NOT A TRICK QUESTION. I can't understand what I'm looking at. It's obviously a picture of him with the words large and bold around him, but . . . what is it *exactly*?

"I thought we were friends. . . ." I don't make the conscious decision to say the words aloud. They're dragged out of me, a harsh, choked whisper.

"*I* thought we were friends. I thought we were—you could have just told me that the apprenticeship wasn't going to happen. You knew from the start it wasn't. You didn't need to distract me with . . ." He waves his hand in my direction, up and down. "All of that."

"I wasn't distracting you!" The thought that I was intentionally stringing him along is laughable. He's been the flirt from day one.

"Okay," he says heavily. He rolls his eyes in a way that genuinely seems like he was trying to hide it from me. "I believe you."

I laugh. I'm not sure what else to do. He's joking. He has to be joking. This is all one unfunny joke. How would he even get in the running this late?

"I figured if I'm not getting anything out of all my hard work for you, I might as well run for myself."

He's *joking*. He *has to be joking*. He told me he didn't want to be student council president. He made *me* run. He's helping *me*.

"We literally made plans for my campaign this past weekend."

"About that. I can't do that anymore." He shrugs. "You understand. Can't help my opposition."

My heart stutters in my chest and it feels like the oxygen has been pulled from my lungs. I thought I was getting my first boyfriend today, not having my presidency stolen out from under me by the guy who helped me win it in the first place.

"Patrick, you're talented. I'm sure my mother would have mentored you, or written a referral letter—something. You didn't even give me a chance—"

"This way is a guarantee, though."

"What? How?"

"If I win this stupid election, my dad is footing the bill for the first year of culinary school. I was his backup plan, apparently, if Thomas cracked under the pressure. He put my name on the list of candidates after you got the election reopened."

I feel like I've been slapped. We were going to change the school and now, with Thomas out of the picture, that fantasy was becoming a reality. The whole point of us fake dating was to win over the student population, but if Patrick is a candidate, no one will give me a second glance. And worst of all, his dad will have so much power over Patrick, and things will stay exactly the same as they are. Clearly, he can be bribed.

"It's not stupid to me," I say. "The election. It's important."

"Yeah, well, my dad finally supporting me is important, too."

"He's supporting you with strings attached."

"How is that any different from you?"

I blink, then shake my head in disbelief. Nothing changes.

I'm really seeing this, really hearing it. "I don't know how you can even believe that."

"It's just this small thing for him, but it's a huge one for me. How was I supposed to say no?"

"No."

He furrows his brow. "No what?"

"That's how you say no," I bite out.

"It's a little too late, isn't it? Saying no could have stopped this whole problem from happening in the first place." He straightens. "I'm sorry things had to go like this. Just take your loss in stride."

"*About that*," I say, mocking him. "I can't do that."

I turn on my heel, abandon any hopes of eating lunch because my stomach is in absolute knots, and make a beeline for—where? Where can I go to calm down from this total one-eighty Patrick has made? Was lying about an apprentice-ship opportunity *that* bad? He wasn't guaranteed it, anyway. Of course, lying is not great in general, but I was going to figure it out. I wasn't just using him. But *he* lied. He betrayed me.

"Heard the news, huh?" a smug voice asks.

I look up to find Thomas standing in the middle of the hallway. He is not who I want to see right now. I imagine I'm so angry that I could run right through him.

"What news?"

"About your boyfriend—or ex-boyfriend?" He bites his lip to hold in a laugh. "I'm actually pleasantly surprised by his tenacity."

"I'm not."

"You're not the first he's ditched so unceremoniously. You'll get over it. You'll find better. His last did." He smooths a wrinkle from his collared shirt.

I try to walk past him but he sidesteps to block my way. "Move," I grunt.

"Don't be so surprised it happened to you. It happened to all of them," he says sharply. "Everyone he shows any interest in is tossed to the side as soon as the next best thing comes along. When Nadia even breathed in my direction while she was with him, he threw her out like rotten leftovers and then rebounded with you as soon as you showed up. She never cheated, but he didn't believe her."

"Nadia clearly has poor taste, so . . . this is kind of a wasted conversation on me. Like every conversation you have with me." I step around him and continue to the school library—the thought of sitting in the cafeteria and holding it together right now makes me nauseous.

"I thought it was you, you know," he calls after me. His voice echoes in the empty hall. "I thought it was you who got me kicked out of the running."

I ignore him, my insides ice-cold. *Play it cool. Now is not the time to ruin everything with an admission of guilt.*

"You don't have the balls for that level of dirty work. Or the connections." He taps his temple. "The truth is adding up now, though."

"Is it? I'm not very good at math," I call over my shoulder, tense. "But then again, neither are you, apparently."

I ignore his attempts to rope me back into conversation by

walking away and trying to recite in my head as many items off the Ashes menu as I can remember. My stomach still in shambles but the thought of food on my mind, I buy a bag of pretzels from the closest vending machine before sneaking into the small school library and wait for my nerves to subside before quietly snacking on them. In a notebook, I begin scribbling a to-do list that ends up being only one action item long:

Keep doing what I'm doing.

But then I end up crumpling it into a ball and tossing it into the trash because, without Patrick, even that one thing feels impossible.

Sixteen

I'm in a mood the rest of the day, but I think I'm justified. I mean, I just broke up with my boyfriend—fake or not, it counts—because he lied to me (this is how I'm spinning it in my head). And on top of that, I found out I have a new opponent for student council after I was convinced I had the presidency in the bag. And worst, my friend, someone I perhaps naively trusted, betrayed that trust and made me feel like a fool.

So I'd say I'm warranted the attitude I can't seem to shake, no matter what Connie says.

"Del-a-waaaaare," she draws out now. I glance up from my broccoli fettuccine alfredo and raise an eyebrow. "Pass the Parm."

I slap my hand on top of it, hating this vegan grated cheese with a passion tonight. "What's the magic word?"

"Maybe if you were paying attention, you would have heard me ask the three times before. I did it ever so sweetly."

Brat.

I hand her the container, but I make her work for it a little, keeping it just out of her lazy reach. We used to do this to each other constantly when we were younger, along with that infuriating "I'm not touching you" game. The difference, though, is that we used to both be laughing.

"What's up, El?" Dad asks through chewing. "You're not very present."

"Bad day," I grunt.

"How bad can it really be?" Connie points her fork at me. "You have the hottest guy in school as your fake boyfriend *and* you're actually in love."

I freeze at her words. I can't come up with a single thing to say to refute that without breaking down into tears before my mom bursts in, having been watching us like a daytime soap opera. I don't even have a moment to fully process that Connie is slow on the uptake as usual. She must have missed all his campaign posters because she had her head in her laptop.

"Wait, wait. Fake boyfriend? Love?" My mom's eyes bounce between Connie and me.

"There is no fake boyfriend, and there definitely isn't any love." As if I could ever. I didn't even really *know* Patrick.

"What?" Connie asks quietly. "What do you mean?"

"We're done doing that." At this point, I'm not even sure we should have started. The fact that he could easily tell everyone he had won to my side that we were faking doesn't sit well with me. Not that he would need to. He'll win them all in this divorce.

"Done doing what?" Mom asks. "Someone tell us old people

what we're missing with the hip young ones."

"Why didn't we meet this mysterious boyfriend?" Dad sets down his silverware and clasps his hands, ready for the sex talk or, now, the ex talk, or something equally painful and embarrassing that will leave me with emotional scars.

My sister's mouth is open before mine, which means no matter what I say or how loud I say it, my parents will only be focused on her. "She and Patrick were dating to get votes for student council—"

"He's running for student council?"

"No," Connie says.

"Yes," I say, seething into my gluten-free pasta.

"*What?*" Connie asks. "No."

"*You're* running for student council?" Mom props her chin in her palm. "When did this happen?"

"Like the first day of school. They sent an email about it. We literally were working on posters for it at the restaurant," Connie says with an eye roll. "But she was dating Patrick—"

My dad pulls his phone out. "What's this Patrick's last name? I want to google him on Instagram."

"How about everyone shuts up?" I practically scream. I take a deep breath, surveying the startled glances surrounding me at the table. "We fake-dated to get votes. We're not doing that anymore. He's running for the same seat as me." I swallow and add, "Because his dad wants him to. End of story."

It feels better to add the caveat. It feels less like it was a personal attack, even though I know it certainly was. And after what Thomas said to me, it seems like something Patrick's used to doing. I was just hoping I wasn't part of the pack on this one.

Connie gapes at me. "But . . . not really?"

"Connie, what do you mean?" I ask, exasperated. I push my chair out from under the table. "Really."

"But . . ." She glances at my mom and dad, then levels her stare at me. Her voice is quieter this time, as if they won't hear what she has to say even though they're only a few feet away. "But you guys were gonna fall in love. That's how the trope works."

"This isn't a trope. This is real life."

"Ella," Mom says with a stern frown that looks out of place when she's addressing me. She's talking to me how she talks to Andrew or Taylor after they've made a mess. "Don't talk to your sister that way. Look at her." Her eyes flit to Connie, whose lips tremble and eyes blink fast. Like a child trying not to cry after being told she couldn't get a toy.

"It's not my fault she has unrealistic expectations of people." I stand.

"It's not unrealistic," Connie says, wiping her eyes roughly. "It's what happens, every time!"

"In *fiction*!" I want to pull my hair out. How is she not getting this? Who gave her the right to be upset about *my* breakup? "You're delusional if you thought that my fake relationship, just to get votes, was ever going to evolve into—into what? Love? You're naive and I'm tired of having to deal with it—"

"Delaware," Mom and Dad say at the same time. I'm honestly surprised it took them this long. I got out more of what I wanted to say than expected.

"Apologize to your sister," Mom says.

I whirl toward her. "I'm not sorry, though."

"Why is everyone breaking up?" Connie mumbles to herself. "First it was *Avenged*—"

"A fucking TV show?" I ignore Dad's protest at my language. "Get over it! You shouldn't have put all your shipping eggs in the Patrick and Ella basket, because I told you from the beginning that this ship wouldn't sail. I *told you*."

"Okay," Dad says suddenly, standing up. "That's enough. Let's go to your room."

Mom scoots close to Connie and places an arm around her shoulders.

I can't take this anymore. I'm either the daughter who's in charge of taking care of Connie or I'm the terrible, evil influence on her who entices her to the dark side or makes her cry. How can I be both to them? Why do they treat her like she's a child, but not me? I basically just admitted to getting into some fuckery that has seriously messed with my heart and all they care about are Connie's feelings.

"Why do you act like her feelings are more valid than mine?" I ask in a wobbly, low voice.

Dad stares at me, hands clenched over the back of his dining chair. "What are you talking about?"

"I just went through a breakup. You guys don't even care that I'm running for student council, *for Connie*. To make sure she'll be okay when I graduate. And instead of treating her like the almost-fifteen-year-old she is, you treat her like an infant and act like I've just kicked her or something. I'm tired of it."

I don't wait for the excuses. I know they'll come. They always do.

Your sister is sensitive. She's an optimist, like your mother. She puts her whole heart into things. She's impressionable. Connie needs extra care.

No. Not this time.

I storm to my bedroom without my dad needing to walk me up like a prisoner and slam the door shut.

Seventeen

I do my best to avoid Patrick like Connie avoids unfinished fics. The irony is not lost on me.

At school the next day, he catches me off guard a few times in the hallway, just walking by and ignoring me, and he even dares to approach my table at lunch to ask Stevie for notes, probably because he's going all in on this new Good Student persona, and because he wants to rattle me with his presence. To her credit, Stevie does not provide him said notes, at least not in front of me. I notice he's still wearing his uniform correctly, he doesn't dawdle in the halls, and I even witness him fist-bump Todd and Dean—undoubtedly at his dad's request. Patrick once told me they reminded him of negative Yelp reviews accidentally posted twice, so I know it wasn't his call to be friendly toward them. Everything feels futile knowing how much power and pull Principal Logan has.

But then I run into a traffic jam of fellow seniors between classes, taste the poor excuse for hastily made lunch, and nearly bowl someone over in my attempt to run to the girls' bathroom between classes.

No, it's not futile, and it's not pointless. I have to see my run the whole way through to the election.

Shortly after last period, a revised schedule of student council events ends up in my email inbox. The subject line has a suspicious amount of red flag junk buzzwords, which I think is intentional so that I might miss the email, and it indicates that my presence is still required at the upcoming car wash fundraiser for homecoming, and there will be an additional moment for remarks to accommodate Patrick having missed the debate. How . . . *accommodating.* If I had missed the debate, Principal Logan would not be scheduling a time for me to speak to the school and claiming it's only fair.

I arrive home from school with my heart in my throat and a migraine pounding behind my eyes. Stevie stops in, wanting to drag me to the mall for retail therapy after I text her the debate news, but even if I wanted to go, I couldn't. I'm stuck in our kitchen, being forced into helping my mom prep desserts for a book club event she agreed to cater for a friend.

"Ooh," Mom says, her hands punching some tough gluten-free dough, her eyes lighting up at the mention of shopping. "Maybe we should go."

"I don't recall Stevie inviting you," I say with a tight smile. If I'm being punished, so is she.

Stevie's brown eyes grow wide. I've learned she's a parent pleaser, and I've just declared war on her reputation with my parents.

"No, oh my god," Stevie says with a laugh. "Of course you're invited, Ms. Parker."

My mom's expression goes from polite to annoyed as soon as she turns back to me. "Thanks, Stevie, but I forgot we're punishing my daughter for her mouth. It doesn't seem she's learned her lesson yet."

I wish *I* were the one punching dough right now.

"You can feel free to stay, though," she says with a smile in Stevie's direction. "I can always use an extra pair of hands in the kitchen."

"Run," I warn Stevie.

Instead, she rolls up the sleeves of her cardigan and washes her hands. We begin a clumsy little dance in the kitchen: Stevie does whatever my mom asks and I clean up scraps, tools, and surfaces.

It's probably just how raw I'm feeling, but the way Stevie is wrapped around my mom's finger rubs me the wrong way. When my mom moves, she moves. When my mom laughs, she laughs. It's like having another Connie around, except this one insists on taking TikTok dance breaks . . . with my mom.

I feel like I'm watching it all happen from behind a cloudy, smog-filled bubble, but maybe that's the migraine talking.

"Brilliant idea," Stevie says, whirling around to face me. She holds a silicon spatula in her hand and batter threatens to drip off it with every movement.

"What is?"

"Weren't you—you weren't listening?" She frowns and then perks up when my mom comes to stand next to her. They're both on one side of the kitchen island, with me on the other. Alone. Stranded.

"Got a lot on my mind," I say, shrugging.

"Well, this could help!" Stevie finally puts the spatula down. "We'll bake snacks for—"

"I'm not trying to bribe people." I'm more determined than ever to win this the right way. The win will be all the sweeter.

"It's not bribery, Ella," my mom says. "It's using what you've got."

"Well, I don't got snacks. I can't make snacks. I don't bake or cook or want people to vote for me because of any of that. I want them to care about what I have to say and my plans to help the school."

The two of them pause, and then exchange a glance.

"If you don't think Patrick's using his dad's power to win . . ." Stevie worries her bottom lip. "This could get them to listen?"

"Oh yeah," my mom says in a cocky tone. "I call these brownies my Silencers. So chewy and good, you have to take a moment to shut up."

"Love that," Stevie says in awe. "Definitely the brownies, then."

"Are you even listening to me?" I ask.

"How about cupcakes?" Stevie asks my mom.

"I could make cupcake versions of my Have It Three Ways Cake—"

"No freaking way. Who would dare vote for Patrick then?"

I blink, watching this unfold without my approval. I shouldn't be fighting against my team, my family. Patrick steps out of line and everyone else in my life follows suit, even the people who didn't know him.

"Am I suddenly invisible? You can't hear me? Hello?" I wave my arms around and accidentally upend a bowl. Leftover batter shoots out and onto my school polo. I hadn't had the energy to change shirts. The symbolism is, pun intended, chef's kiss.

They don't care, though. My mom and Stevie are stuck in a brainstorm tunnel together, spiraling ideas back and forth into each other's face. Stevie pulls out her ancient phone and starts typing notes.

"We need to capitalize that you were on *Nailed It!* If that's okay with you, of course."

What about me.

What about if it's okay with *me*.

"Yeah, I had a blast doing that—between you and me," my mom says with a secretive smile, "they asked me to come back."

"Maybe we can hold a little rally with the cupcakes and you could announce—"

"*What about me?*" I basically roar toward their echo chamber. My shout must pierce the exterior because they both turn to me, stunned expressions on their faces.

"What do you mean?" Stevie asks. "This is *for* you."

"It might be for me, but it's not me. I don't like it, and you didn't ask my opinion, or even mention when I'd be speaking at this stupid little supposed rally."

Stevie blinks, obviously taken aback. But because my mom is here, she won't say anything. Her presence doesn't stop my mom, though.

"Delaware, what has gotten into you lately?" She uses the

clean back of her hand to push away an errant strand of hair.

"I feel like everyone has forgotten that *I'm* the one running. I don't want to suck up with sweets; Patrick won't need to cheat like that. I don't want to lean on my maybe-famous mother; Patrick—"

"—*will be using his dad.*" Stevie's wide eyes beg me to see her reasoning.

"I just want to remind everyone that this is me. I'm in charge." I cross my arms over my soiled shirt.

Stevie matches my pose. "And I'm your campaign manager."

"You were just supposed to help me with social media."

"I have, and more. I've done everything you've asked."

"This whole thing is so cute," my mom says quietly, mostly to herself. But I can hear it.

"It's not, Mom. It's serious." I throw the microfiber cloth I'd been cleaning with into the basket by the island.

"Sure, sure," she says quickly.

"You have to trust me, Ella. I know what I'm doing." Stevie offers a smile.

I want to ask her what makes her think she's qualified for this. Several thousands of followers and product placements do not equal a bid for student council. Maybe I just need some time to calm down. A moment of silence to process everything. To regroup and replan.

I exhale a deep, long breath and let go of the doubts clouding my vision. I have to get a grip on this runaway train or else Patrick gets what he wants—*Principal Logan* gets what he wants. A derailment.

"I'm sorry for yelling," I say, only meaning it to the extent of actually yelling—not apologizing for what I said when I yelled. My head is throbbing. "I have a migraine and I'm stressed."

"Period?" my mom asks sympathetically. "I can make you a chocolate shake with fruits and veggies."

"I think I just need to lie down."

"Okay." My mom turns to crack open the oven. The scent of chocolate wafts toward me. "I can bring you a brownie when they're done."

"And I'll help you clean up the rest of this," Stevie says. "Sorry, Ella. I was just excited about all the possibilities."

"Thanks." I grimace back. "Thank you. I appreciate all of your help."

I just don't feel very in control of this whole thing since Patrick switched sides, but I'm not sure I'm ready to admit it out loud.

She nods, a frown marring her pretty features. "We'll figure it out."

I excuse myself upstairs and stay there, because I don't hear Stevie leave for a while. The sounds of her and my mom chatting carry up to my room, but I can't distinguish any words. Finally, I hear the front door close and bury myself under the blankets. When my mom comes into my room, she sets a plate with a brownie on it and cup of almond milk down on my side table. She tries to talk to me, but I pretend to be sleeping.

"I'm sorry," she whispers. "I think I should have asked Stevie to leave so we could have one-on-one time. Just you and me."

It wasn't that. I just wanted to be heard.

She leaves me when I don't stir. I slide my hand, still

wrapped around my phone, out from under my pillow and keep scrolling.

But then I stop on a video Stevie posted of her dancing with my mom in the kitchen while they stirred batter. I'm seen scowling in the background, cleaning spray clenched in my hand like a murder weapon. Naturally, Stevie hashtagged the shit out of it for visibility, for herself. The views and likes are stacking up; the shares seem to multiple by the minute. I don't have it in me to start another battle with someone I trusted because they went behind my back to do something I obviously didn't want them to do. I don't even have the energy to roll my eyes.

But . . . I didn't tell her to not post content with my mom. It's up to me to make very clear boundaries as soon as I'm feeling more motivated. She can't know what I don't tell her.

Her caption reads: **cooking things up for this election with ella's mom. maybe if you vote the right way, we can get these daily in the cafeteria.**

The comments section mostly roots for me, which is the only nice thing I have to grasp at:

Vote for Ella!

Wait Ella's mom was on nailed it

She like makes really good food right?

W Ella

I knew I had a sweet tooth for Ella

I put my phone back under my pillow and exhale, like I could blow out everyone's thoughts and opinions. The only that matter right now are mine. I'm done letting Stevie—and obviously, Patrick—dictate the way I behave during this campaign.

I'm even done doing this for revenge against Thomas.

I'm doing this for me. My whole life I haven't felt seen or heard, and this election has made me realize it. I don't want to be a final approval on something. I don't want to be the last person considered. I don't want to be an afterthought. I want to be the one in charge. And I will be.

Eighteen

As if this school needs more sports equipment.

The administration could be repaving the cracked parking lot, adding ramps for wheelchairs, or investing in better lunch options. It could be doing a number of extremely useful things, in fact, but instead, it's holding a car wash for new sports equipment—new treadmills. The last time the football team's treadmills were replaced? Three years ago. Maybe if they ran on the track or field sometimes, they would last *four* years.

And maybe if they cared for the thousand-dollar machines, I wouldn't be sitting next to Patrick at our Countdown to Homecoming fundraiser on Saturday morning.

The fundraiser is technically held by the football team—they're washing cars (badly, I might add) in the school parking lot—but representatives from the student council are supposed to be present to handle the money and keep the show running smoothly alongside the coach. Since we don't technically have a student council firmly in place, we are a mishmash of parts today. Kat Simms is carrying around a lockbox and taking the funds every time someone pulls into the lot. Dean, who's running for the same position, didn't see the point in coming if Kat was already going to be here, and I couldn't leave Kat to handle this alone, nor could I let Patrick show up as the sole representative for president. The people cannot forget about me. Now more than ever, I need to be in their faces and on their minds.

I slide my sunglasses up my nose and sigh.

"Stop sighing and just spit it out," Patrick mumbles into his arms. His head is down on the table we're sitting at and he's been that way for a good thirty minutes. His neck probably hurts. If it doesn't now, it will later—with his new haircut, the skin on his neck is seeing the sunlight for the first time in who knows how long. I'm forecasting a sunburn. And if sunburn didn't cause cancer or whatever, I'd wish it upon him. It's the least he deserves for lying to me and then being mad that I lied less than him.

"I don't know what you're talking about." I cross my arms, leaning back in my school-provided, wobbly chair. Kat gives me a thumbs-up from across a truck bed, like the amount of money we raise is some kind of reflection on us as candidates. I return it.

Patrick comes out of his arm cocoon with fake shock written in his eyes. I think I hear his spine give a halfhearted crack. "She speaks!"

"Don't be so happy about it. You might not like what I have to say."

He raises an eyebrow. "I thought you didn't know what I was talking about?"

I sigh again.

"Come on, Ella." He scoots his chair closer to mine, so similar to that first day in detention that my heart aches. It's not fair that he's doing this to me. "We're here for four hours today."

"And they'd go by so much faster if you were silent, or gone." I pretend to dust something off my school skirt, which I rolled an extra two times at the waist today. It's hot, and that's the only reason why.

"*I'm* the one who should be mad here."

"Yes, well, finding out our fake relationship was a rebound to get back at your ex and Thomas in addition to an apprenticeship we agreed on leaves a bit of a sour taste on my tongue—kind of like your homemade tomato sauce." It's a lie. His sauce was sweet and perfectly acidic. "It's all feeling a bit unfair, and I guess we just have to accept it."

I turn toward him now, on a roll. "You know, if you had just told me, we could have worked with that. We could have been a team—but you hid it and tried to get more from me than I agreed to—and now . . . We—you know. Why—I don't want to talk."

"I didn't lie." He fluffs the back of his hair, getting some airflow in the early-morning humidity. "It's not like we disclosed our previous relationships and I hid that."

"You knew I had never been in a relationship before," I whisper, venom in my words. "And when we were talking about how we don't like Thomas, you never brought up the fact that he *stole your girlfriend*."

"He did *not*—"

"You accused her of cheating." I watch his expression turn

frantic and then glaze over into a semblance of control. "*Thomas* told me."

He faces forward, crossing his own arms. "If we're hitting each other where it hurts, when are you going to admit that you're doing this whole thing for *you* and not Connie?"

"Nice try. I've already come to that conclusion. I can run for president for multiple reasons. For example, I now want to win this thing just so *you* can't."

Kat drops the lockbox onto the table. "Special request from the black SUV over there." They point at a Ford parked away from the rest of the soapy, wet pack. "For Patrick."

"I'm not cleaning cars," he says without looking.

"That would be beneath him. I'll do it. I need to cool down anyway." The window on the SUV rolls down and *Nadia's* head leans out. "Actually, I think he's going to change his mind."

Patrick follows our gazes, pushing back in his seat and standing. I cannot believe this guy was kissing me the other day. I wonder if me falling for him was part of his plan to really sell our fake relationship. Clearly seeing us together had an effect on Nadia.

"I'm going to send her away," he says, as if he owes me an explanation.

"Why? Kat, go with him. Make sure he charges her the full amount, please." Or better yet— "No, wait, I'll go with him. You deserve a break, Kat."

I ask them to watch my iPad, which I tuck under my bag, and grab the lockbox before following Patrick. In the *sigh*-lence of earlier, I had been working on photos for Stevie's

Instagram—her thing this week is model-esque photos of her with neon designs overlaid. I actually really like how they've turned out so far. I'll probably do some for myself. My follower count has jumped an alarming amount since we started this account, and it's been fun incorporating art into my posts and seeing people's reactions.

"Hail to the chief," resident jock John Briar calls from the rims of a Mustang, saluting Patrick. He pauses. "Or whatever they say."

Patrick stalls a few feet from Nadia's car. "I'm not president yet."

"Oh, shit." He wipes his wet hands on his soaked Courtland Academy soccer T-shirt. He's on every sports team. "I thought you were president and she was VP." He wiggles his copper eyebrows. "Or your First Lady. Second Lady? Who are you with right now?"

Sunglasses are a marvelous invention. They make it so this asshole can't tell I'm glaring at him.

"We, uh, broke up," Patrick says awkwardly, eyes flitting from me to Nadia. Right. Because *that* was the thing to latch on to and run with.

"The election hasn't happened yet," I say. "It's next week. You can vote for me on Friday." My heart rate kicks up when I say it aloud. It's so close and Patrick has thrown a hundred wrenches into it. I deliver a sweet—but very cynical—smile that seems to go over John's head because he shoots me a confused grin.

"Oh right! Stevie Hernández said there will be cupcakes."

I grit my teeth. "Apparently."

He rises from his squat. "Red velvet?"

I force a smile. "Sure."

"With cream cheese icing?"

"Just for you." The smile hurts.

"You really should vote for her," Patrick adds with a kinder smile to him. He turns to me and whispers, "Idiots susceptible to bribery aren't really my demographic, so you can have him."

"And you can have Nadia—oh, wait. She's with Thomas." I push ahead of him, lockbox between my sweaty hands, and meet her at the window. "Hi, Nadia. I'm Ella. We met at Peter's party."

"Yeah," she says with a small smile. "I obviously know you. You left quite the memorable impression." Her cheeks bloom into a pink haze when she glances over my shoulder. I can tell by the steps against the loose gravel that Patrick has joined us. "Hi, Patrick."

"Hey," he says stiffly. "You need your car washed?"

"No. I was actually hoping to talk to you." Her brown eyes flit to mine and then up to his. "If that's okay."

"No worries," I say, my fake smile practically cemented into place at this point. I step back, into Patrick's chest by accident. "But from one ex to another, you can do better."

I glance up into Patrick's angry face.

"But can you? Do better?" he asks me quietly, his breath tickling my cheeks.

"Can't be hard to go up from here. At least it'll be real." I push past him, shoving the lockbox into his hands.

I try taking deep breaths on my way back to the table, but John cuts me off.

"Yo, Ellie."

"It's Ella."

He throws a thumb over his shoulder, where a few of the guys are hunched over the hose and a bucket. "We got a problem. The water stopped."

"Did it run out?" Mike Daniels asks, appearing from behind a truck.

I give in to my eye roll because they can't see it and step closer. "No."

"Well, we don't have water anymore."

John crosses his arms, taking the spot next to me. He has about a foot—maybe a foot and a half—on my height, and he's almost twice as thick as me. He's exactly what you think of when you hear the words "football player." "Maybe we should get Coach."

All of our gazes fall to Coach Finstock. He's been actively flirting with someone's mom for about an hour now and no one wants to be the one to interrupt him. He's been there, leaned against her Acura, so long that his elbow has probably left a dent. She doesn't seem to mind.

I grab the hose from one guy and follow it toward the source, looking for any kinks that would stall the flow. With each step, I fight the urge to glance at Patrick and Nadia. It's not an easy task. Definitely harder than finding the problem with the hose, which the guys, if they had given it a second of thought, would have discovered had come loose from the wall of the school.

Water flows freely and wildly out of the faucet. I turn the nozzle and reattach the hose. When I crank it back on, the guys cheer wildly behind me.

When I confirm the water is flowing out of the hose and filling the buckets, crisis averted, John sidles up to me again. "Thanks, Ellie. But, hey, we were wondering."

"Yes?" I hate how easily he gets my hopes up that he'll ask me a question, something about how I plan to change the school, how my vision is different from Patrick's. Or at least about other cupcake options.

"If we vote for you, what are the chances you ditch the power suit for your birthday suit?" The guys behind him start laughing.

I stand there in shock for a moment, a burst of cold adrenaline crashing into every limb despite the heat of the sunny morning. I had gotten so comfortable with Patrick on my arm that I forgot he was armor. My shield. From comments like this.

"You're not going to talk to me like that," I say in a shaky voice. I think about punching him. I think about not punching him. There's no way I could do any damage, and I couldn't get to all these guys before someone pulled me off, and not completing the set might cause me personal agony. "You're not going to talk *about* me like that, and you *are* going to vote for me on Friday."

John laughs. "Yeah, but like . . . no. Thomas says we should vote for Patrick since we can't vote for him—he'll make sure things stay the same, because of his dad and all, and he's chill. So, I'm going to vote for him. I'll still take a cupcake, though."

I step forward, my fists clenched. Violence isn't the answer. Violence isn't the answer. Do *not* punch him. Think of the election. Think of every reason why I need to win, why I'm even running.

To change things like this.

I fight back a primal scream and grunt out, "Red velvet with cream cheese is so fucking mundane, you misogynistic football for brains!"

I stalk back to the table and swipe my bag, Kat's heavy gaze tracking my movements. Somewhere behind me, Patrick shouts my name, but it's hard to hear over my blood boiling.

Nineteen

"Wait, I need my portable charger," Stevie says, throwing open her back door.

I stand next to the hood and keep a lookout while she pushes aside several half-opened packages of stuff she was sent to promote on her accounts. Even though I'm skeptical that a scavenger hunt is actually happening at the school tonight, I still don't want to be late. It could be a great opportunity to kick Patrick's ass and show my classmates who is the better choice for president, who knows the place better. Especially since we haven't spoken since the car wash.

The event was pitched to me today via mysterious handwritten note slipped onto my lunch table by some random walking past. I insisted Stevie come with me to document my win because Stevie Hernández doesn't miss shenanigans. She said she was already planning to be here.

"What do you need that for?" I ask as she continues to rifle through her items. A breeze picks up the slight chill in the air and it brushes against my uncovered legs. An essential part of psychological warfare against Patrick: showing some skin to maybe distract him. After school, I put on some short shorts, some knee-high socks, and an oversize sweater. Because it's cold. "We're going to be late. The invite said eight o'clock."

"Found it!" She flicks her head back and thrusts the device into the air. "I need it to film. You know my phone's shit. It'll die after a minute if I'm not pumping it full of juice while live streaming."

"Do you think this is really happening?" We walk arm in arm toward the back entrance, as specified by the invite. I freeze, dragging Stevie back a step. "You're *positive* it's not a setup?"

"No. It's not." She points to the broad glass vestibule. "Look, there's a light on inside."

"Yeah, it's probably a janitor. Not people here for a scavenger hunt."

"No, Ella. I did a lot of digging and asked all the nepo babies, and this used to be a real thing back when elections weren't just swearing in the one and only person in the running. It's real. Not a scam."

I take a deep breath and let her guide me inside. "Okay. Yeah. I'm just so close; I can't get kicked out of the running now."

It's eerie how silent and still the school is when it's not packed to the ceiling with students. There's no familiar soundtrack of chaos: lockers slamming, music playing off phones, teenagers tripping, stomping, and running. It even smells a little different, but that's probably because it's just been cleaned.

"Where are we supposed to go again?" I ask.

"The invite said the auditorium." Stevie plugs her phone into her charger. "Let's go before a ghost gets us."

"That's not funny," I say, picking up the pace. She giggles, trailing on my heels and poking my sides.

We make it to the auditorium without spotting anyone else—or vice versa—and it makes me wonder again if I'm being set up, if this is another thing Stevie will accidentally feed me to the wolves for, all in the name of content. It feels too easy. I'll probably walk into the room and be welcomed by Principal Logan and a cop, and all my dreams of allocating the pointless landscaping budget into better elective choices will fade away.

I take a deep breath and tug on the auditorium door. It swings wide to reveal a small group of our classmates seated near the stage. Surprisingly, Lila, Connie, and Sasha are front and center. I don't even know how Connie found out about this, or how she got here, which sends a tingle of panic down my spine, but she gives me a discreet thumbs-up when I walk down the side aisle to the stage, and some of my worry dissipates. She really *isn't* the only reason I'm doing this anymore, because she's okay. Because I can focus on me now.

At the front, Patrick stands a few feet away from Tana, Kat, Todd, and Dean, like he has no allegiance to any of them and, even though it's his own doing, my heart hurts at the thought of him being alone in all of this. He's popular, the clear winner, but he has no one. Tana, Kat, and I are not officially tied together on the voting ballot, but it's been made clear that we are working together and our visions align. Patrick's, unless they've changed with his appearance and attitude, do not mesh well with Todd and Dean, who were along for the Thomas Hayworth ride more than anything. I'm not sure they have their own opinions. They give off the vibes that they want to *be* on the council, but not *work* on the council.

Stevie takes a seat next to Lila, greeting her with a kiss. I'm about to break away to join the other candidates, my heart racing, when the door opens again. It's Nadia.

Stevie's gaze flicks from her to me. "Oh, so maybe I forgot to mention that."

I meet her panicked eyes and sigh, "*Stevie.* What?"

"I didn't want to distract you!" She lowers her voice. "Nadia and Thomas broke up."

My skin prickles, all too aware that with every step Nadia takes, the distance closes between her and Patrick, not just physically, but perhaps also emotionally. If they get back together again . . . I can't risk thinking about it more.

I watch as Nadia takes a seat among some of our classmates, her shoulders slouched forward as she tries to make herself smaller. When I shift my focus to Patrick, he's staring at me.

To Stevie, I ask, "And?"

"That's all. It's barely noteworthy. Nadia finally came to her senses."

"I heard that her dad is friends with Thomas's dad and that's the only reason they dated," Lila adds unhelpfully.

Great. So. She didn't even have feelings for Thomas and yet she abandoned Patrick? And now she's single and he's single— *no.* Focus.

Tana addresses the group. "Thanks for joining us tonight, everyone."

The door at the back of the room flies open, stealing everyone's attention again. Thomas strolls in with a smirk on his face.

"Sorry I'm late."

I cross my arms, standing next to Tana. "No you aren't."

He drops into an empty seat at the back of the theater, nowhere near anyone else. "You're right. When you look like me, and you *are* me, you deserve an entrance."

"That's not all you deserve," I mutter without looking at him. Stevie snorts to herself, her phone in hand and elbow propped up on the armrest between her and Lila's seats. She's begun to live stream.

"I thought we were friends now," Thomas says, sickly sweet. He smirks at me, then Patrick. "Since you've had a vacancy on your roster."

"I know that *you* think people are replaceable, but I don't. I'd rather be by myself than with you. I'm not that desperate, Thom-ass." I make my voice as sweet as I can muster in the moment. My nerves jangle about inside my stomach.

"Let's focus," Tana says, snapping. "We didn't spend all this time prepping to be shut down five minutes in."

My shoulders tense. I was so distracted at school, then at a shift at Ashes, that I didn't think to wonder who set this whole thing up, if Patrick or maybe even *Thomas* had a hand in it.

"First," Tana says, raising an index card so she can read from it, "for the sake of fairness, my name was pulled out of a hat by the freshmen to deliver the rules."

I instantly relax. Rules, I can get behind. I like structure, and things with restrictions and instructions can't be part of a conspiracy to remove me from the running.

She starts reciting them. "Rule one: We must all be very quiet. Despite this time-honored tradition, we are not supposed to be here."

I listen to Tana, but my focus is on Stevie's phone. Shit. She shouldn't be recording. Trivia was after-hours, off-campus, and we still got in trouble. This will definitely get us in trouble, and even though she's live streaming, someone could be screen-recording. Even if she gets Patrick's face and his cooperation in frame, there are ways for Principal Logan to swing this so it's only my fault. I gesture to Stevie to put her phone down, but she's too glued to the screen to see my movement.

"Rule two," Tana continues. "No one is allowed to help the candidates. We have to figure this stuff out on our own, and though we're allowing live streaming for viewers at home, we cannot mine the comments for clues or receive assistance from anyone in person. Candidates can help other candidates, but, like, why would we actually do that?"

The list goes on:

Rule three: Don't get caught by janitorial staff or whoever else might be in the building.

Rule three and a half: Don't rat everyone else out if you *do* get caught.

"The potential presidents, vice presidents, and secretary/treasurers will be given different clues to ensure we don't run into any case of someone following hot on the heels of someone else and then usurping the win last-minute like a blue shell in *Mario Kart*."

"Um," I interject. "Where did these clues come from?"

Tana nearly laughs. "Don't worry. An impartial set of judges put them together." To me, she leans in and whispers, "Freshmen. Very eager."

I nod, though I'm not feeling any more confident from her answer.

In a louder voice, she announces, "We tapped freshmen from Ms. Peters's creative writing class to come up with the clues to avoid any favoritism or hints."

I nearly snort. I wonder if it was Connie's class. It would explain why she's here of all people, but it doesn't exactly make me any more confident about unbiased clue creation.

Tana hands one folded paper to Patrick, then one to me. "We're going to go in waves to reduce the chance of getting caught. First the presidents, then the VPs, then secretary/treasurers. When I say go, Ella and Patrick can check out the clues and get a move on. The first one to return here with the correct item is the winner."

"What do we win?" Patrick asks, twisting his paper in his hands.

"You get a pat on the back," Tana says with a shrug. "Now, show us why we should vote for you. Go!"

I unfold my paper so quickly it tears at the corner. *What you seek is what you'll get at the end of the year. Where you seek is where a lot of us fear.*

Rhyming, unhelpful clues.

Despite having no idea where to go yet, I take off out of the auditorium, with Stevie, Lila, Connie, and Sasha hot on my heels. Patrick frowns at his clue and then runs toward the side exit, a few other people following him. I have no reason to believe they won't help him—or that he doesn't already know the answer—but I'm going to follow the rules. As soon as Stevie opens her mouth, I hold up a hand and shush her.

"No help. Be quiet."

"But—"

"Nope."

Stevie angles her phone's camera at her face for one sad, pouty moment and then faces it back to me.

"Don't live stream," I say.

"What? Why? That's why I'm here."

"We can't chance someone in the comments helping, or Principal Logan seeing."

She rolls her eyes. "I'm literally here to live stream. Were you even listening to Tana?"

I realize now that this is part of the hunt, and not just Stevie doing her duties as my friend and campaign manager. I glance over her shoulder like I might see a crew of people with cameras following Patrick. "Well, who's streaming Patrick?"

"Some junior with fewer followers than me." She points the camera back at herself again. "Sorry, no offense; it's just facts."

"I set up the projector in the auditorium with both of their feeds so people in there could watch," Sasha adds with a smile. "And yet the tech club is still mysteriously *full* with only three members and won't let me join."

"Is everyone here for a reason?" I ask, glancing between Lila and Connie.

"Kind of," Lila says with a shrug. "I'm the influencer's assistant."

"And you?" I ask Connie.

"I got to come up with one of the VP riddles!" She looks so proud, but I'm crushed. I had no idea.

"That's awesome." I try to shake off my nerves. "Okay. I'm going to say what my riddle is, but I don't want any input or hints, okay?" I read the clues to the camera. "I think I'm looking for . . . I don't know." My heart stutters in my chest. "What do I get at the end of the year?"

My first thought is a kiss at midnight. But tied to the other clue, it doesn't make much sense. Plus, how would I bring a kiss back to the auditorium?

I blush from the first image that pops into my head.

"A calendar?" I ask myself aloud. Stevie pulls a face. "Don't help me!"

"I didn't!"

"Your face was so loud," I say.

"Be quiet," Connie reminds all of us in a whisper. Sasha and Lila both look different ways, checking that the hall is clear. Whatever Patrick's riddle said, it took him in the opposite direction.

"Let's hide somewhere so we don't get caught in the meantime," I say, navigating us to the closest classroom. It smells of artificial lemons and the floor tries to cling to my shoes with each step. "Things you get at the end of the year: midnight kisses, a new calendar, um. Or maybe I start with the where first. Where do students fear?"

I go to the whiteboard and use a dry-erase marker to start scribbling. I know I told them not to help me, but their silence is unnerving.

Detention—but the detention classroom changes; there isn't a designated one.

Guidance counselor's office—but the whole point of a guidance counselor is to put students at ease.

Metaphorical place of fear? Failure? Isolation? The cafeteria? Principal's office—

"Oh my god." I cap the marker and throw it back on the holder. "One of you erase that, please," I whisper-yell over my shoulder before running from the room with Stevie following.

I navigate through the halls to Mr. Logan's office. A place we fear: the principal's office.

Rounding a corner, I come to a sudden stop, Stevie slamming into my back, when I see the janitor mopping the floor between us and the administrative offices. I push her back behind the corner and mentally map out another way. If I'm lucky, Patrick hasn't figured out what he's looking for yet. I reroute us to the next-closest hallway and speed down the glossy floors. Only two turns stand between me and—a locked office.

I stall, catching my breath. Patrick and I hadn't needed a key when we used Mr. Logan's computer before because the door was already open. What had helped us in that situation was . . . tears.

My eyes flick to Stevie's. She worries her lips as Lila, Connie, and Sasha catch up to us. "I need one of you to punch me, hard."

"What?" Connie hisses with wide eyes. "No."

"I'll do it," Lila says with zero hesitation. She takes a step toward me and before I can say where or when, she launches her fist into my face. She narrowly misses my nose, hitting my eye. I fall back into the wall, gripping my face as Connie and Sasha rush forward to help me. Stevie watches the whole thing from behind her phone, riveted like it's not actually happening a few feet in front of her.

"Oh my god," Connie whispers, grabbing my arm and yanking my hand from my face. "What the hell?" She turns to Lila. "Why would you do that?"

"She said—"

"You don't just punch someone like that!" Sasha interjects. "In the *face*."

"Quiet," I mumble through my splitting headache. This works to my benefit. I didn't want a broken nose, but the force was still enough to make my eyes water. "Back to work. You guys can't be seen."

I use my sister and Sasha to thrust myself onto my feet and say into Stevie's camera, "I'm going in."

"Wait, take this with you. Put it in your pocket." Stevie places her battery in my one shorts pocket and her phone in the other, positioned just right so that the camera sticks up over the fabric.

Without another word, I head to the hallway outside the offices. My tears are already building in my eyes, and I think about how mad I've been lately and let go. I weep, my face throbbing with each jagged inhale.

The janitor stops mopping, removing an earbud. "Are you okay?" she asks.

When she turns to me, the keys on her belt loop jingle. The keys I need.

"Where'd you come from?" she asks quietly, reluctant to put her hand on my shoulder. But she does when I release a wild sob.

"I—I was in Mr. Logan's office earlier today and I forgot—I forgot my inhaler and—"

"Oh, Jesus," she says, rushing to find the right key. "Come on."

"My mom will—if I don't *die*—she'll kill me—they're so expensive."

"My daughter has an EpiPen. I get it." We head down the hall at a brisk pace, her mopping abandoned. Now I just have to figure out how I'm going to walk in there for an inhaler and walk out with . . . whatever I'm supposed to be getting. I haven't gotten there yet.

A thing we get at the end of the school year. In the principal's office.

It's not a calendar year. A school year.

We get a degree.

His degree.

Inside the annex of offices, we bypass the front desk and walk to the principal's office. She lets me in without a word and I fall to my knees searching for an imaginary inhaler. After a minute of fake sobbing and searching, I stand up and face her, eyes wide.

A lie will come in three . . . two . . . one . . .

Okay, zero . . . negative one.

"Not here?" she asks in a sympathetic tone. "Maybe it's in the nurses' office? If they found it—"

"Lost and found!" I take a step forward, my fingers locking in front of my stomach. "Is there a lost and found?"

"Yes, by the front desk." She moves out of the doorframe so I can follow her—most likely so she can lock up behind me—so I throw myself into the seat by the desk.

"I . . ." I inhale long and deep. "I need to sit for a moment. Thank you so much; you've been so nice. My mom is so mad."

"I'll go get it. You sit right there." She rushes toward the front of the office and I whip around the desk to pull the degree off the wall. I can't very well walk out of here with it, so I tuck it behind a potted plant outside the office and then pull out my phone. I join her near the front.

"Oh my god, I am so—you're going to hate me and think I'm dramatic." I exhale. "My friend says she has it."

The janitor sighs with relief, a smile on her face even as she's elbow-deep in other people's lost junk for me. "Good. Are you okay? Do you need to do some breathing exercises?"

"Honestly, I just think I need to get out of your hair. Thank you so much." I flee toward the hall and wait her out. When she finally leaves the grouping of offices to resume her mopping, I head back in and grab the degree. As I'm flying out, my heart racing, Stevie and the others appear from behind a turn.

They squeal as quietly as they can. It's hard not to join them. I hand off Stevie's phone and battery, and then I run toward the auditorium. I hope intentionally revealing myself but not getting into trouble doesn't count against me. I don't *think* I broke the rules. At least not any rules of the scavenger hunt. Courtland Academy rules . . . that's another thing.

On the way, I spot Tana inside one of the art rooms, a small group of people around her. She's riffling through a box full of bottled paint, occasionally pulling one free and then placing it back inside. She catches my eye, and hers are wide. I could stop and help her, but then I might lose to Patrick.

But I have my item—I think I do, at least—and isn't my whole platform about helping each other? Becoming a more connected school?

"Ella, what are you doing?" Stevie asks from behind her phone. "We have to go."

"Tana needs help."

"She'll manage. You have to beat Patrick."

"He might not have even found his item yet," I say, stepping into the art room. "Do you need help, Tana? I can help you, right?"

"Uh." She blinks, elbows deep in the box. "Yeah. If you're sure."

"It's not against the rules?"

"No. Not for you."

And maybe there's a reason we're allowed to help each other in this. Maybe we're *supposed* to.

"What are you looking for?"

"A bottle of wine." She pulls her arms free. "I've searched through two boxes already."

"Wine?"

She laughs, the first sign of relief since I said I would help her. "The color."

"Can we . . . make the color?"

For a second, we stare at each other. Then, like speaking some silent language that rides along our brain waves, we decide that we can.

I grab an empty bottle from next to the messy, paint-stained industrial sink while Tana frees red, black, and white paint. When I meet her back at the table, I quickly replace the red and black bottles with orange and a purple I find buried at the bottom of the box. Without even questioning my changes, we squirt and mix and force the combination into the bottle. Our audience is squirming in their silence and it makes me wonder what they know from checking the other live streams. Maybe Patrick or Todd already got their item and returned. If this detour leads to one or both of us losing, is it worth it?

I decide that it is.

Before I even return, before I even find Patrick standing empty-handed and defeated in front of the auditorium doors, I decide yes, it's worth it. Because not only am I celebrating my own win, but I helped Tana secure her win, and I can't think of anything, aside from maybe tracking down Kat and helping them win, that would so perfectly show what I stand for, what I have to offer this school, what I *want* for this school.

Patrick's shoulders sink at the sight of me, maybe in relief, maybe in regret. A part of me is happy he's still alone, no Nadia cheering him on, and the other part of me, the part that refuses to stop caring about him, is sad that I couldn't be the one cheering him on, that he wasn't with us while I removed his father's degree from the wall.

But he chose this.

Wearing a smirk probably better suited to his face than mine—especially with a bruising eye—I walk up to him, my growing confidence adding a sway to my hips. For a second, what might be concern flashes in his dark eyes, but then I'm tapping him on the chest with the corner of the degree. He tenses, recognizing it. I pass him without a word and enter the auditorium to applause. I refuse to make this easy for him.

Twenty

My eye may be bruised, but my ego isn't.

Walking into school the Tuesday before the election, I don't bother hiding my black eye—I wear it like a badge of honor, and my classmates treat it as such, especially as the day goes on and the word of my victory spreads. People imitate Lila punching me in slow motion as I pass through the halls, clap my back, ask if I kept Principal Logan's degree—the coolest thing is when they say I was a good person for helping Tana. It seems that everyone's seen the live, or the parts people screen-recorded and uploaded themselves—mostly Lila punching me—and, while I can't say everyone is voting for me, I think I've won back a ton of the votes I lost when Patrick betrayed me. For every person congratulating me, I extend an invite to come talk during lunch.

I basically strut through school, my tie loose in a way that I hope looks cool. It was a last-minute choice this morning and the first time I've worn this part of my uniform. I feel awkward but do my best to play it off as humble. Past Ella might have been afraid to be this confident in Courtland, especially after the rule breaking last night, but there's basically zero chance of any blowback because Principal Logan would definitely need to punish Patrick too this time. There are more fan edits of him rolling through the halls on a teacher's desk chair than anything I did—I think he had no idea how to solve the clue and decided to just be charming, *ugh*. Patrick is his dad's last chance, so the administration will stay quiet this time. I'm sure of it.

This morning, Connie, who told me after the scavenger hunt that she forgave me—*even though she had nothing to be mad at me for in the first place*—begged Dad to make chocolate chip waffles and bacon for us before school because she knows they're my favorite. She even explained the eye situation to my parents in the sort of excruciating detail and with dramatic descriptions that only a writer could come up with. She must have realized that they wouldn't believe me if I had said I didn't instigate some fight.

But.

Despite the wins.

I can't help but still focus on the loss I've suffered.

"Delaware?" Later in the day, my mom stops just outside the kitchen and takes in the scene: me hunched over the island with my phone in hand because I can't find my iPad, red sauce bubbling and spitting on the stove, smoke billowing from the oven, and the fire extinguisher an unhelpful foot away from my mess. Used towels and utensils cover every surface as thoroughly as flour coats my fingers.

"Yes?" I ask, distracted.

"What are you making?" Her question is full of caution. She steps closer the way one might approach a lion loose from its enclosure.

"Stupid freaking eggplant freaking Parmesan—but I don't have any real Parmesan so I'm looking for an alternative."

"And you burned the eggplant?" She cracks open the oven and more smoke pours out.

"I was just trying to dry it out a little!" The smoke detector starts whining at the same time as me.

She climbs onto the counter to hit the button and cease its yelling. "And what's the thing at the back of the oven?"

I check to see what she's referring to. A brick of charred blackness rests behind the pan of scorched eggplant, which might have been salvageable if it hadn't been soaking in the smoke from—

"My garlic bread." I forgot all about it. The multitasking is too much, and I'm sure my accidental five-minute spiral down the rabbit hole of Patrick's Stories wasn't helpful. He's posting highlights from his loss last night, spinning it so people forget *I* won. That's a move *we* would have done, together.

My mom rarely has time off from Ashes, so I feel bad for pulling her into my orbit, but also so grateful she's here without me having to beg her. No, I'm not often impressed with food, but I know, technically, she is skilled in the kitchen. She can help me.

"Okay," she says, clapping her hands together. "Okay."

This is her recalibration mode. I've been in the Ashes kitchen enough times to see it in action with Andrew and Taylor. She takes a second, gathers the troops, and makes a plan.

"What were you making this for? Should I call Pane Caldo and put an order in for pickup?"

"I was just craving it," I mumble, my stomach growling. "Never mind. It's stupid. I'm going to start cleaning up."

I remember the sauce when a particularly hot bit of it pops out of the pot and onto my arm. Maybe I will start with turning the heat off. Of everything.

"No, don't do that." She pauses when she sees the disaster I've made on the stove. "Or . . . yes. Just take that off the heat."

I do as instructed and eagerly await more directions. I'm feeling all drained out, like there isn't much left of me to give. I just wanted to eat something that made me feel good, but I messed it all up. I don't know what I was expecting; I'm not Mom, I'm not Connie. I'm not Patrick.

"Can I help you salvage this?" She places a lid over the sauce-pot. "Or do you want help cleaning up?"

I full-body sigh, crumpling onto the stool at the island. "I don't know."

"Do you want to talk?"

I tuck my head into my arms. "I don't know."

"Okay . . ."

A nagging little voice in my head reminds me that I want to be heard so desperately that I've been lashing out and yelling at people, so I shouldn't squander this opportunity!

Sitting up straight, I say, "I was trying to replicate a meal that a friend made."

It hurts to call him a friend. But he was a friend at that point.

At least, I thought he was. It's almost comical that, back then, I was confused if he was my friend or my boyfriend, and now I'm wondering if he was anything to me at all.

"A former friend," I amend.

"The guy," she says, nodding. "Connie says his name is Patrick?"

"Yeah. He made this—" I don't want to compliment him! His skills! His food! But . . . "He made this amazing eggplant Parmesan. Everything from scratch. He—he loves cooking. He was actually really, really annoyingly excited to find out you're my mom."

"Wow, what a nerd," she says, taking the seat next to me. "It won't taste like his, especially with the quality of our ingredients now, but I can help you make something. Connie is out with Sasha again, so it's just you and me for dinner anyway."

I watch her watch me for a second. "I would appreciate that."

She smiles, standing to grab her apron from the hook on the wall, and washes her hands. All without an order, without a please.

"I'm sorry for my outburst . . . s. All of them. I've been a little stressed lately, but that's not your fault."

She looks over her shoulder as she towels her hands dry. "No, *I'm* sorry. It kind of was my fault. I was putting too much pressure on you to be this perfect role model for your sister—I hope that's not actually why you're running for student council."

"Yeah, you kind of suck."

Her laugh is a welcome sound, but she leaves space for me to answer the question.

"I thought Connie was the reason at first, but then I realized I wanted it—I want to be student council president. I could really make a difference."

"Want to talk about everything? It's really cool that you're into student government. I wouldn't have thought that would be your thing." She pulls the burnt crisp of my garlic bread from the oven and dumps it straight into the trash.

"Why not?"

She frowns. "Why not what?"

"Why wouldn't it be my thing?"

Her laugh is a huff of air. "You don't like public speaking, to start."

"True."

"And you just—you seem—I don't know." Watching her fail at coming up with words to describe me is like a paring knife to the heart. She wouldn't struggle with Connie. She finishes, more confidently, "You take instructions really well."

"But . . . I don't give them well?"

"No, of course not. You're so good with Connie and at the restaurant."

"Then what?"

"You've always seemed *comfortable* that way. Following."

I bristle at the insinuation. "I'm not."

It surprises me how easily the words come out. I'm *not* comfortable taking orders. I want to come up with the plans, put them into action.

"I want to be heard," I say. "I want to be listened to. Not the other way around."

"Of course." She nods. "I don't want you to let it stress you, though."

"It all just kind of happened. And stress has been the result. Not the end goal." It's not my place to tell her what happened between Connie and Thomas that first day, and I'm not ready to tell her the lengths I went to in order to get him out of the running. I'm not proud. "I . . . I might have a shot, though. At winning. Maybe."

"Of course you do!"

"You have to say that because you're my mom and you don't want me to burn down your kitchen."

I follow her movements as she regards the eggplant. She takes the disks I made and cuts them into smaller pieces, throws them into a bowl with olive oil and salt, and shakes to coat them all.

"You got me there," she says to the bowl, laughing to herself. "There's a reason you're a waitress and not a cook."

"Hilarious. As if I even applied to be a waitress. I think I was conscripted."

"Guilty. I need you around!" She nudges her hip into mine playfully. "How about while we finish roasting this, we work on the sauce and cheese situation? Not all hope is lost. And since we don't have *any freaking Parmesan*," she says, copying my word choice from earlier, "let's go with mozzarella, then." She grabs a new bag of vegan shredded cheese from the refrigerator.

I nod and accept the bag. "What do I do with it, though?"

She holds back a laugh, no doubt used to Connie's quick thinking in the kitchen, and guides me through making roasted eggplant with marinara sauce and garlic mozzarella cheese dip.

When the pots are piled high in the sink and the smell of garlic overpowers the smell of smoke, we eat together in silence, just enjoying the results of the mess we made—and also delaying the process of cleaning up.

"So your friend made you some good eggplant Parmesan?" she asks with a full mouth.

"Yes. But this is really good, too." I dab my napkin at the corners of my mouth. "And you just came up with it on the spot."

"Don't sound so impressed," she says jokingly. "But seriously. Don't. I've had years of scraping together something out of my mistakes. It was a relief to do it for someone else instead."

"Even on your night off?"

"I was looking forward to ordering some Chinese and putting on a movie, but I doubt you would have stuck around if I did." She sets her fork down. "It's nice to have some time with you."

"We work together," I remind her.

"That doesn't count. It's not the same." She takes our empty plates and puts them into the dishwasher, so her eyes aren't on me when she continues. "I'm always busy in the kitchen with the guys, and you barely pop in to grab meals, *and* your work schedule is slashed to a third of the hours now because of school."

"Well, we *live* together."

"We're on such different schedules!" She turns to me, finally facing me. "Are we going to talk about the friend? The boy? Or are we avoiding the subject still?"

"Not much to say." Now it's my turn to hide—I start gathering all the utensils I dirtied and put them in the sink. I take a deep breath. "We joined forces so I could defeat the villain, only for me to be betrayed and find out I was working with the villain all along."

It sounded good, all dramatic like that. Connie would eat it up in anyone else's story.

"Except. We agreed to work together. He would help me get votes and in exchange for that . . . I promised to help him maybe get one of the apprenticeship roles at Ashes."

"The ones that are currently filled and exhausting me to my core so I swore I would never do them again many, *many* times?"

"Yes." I toss a rag toward the hamper and miss. "I promised him something that I couldn't give him, knowing I couldn't give it to him, and then he found out."

"Ella."

"*But*," I start with wide, mad eyes, "he conveniently didn't tell me that the guy we were trying to overthrow stole his girlfriend, so he had motive and he was getting more from a fake relationship than I was!"

"He was probably embarrassed."

"And I wasn't? I've never had a boyfriend before and I had to use him to get people to like me. I put it all on the line and he didn't tell me the one thing that would have changed . . . changed how I was . . . starting to feel about him." I bite my lip. "So now we're angry with each other because we both lied."

"Any chance that two lies cancel each other out?"

"They don't."

"Did you ask?"

"I didn't have to." I steel myself for the reaction I know is coming. "He's running for the seat he was supposed to help me win."

She braces herself against the counter. "*Oh.*"

I glance around at the kitchen. Despite us starting to clean up, it's still a—

"Mess. It's all a mess." I face her, leaning my hip against the counter.

"And I've been no help with any of it. I'm sorry."

"No, you're fine. Stevie ticked me off the other day, though. She was telling everyone that I'm going to have desserts available for anyone who can prove they voted for me on election day."

She mimics my position. "Yeah, before she left, we made plans, but I didn't think it was a problem. You know, I don't mind doing it. I'm sure Connie would gladly help us, too."

"That's not the point. I told her not to do that and she did anyway. How can I be heard as student council president when my friends don't even listen to me?"

My mom sighs. "I'm sorry, honey."

"It's fine. I'll figure it out." I stand straight. "After I clean the kitchen."

She grabs a clean rag for drying. "I'll start on dishes."

It takes twenty minutes, but the two of us get the kitchen back to its original spotless glory, all the dishes washed and drying in the rack. My mom even lights a candle to help mitigate the burnt smell somehow still lingering in the room.

As she's inviting me to watch some old rom-com with her, my phone starts vibrating in my back pocket. I raise my index finger toward her. "Hold, please."

I prepare to answer, assuming it's Stevie, but stop with my phone frozen in front of me. It's *Patrick*.

I glance at my mom in panic, but she's too busy scrolling through Netflix to notice. I quietly hustle up the stairs to my bedroom, holding the ringing phone out in front of me like a live grenade, and clear my throat. My heart pounds forcefully in my chest.

I answer the call with a slide of my thumb over the screen. "You've reached Delaware Parker-Evans, evolved human being who is too kind to decline your call. How can I be of service?"

"Oh, wow," Patrick says sarcastically. I hate that I can hear a smile on his lips. I hate that I know what that sounds like. "I wasn't prepared for this. What kind of services do you offer?"

"Nothing you can afford—wait, I guess you could with all of Daddy's money you're getting now."

Possibly a low blow, but also not *un*true.

There's a pause on the line as he sighs almost out of earshot of the phone.

"I have your iPad," he says suddenly, louder. "You left it at the car wash and I keep forgetting to give it to you."

"Bring it to school tomorrow." It's already been missing for days; what's one more?

"That's the thing. I just said. I keep forgetting to give it to you."

"How is that my problem?"

"How is this *my* problem? I should have just let someone steal it. I'm trying to be nice—"

"Okay, fine. I'll come get it right now." My mouth works before my mind can catch up. Going to Patrick's house for the first time after the date-not-date that ruined it all is a terrible idea. "Is this a trap?"

"What?"

"It feels like a trap."

"The only trap is me being trapped on the phone with you—"

I smash the end-call button, heart still hammering away, and immediately text Stevie for advice on what to wear. My casual clothes won't cut it, even if I am just going to Patrick's to pick up my iPad. Stevie says there's an implied dress code for everything, and I don't need a fashion faux pas on top of my other mistakes, even if it's just Patrick seeing me.

Especially if it's just Patrick seeing me.

Twenty-One

Patrick greets me at the front door, my iPad nowhere in sight. He sports a pair of gray sweatpants slung low on his hips and that SkaLa Land T-shirt haphazardly thrown over his torso. I hate that his outfit was thoughtless while mine was approved by Stevie *and* Lila.

"You did this on purpose," I mutter, pushing past him and into the foyer. My steps echo off the floors, and my eyes narrow as I take in the minimalist and, frankly, expensive styling the house exudes. I was much too nervous the first time around to really take in every detail. A school principal, even at a private school, wouldn't make this much money—and one with such bland fashion sense couldn't have participated in the decorating. I wonder what Patrick's mom does for a living; maybe she's an interior designer.

"Yeah, you got me. I made you flee the scene without a prized possession." He closes the door behind me. "My ADHD is also just a thing I made up to inconvenience you more."

I hadn't factored in his ADHD, to be honest. I just assumed

he was mad at me and being petty by making me come to get it.

I adjust my shorts, almost feeling overdressed in his presence. "I did not flee. I don't flee."

He waits a moment, like he's allowing me to think about all the times I have, in fact, fled. It just makes me madder, because he's right. I flee. When he kissed me; when he basically dismissed me and our fake relationship that morning after his makeover.

Not anymore.

"My iPad?" I cross my arms over my cardigan and wait for him to bring it to me. I will not ask for a tour of his nice house. I will not comment about how comfortable his bed probably looks and feels, or request a song for him to play on guitar. I will not flee and I will not back down.

"Straight to the point, huh? It's in my room—"

"And I'll wait here."

He blinks. "I wasn't inviting you—"

"Can you hurry up?" I cut in, to avoid him pointing out that I'm the one thinking inappropriately. He was never actually interested in me in that way. It was all to steal back Nadia's interest.

"My parents aren't home right now, but they could be back any minute."

My stomach lurches. "There goes your plan to try to seduce me to the dark side."

"Can't convince you to join something you're already the queen of." His socked feet march up the stairs and he disappears from my sight.

The longer Patrick is gone, the flightier I feel. All my

high-and-mighty talk of not fleeing and I am already inching toward the door. I do not want to small talk with the Logans. Having to be fake nice to them will make it harder to be real mean to their evil spawn and the human embodiment of a villain monologue that Mrs. Logan chose to marry.

I start pacing lightly around the foyer, my fingers twisting together in front of me. What is taking him so long to find my iPad? He knew I was coming over for it—*he* called *me*. And the fact that he could have lost it *at all* pisses me off. But I suppose that's his thing—not caring about others (or their belongings). And, yes, someone could make the argument that I also don't care about my belongings since I lost it and then didn't realize it for days, but this is about *Patrick*.

A cat meows. My body reacts before my mind does, turning toward the sound. I can't believe there's a cat here, mostly because it doesn't smell like a cat lives here. The house smells like Patrick—which I guess means that Patrick just smells like his house—all clean, fresh, and citrus. He never mentioned having a pet, and I don't recall seeing it when I was here before. I hate being reminded of all that I don't know about Patrick, even when it's something delightful like this ball of fluff.

I extend my fingers to the cat, a gray, short-haired tabby with dark stripes rolling down its back, and try to call it toward me. "Come here," I whisper. It eyes me from halfway inside a room maybe ten feet away before sliding itself against the door-frame and disappearing.

Listen here, cat. This is unacceptable. I shall be loved and you shall let me love you.

I tread gently past the half bathroom where Stevie and I had our whispered fight last time, and toward the room. Bookshelves stuffed with the "classics" line the walls, and paperwork threatening to teeter to the floor covers every inch of the large brown desk in the center. It's basically what I'd imagine Principal Logan's office to look like. Messy and cliché.

The cat sits atop the desk, staring at me with unblinking green eyes.

I know I shouldn't go in, but this cat has offended me and must make things right. I toe the threshold and take a deep breath before charging in—but cautiously; I don't want to scare the cat. It watches me approach before delivering one painfully slow and sweet blink. I offer my hand, letting it sniff me, before attempting to pet the side of its head. It leans into my touch and even if I don't win the presidency, I've won over this cat, which, in the moment, feels like the only thing that matters.

"What's your name?" I scratch softly at the back of the cat's ears and smile when it nuzzles into my palm. A red collar graces its neck, but there's only a tag with contact information dangling from it, no name engraved into the metal. "I hope Patrick lost my iPad so I can take you as collateral."

The cat gets really into my scratching and flops down on a massive pile of papers, toppling them just as I hear Patrick stomping down the stairs. I can*not* be caught red-handed snooping when I was *not* snooping, so I crouch down to gather the papers in whatever order they may have fallen in—I stop, my heart beating louder than Patrick's footsteps. He calls my name with a definite question mark at the end, but I can't move because the top paper is Principal Logan's contract renewal terms for Courtland Academy, as stated in the smudged black ink atop the paper. My eyes skim back and forth at lightning speed, barely capturing anything relevant to, well, anything, until . . .

. . . contract renewal finalized during the December 2024 Courtland Academy Board of Directors meeting, location to be announced, wherein the Board, including a Courtland Academy school representative, such as the school-elected Student Council President, shall be in attendance, to vote on passing the renewal and state any grievances or concerns . . .

I snap a few hundred messy pictures of the paper and slide my phone into my pocket just as Patrick enters the room.

"What are you doing in here?" he asks, suspicious. He holds my iPad to the side like he's already forgotten his main reason for seeking me out. His shirt looks less wrinkled than before—maybe he swapped for a different one. He said he had about a hundred to choose from. Not that he would care if he's unkempt in front of me. He probably can tell, and likes, that his appearance is flustering me.

I gather up the papers, trying to avoid direct eye contact. "Your cat knocked these papers over when I was petting it."

"Taters," Patrick groans, stooping to help me. He places the iPad carefully between us. "She's a menace."

Pausing, I finally look at him. "Taters?"

"Her name is Potato." He shuffles the papers together and places them on the desk.

I grab my iPad and stand, my heart still frantically beating. I push away the new information I've learned, an extra layer of potential betrayal, to play it all cool. "Potato."

"The most versatile and universally loved food, Potato." He shrugs, only a bit sheepish. "I named her when I was ten. Do you have a pet?"

"No, just Connie."

Patrick raises an eyebrow. "Want one?"

"If you're offering Potato, then yes."

He scoffs, but it's gentle, unserious. "I wouldn't even give her to someone I liked."

We walk slowly to the hall and I'm grateful for the casualness of it. He may be taking his time because he's comfortable in his own home, but I need to go slow so I can make every step steady or else the weight of my phone in my pocket and what it now holds will topple me. Does he know? Did he know all along? Is this another thing he kept from me? Is this another thing he used me for? I can see no greater way to grind his dad's gears than to date the one person who threatened to dismantle his reign over the school. I bet it gave him the upper hand in negotiations for culinary school.

My heart's already cracked, but if it wasn't, it would break right here and now. Campaign promises are so easily broken.

"My dad wants a dog, but my mom refuses to get a golden retriever." I swallow down my panic. *He's not suspicious.* I just have to make it a few more feet and then I can reread this contract. I can confirm my suspicions that his dad wants someone as student council president who he can pin under his thumb so his contract will get renewed. I would be much too opinionated and honest for his liking. And having his son or the leader of his one-person fan club in charge would be ideal to report to the Board about issues in school.

"You?" Patrick asks, pulling me from my distracted state.

"Me what?"

He raises an eyebrow. "You want a dog or a cat or . . . ?"

"Oh. I'm a cat person through and through. Potato's my people."

He nods and then stops, his hand on the doorknob. "Are you okay?"

"What? Why?"

"You're really pale, and acting weird." His hand drops. "Are you okay to drive?"

"I'm fine. Just happy to have my iPad back and be done with you, until it's time to shake your hand before your concession speech."

"I don't think it's going to happen quite like that."

"Fine, I'll shake your hand after the speech; it's not that big of a deal."

"Funny, but I meant that you're not getting rid of me that easily." He tilts his head to the side, considering, for a moment. He bites his lip, but I can still make out the beginnings of a smirk in the corner of his mouth. "Or that you'll have an acceptance speech, or a moment for anyone to have a concession speech. This is high school."

I roll my eyes, but catch him watching me. He reaches up, like he's about to push some hair back behind my ear—because Stevie *insisted* I wear it down and it's been nothing but a problem since I released it from its hair tie—but then he lets his hand fall. Disappointment thuds low in my stomach.

"Are you allergic to cats or something?" he asks. "You seriously don't look good right now."

Wow.

"No, this sickly reaction is all because of you. If we're done here?" I wait for him to open the door and my exit is flawless. Not fleeing. Not even a walk of shame, which, admittedly, I was worried about when I arrived here. Again, he is *very* attractive and all the improper thoughts were filling my head despite my anger, and it's possible that I imagined what would happen if I consensually jumped him, but no. No. This is a bustle of a girl who hustles, a girl who does not care if he's watching me leave or if he even thinks about me once I'm gone.

But no, that's a lie. I can't help it; I look back.

He's leaning against the doorframe, watching me with dark eyes. When they travel up to meet my gaze, he straightens and shuts the door quickly, having been caught like a deer in my headlights. I'm glad to know that my outfit worked as well on him as his did on me.

Twenty-Two

"We're sitting on a land mine here," Stevie says, zooming into the contract on my phone screen. She hurriedly sends herself every single blurry, panicked shot I took last night. I haven't been able to stop shaking since I found said land mine, certain it's about to blow. "This will change everything."

"It won't change anything except the amount of pissed off we'll be when I lose. No one will care that he's going to use the student council to further his agenda except us." I stuff my phone into my backpack before the lunch monitor can spot it.

"That's pretty negative," she mumbles. "People are going to vote for you."

"Look, just . . . don't do anything with those photos." I make sure to stare pointedly, since the last time I told her not to do something, I was somehow signed up for baking and transporting cupcakes for the entire school.

"But how could I not?" Her eyebrows push together. "This will go viral. People are rooting for you online. If they knew *this*—"

"This isn't about going viral and those random people aren't the ones in the voting booths," I hiss. Everyone else is as absorbed in themselves as we are with this dilemma, but I want to be careful. It sounds like the nearest table is having a debate about banning single-use utensils at school and it's getting rowdy enough to mask any conversation Stevie and I have. I remember the first discussion I overheard at this school—it was about whatever store most recently closed at the local mall. The discussions are getting more specific to what's happening right in front of our faces. I wish I had the energy to be proud, to join them. "This stays between you and me."

"And Lila."

I hesitate. "Yeah, you can tell her."

I only allow this because I know Lila, although ready to punch someone without question, will be on my side that we can't use this information like we couldn't use the video of Principal Logan shit-talking me. The worst part of having this information is that I can't fault Patrick for taking his dad's deal. For how he went about it? Yes. For the actual decision he made, to pursue his dreams? No. It's no secret that I'm not the most passionate person. I don't shout my likes and dislikes, my talents, from the rooftops. But if I did, my parents would support me wholeheartedly. I don't know what it's like to be shut down like Patrick has been.

I just wish he hadn't lied about it all. I wish I didn't look at him and feel used, and like I still owe it to him to keep this secret.

Stevie taps her fingernails against the table, pulling my attention back to the present. "If you won't let me release the information and the video now, can we agree to do it if you lose the election? Or after the election, regardless? We can't just sit on this."

"Yes, we can."

The students should know the power their elected president will wield. They should know and trust that the president will be their voice. But I feel like I need to win this whole thing fairly. If getting Thomas out of the way felt good, beating Perfect Patrick and saving the future of the school will feel even better, especially if I don't tamper with his dad's job beforehand. I will not sink to their level, and I will not hurt him more.

She raises an eyebrow. "You're the one who wants to do the right thing and protect Connie, blah blah blah—"

"Yeah? *You're* the one who's only doing this to get internet famous."

Lila stops short behind Stevie, her eyes wide when they land on me. "What's going on?"

"I'm posting them," Stevie says, standing and gathering her things. "It's the right thing to do. I don't want a president who's keeping secrets."

My heart rate kicks up a notch and I stand so I'm face-to-face with her, not letting her loom over me like she has all the power. "You'll get one either way. This won't do anything except make the people scared of change double down on their votes for Patrick. If there's going to be more shady campaign practices happening, I want it to be for my benefit instead of his."

"Is that what you're worried about? That you can't win?" She pulls her phone to her face and begins typing quickly. About to reveal everything, no doubt, for likes and views and fading acclaim. Like with the video of me talking to Principal Logan at the assembly. The posts she made exposing who my mom is. She's just going to take another thing from me, use me, and then wring me out for more. I said no. I say no. No.

I snatch the phone out of her hand and throw it . . . accidentally against the wall. If the cafeteria hadn't already been silent as everyone began watching our shit show, it would have been at the sound of Stevie's iPhone screen cracking against concrete.

Her eyes widen to match Lila's as she stares at me, her cheeks blooming in red, blotchy spots that she'd never show on camera.

"Delaware Parker-Evans," she gasps, her hands reaching out to me, "what the hell did you just do?"

She latches onto my blazer and pulls me close, deep breathing to calm herself down, but it's not working.

"Whoa, what's happening here?" Patrick arrives suddenly, stopping next to Lila, his own hands outstretched like he can ward off the potential fight about to happen. The only thing he can possibly do is make things worse.

"Nothing that can be prevented, I think," Lila says. "It's been brewing."

"Go away, Patrick," Stevie grunts in his direction before facing me again. With her pupils dilated in rage, nearly all the brown of her irises disappears.

"Hopefully they take their tops off and wrestle," Thomas adds, sliding up to the scene out of nowhere.

"Could you be any more of a cliché?" Patrick asks. "Back off."

"I don't think I will," he says with a smirk. "She's not your girlfriend anymore and, as you know, I don't mind your left-overs."

"What the fuck did you just say—" Patrick surges forward, Lila unable to catch him by his arm, and he swings on Thomas, who blocks with his lunch tray. All his food falls to the ground between them.

Meanwhile, I pull free from Stevie's grasp and shuffle backward, bumping into classmates and trays and banging my calves off chair legs in an attempt to keep out of her reach.

"Ella," she seethes, "all I do is help you—all I wanted to do now was help you—"

"You were going to make things way worse. I said *no*." I trip over someone's backpack, but thankfully don't fall. I spin around a guy dumping his trash in the bin and circle back to our table, hoping Lila can calm Stevie down.

She's hot on my heels. "That's not an excuse for you to break my phone, my livelihood!"

"Get a real job!" I call over my shoulder.

"I'd still need a phone!"

"Not one with a camera or internet! Not everything needs to be live streamed or shared for likes. I'm so sick of you putting that stupid thing in my face and telling me it's for my own good!"

She swipes at me, but I dodge her by hiding behind a free-standing bulletin board boasting after-school activities and sports game schedules.

"Oh, excuse *me*, I forgot you were so evolved and social media is so beneath you," she drawls out.

Before I can say anything to defend myself, someone yanks on the back of my shirt and tugs me to the floor with a loud smack. A bolt of pain shoots through my spine before Thomas's body falls onto mine—the culprit—and the air pushes out of my lungs in a silent scream. In what appears to be an attempt to pull Thomas off me, Patrick slips on splattered mashed potatoes and joins us on the dogpile.

When the pain ebbs away enough that I can see straight again, I spot Lila holding back Stevie, though it looks like the fight has left her. Finally, three teachers arrive on the scene—I think the lunch monitor was waiting for backup, which was probably smart. Lila raises her hands in the air, trying to establish that she is *not* part of this mess—she only punches when asked. The one Courtland Academy art teacher steps between Stevie and the mess of us jumbled and tangled up on the floor.

Once everyone has been yanked onto their feet, Thomas says something quietly that upsets Patrick and then he's flailing toward Thomas, despite two of the larger teachers, including the one that was on lunch duty, trying their hardest to separate them.

I watch them, rubbing my lower back with my one hand not covered in Thomas's spilled lunch. All this over a remark about Nadia? I get angry all over again, thinking of how he didn't tell me this massive grudge he was holding against Thomas. How *no one* told me. How it was better for everyone if I stayed in the dark.

The principal storms into the cafeteria, somehow drawing everyone's attention even though he makes no noise. He breaks past the group of students surrounding us and his eyes land on Patrick first.

He really puts a kink in all of this for our dear principal.

How will he handle our punishment? Principal Logan could get me suspended, which would kick me out of the running, but I only broke Stevie's property. Patrick, on the other hand, his star player in this election, is the one snarling and—oh, holy shit—*bleeding* after getting into a fistfight in front of everyone, with absolutely no way of lying his way out of it. No amount of nepotism or loopholes can prevent Patrick from getting in trouble.

So, what'll it be, Mr. Logan? Will you show your favoritism or hold us all accountable for our actions?

I watch him yank at his tie as he fumbles for something he can declare loud and clear to the cafeteria. It's too late for anyone to jump into this election—and who would want to? His two best bets have been proven otherwise and they were basically bribed into running from the start. There's no one else.

What will you do, Principal Logan?

He glances between Patrick and me. "All of you," he says, his voice shaking. "Come with me."

Unsurprisingly, because of Patrick, not a single person is so much as suspended, despite the code of conduct's zero tolerance for violence. Instead, we're silent, if you don't count the complaining we do to ourselves as we clean all twenty lunch tables at the end of the day. Each grade has thoroughly destroyed the cafeteria today with little regard for the people who usually have to clean it, so we have our work cut out for us.

We're missing last period to do this, taking zeros on any homework we don't get to turn in or quizzes and tests we may be missing, but I guess it beats the other option.

Then again, as I scrape off dried meat—meat?—of some variety from the table, I'm not sure it does. Changing this school for the better seems impossible now, more than it ever did before because it's literally rigged into contracts I'm unable to rewrite, and I'm exhausted from trying. It's left me best friendless, fake boyfriendless, and I've been so distracted by everything that I don't even know what's going on with Connie lately. This was all for her originally. I know it became a Me Thing, but I really do want to make things better for her. But I don't see a way to do that if *I'm* not better. If anything, I've gotten worse.

"Watch it," Stevie groans when a piece of my mystery meat flies toward her almost-clean part of the table.

We're tackling them as a team so we can make sure we're not missing any spots, but even several feet apart is too close when the tension we each radiate feels like walls closing in on us. On the one end, Thomas scrubs a pasta sauce stain like he's getting revenge on Patrick for putting him here; next to him is Stevie, who probably shouldn't be so near me for selfish safety reasons; and then on my other side, Patrick alternates between cleaning the same circle of tabletop and dabbing at his nose. I'd be angrier to be stuck between the two of them if my other option weren't to be stuck between Stevie and *Thomas*.

"No talking," Mr. Carpenter says from the little lunch monitor desk behind us. He's got his feet propped up—his natural state—his phone clenched between his hands as he plugs in earbuds and places them in one ear, then the next. I seethe over the fact that we have enough money for Mr. Carpenter to be available randomly for babysitting, but not to fix the one tile of flooring that I trip on outside the gym nearly every day.

"Mr. C," Patrick says with his tissue pressed against his nose. "Hey, Mr. C."

Mr. Carpenter removes an earbud when Patrick waves for his attention.

"I'm going to need more tissues soon." Patrick holds up the wad of clean tissue he has left.

"Do you need them now?"

"No."

"Then quiet." He puts the earbud back in and closes his eyes.

Patrick throws out his used paper towels and tissues in the trash can next to him. His nose is red, but for now he's not actively bleeding, and because of that, I look away and get back to my cleaning.

"Delaware," Stevie grits out when another piece of food zooms into her space.

"I'm not trying," I whisper. "Sorry."

"Wow, wish you could have said that earlier, like, when you broke my thousand-dollar phone." She stalks past me to throw out her own used paper towels. "Can you even process how much money a thousand dollars is?"

"Well, I'm sure you can just post a picture to get some more money for a new one. That's what you call work, right?"

"Not without a phone."

"I believe Mr. Carpenter said no talking," Thomas says,

joining Stevie at the trash can. He sidesteps Patrick, holding up his bruised hands like he's afraid Patrick might swing again.

"Then why are you?" Patrick asks in a low voice, eyes focused on the table.

"He's just jealous none of us like him enough to even argue with him right now," Stevie says under her breath. The only one to not hear her, though, is Mr. Carpenter. Patrick fist-bumps her as she passes him. I hate that me fighting with both of them has brought them closer.

"Hey, separate," Mr. Carpenter barks, making all four of us jump. We face him. "No touching. You two—" He points to Patrick and me, and then the table nearest the cafeteria kitchen. "You two go over there."

We move with small sighs, but little else. I start spraying the table down just as Patrick goes to sweep crumbs and other loose bits off. Naturally, the cleaner ends up on his hands.

He wipes them off without a single word, not even giving me a half-assed eye roll in response. And, even though it had been an accident, his non-reaction causes me to react in a way I know I shouldn't. I spray his hands again when he attempts, once more, to clear off the crumbs.

"Ella," he growls.

He doesn't even get a chance for attempt number three. I spray him square in the chest.

He tries to wrestle the bottle away from me. In the meantime, I keep hitting him with this overpriced "all-natural" cleaner that smells more like Clorox. "Knock it off! You'll get it in my eyes!"

Mr. Carpenter doesn't notice our struggle. Stevie stops

cleaning to watch; I know she's itching for a phone to grab so she can record this. Finally, Patrick gets the cleaner out of my hands and sprays me three times before tossing the bottle into the kitchen.

"Whoops," he says heavily, "guess we better go get that."

He drags me into the kitchen by one wrist and only lets go once the door swings shut behind us. "What's your problem, Parker-Evans?"

"Are you kidding me? You!" I shove a finger in his face. "Stop trying to reduce what you did, what you're *doing* to me, and stop making me into the bad guy here."

"I didn't *do* anything to you." He seems to reconsider quickly. "Except I stood up for you today. That? You're mad that I stood up for you?"

"No—what? You didn't stand up for me. You stood up for Nadia." I cross my arms over the wet spot on my school shirt. "I'm obviously talking about you betraying me in a thousand different ways."

"Because *you* betrayed me!" He mirrors my action. "And it wasn't about Nadia—not entirely. I was defending you, too."

"In case you forgot, we weren't dating, so I don't need you to defend me, and I'm not your—whatever he said. Leftovers? You never had me."

He pauses, mouth tight. "Yeah." He nods, tonguing his cheek while he works out his next words. "Yeah. You're right. Because that was all fake."

"Yeah. All of it." I glance down at his bruised hands. A bit of blood pooled between his knuckles and dried. "You getting into a fight with Thomas was for you more than anyone else, especially not me. Don't use me as an excuse."

"You're making me into some kind of monster for reacting to you breaking our promise—"

"It was more than a promise. It was a deal. And I intended to follow through somehow."

He tugs his shirtsleeves up aggressively. They're visibly drenched with cleaner. "All right, fine. Contact my lawyer, then. I'm tired of running in circles trying to get you to understand that you hurt me."

The final words slip out in a strangled voice, like he didn't mean to say them. He rolls his eyes to the ceiling and takes a deep breath.

"You hurt me, too," I say in a soft voice. Hot tears threaten to fall from my eyes. "I thought we were friends. I thought— we could be something else, maybe, but then you—"

"But then *you*," he cuts in. "You."

He steps forward and pushes a stray hair behind my ear. "All deals are null and void when you make them under false pretenses, Parker-Evans." He sucks in a breath, a half laugh and half scoff. "I wanted everything. With you. Just say you're sorry."

"I'm sorry," I finally say, barely a breath above a whisper.

"Mean it," he implores. "Please."

"You were wrong, too." And now, with his dad's contract burning a hole in my mind, even if Patrick hadn't left out his grudge against Thomas, we'd still be here. We were always going to end up here, on opposite sides.

His body slumps, his hands dropping to his sides. I've never seen a blanker face.

"I just wish we had both been more honest from the beginning," I say. "I wish you would have told me about Nadia, about what your dad offered you to run—I saw his contract. I know the president gets a seat at Board meetings. We could have made a plan. We—we worked well together. Didn't we?"

He frowns. "I don't know what you mean."

I sigh. "Please stop lying. There's no need for it anymore."

"It's too late for that," he says, monotone, eyes focused on the floor or maybe someplace much farther away. "Good luck at the election."

I don't turn as he passes and opens the kitchen door. Maybe his dad will just rig this whole thing. "You too."

"You'll probably need it more than me."

Don't I know it. . . .

Twenty-Three

I wait for Connie after school in the shade of a tree lining the parking lot. She doesn't say hi, but instead, "Everyone's talking about the fight."

This will surely be a miserable walk home.

It takes me a second to realize she means the physical fight and not what happened most recently with Patrick. Relief washes over me for the briefest moment. The last thing Connie needs to know is that Patrick might? still? reciprocate? feelings? and that we're both too stubborn to do anything about it. But is it stubbornness when what's keeping us apart is a lack of respect for the other?

"Did you see it?" she asks when I start walking home instead of acknowledging her. No Stevie or Patrick on my side means no more free rides. Our house is only two miles away and most of the journey is on sidewalk anyway. If we hadn't changed schools, I would have had to call my parents for one of them to pick us up. We live too close to the school to be put on the bus route and Courtland Academy doesn't care if it's raining or snowing or we don't have cars or licenses. If you're affording the tuition, you probably have a ride, right?

"What do you mean?" I try to keep the steel from my voice, but a little slips through.

"The fight between Patrick and Thomas. What happened?" Her eyes are wide, hungry for gossip, and full of a certain mania I haven't seen in her bookworm-sleepy expressions before. I watch her walking next to me, hands clenched around her backpack straps, her blazer rolled up to her elbows. At some point, she added a GSA pin to her lapel.

We're not the same girls who started Courtland together this school year. I feel so out of touch with Connie and who she's become.

I frown, the ache in my back more present now after leaning over the lunch tables for an hour than it was as soon as I hit the ground during the fight. "Yeah, I saw it. I was part of it."

She stops and flings an arm out to stop me. "Wait, what?"

"Patrick and Thomas fought, but . . ." I hesitate before saying it, like not giving life to the truth out loud will somehow make it less real. I decide to keep walking and she follows. "Stevie and I got into a . . . disagreement, and the boys knocked me over accidentally. All four of us had to clean the cafeteria last period."

She tightens her grip on her backpack with a scoff. "What could you and Stevie possibly have to fight about?"

I'm about maxed out on talking and the heat makes my blood boil again. I want to roll my eyes at her tone, at her assumption that Stevie and I don't have our own issues, that we can't possibly fight about things, but I'm too tired from the day.

"Friends fight sometimes," I say, unable to stop the condescension in my tone.

"Not Sasha and me."

"Well, that's great for Sasha and you, but Stevie and I have real issues to deal with, not just a mean review on fan fiction or whose parent will drive you to the movies."

She takes a step away from me, my annoyance palpable enough to drive her away. "What's with you? It's not like I was the one you got into a fight with."

"Sorry."

"And we don't fight because we know how to communicate. We don't let things build up so that we resent each other. We're honest and we have boundaries. Get off your high horse and kick rocks, Delaware." She ends her speech by actually kicking a rock off the path in front of us and onto the road.

"Not every relationship is going to be perfect like your silly little stories," I end up mumbling. In my imagination, I was going to scream at her, but in reality, it's not even necessary to say, especially when she's right.

"I didn't say they were," she says, facing me. Her cheeks have reddened, and I know it's not from the sun. "You've been so mean since we changed schools—definitely since Patrick broke up with you—and it's starting to feel like your only redeeming quality is your friends, but they appear to be dwindling away."

I blink, and then muster up the words. "I don't want to hear that from someone who essentially has a built-in best friend and babysitter for a sister. You wouldn't know what it's like to be alone because you've always had me here. Before Sasha, who was the person you hung out with the most?" I don't let her answer because we both know it was me. "Don't you dare criticize my relationships when the one you've maintained the longest has been because I was *forced* into it."

"I never forced you—"

"Ella, play with me. Ella, watch TV with me. Ella, read this. Ella, do that. Ella, hold my hand and wipe my butt and take all the blame for everything I do wrong because I'm baby. I'm baby, Ella—"

She punches me in the arm, the hit reverberating sharply up to my shoulder, and stalks off, tears choking her words. "You're the one who literally has nobody without me! I never wanted you to be my babysitter, just my sister!"

I stalk after her, rubbing my arm. "Then you should have said something to Mom and Dad because they're delusional and think you need constant supervision."

"I've tried." She clears her throat, a tear sliding down her cheek. "I don't want to be treated like a little kid anymore. I don't need you watching over me! I've tried to make it better lately! It was better."

For a moment, I just stare. It contradicts everything I've ever been taught, every feeling I've had since the day she was born. My parents told me then, in the delivery room, when I could barely comprehend that suddenly there was a new person in our family, that I must always look out for Connie. I guess in a way, I wasn't looking out for her by doing what my parents wanted, for treating her like a kid instead of the teenager she's grown into. I never gave her the chance to prove me wrong.

"Fine." I walk a few feet forward, and settle on a bench by the local bus stop. "Okay."

"What, you're just not going home?" she calls.

"Don't feel like it," I lie, new sweat blooming across my forehead in the direct sunlight.

"I can't walk home alone," she says slowly, like she's spelling out each word for me. "I could get kidnapped."

"They'd give you back." I place my bag next to me and pull out my phone. I don't exactly have anyone to text at this point, but I open and close the app a few times so I look nonchalant to her. "Besides, you don't want to be treated like a little kid anymore."

"*Whatever*," she says, gripping onto her backpack straps again and . . . heading in the wrong direction. She's taking the long way home, probably to make me metaphorically sweat. Once she's out of my sight, I sigh and stand. No, of course I can't just let her go on her own. Not like this.

I don't say anything when she cuts through the grass of the baseball field in the local park, or when she scowls at me over her shoulder. She's making her own way, and I'm letting her. Sometimes, instead of fleeing from my problems, I have to chase them down. Or keep a steady pace behind them.

Silence blankets us for a good five minutes before I finally speak up.

"I'm sorry," I say.

She has her head down, but she angles her ear my way.

"I'm sorry for being mean and for not talking to you about how annoying Mom and Dad were for always making me watch you—and for how annoying it must be to have me always watching you, like, I honestly can't even imagine. I would have exploded to be micromanaged like that."

I've never once considered that Connie would be bothered to be babysat, mostly because she's always so positive, so eager to be around me, but it feels so ridiculously clear now—like, I should have seen this a million years ago—that she would have liked to be left alone sometimes. She would have liked to be treated like a person with a voice, a say in the matter.

Just like me.

"It was a lot." She slows her steps until I meet up with her, and then we walk next to each other. "Sasha has helped; she gave me some good advice about talking to Mom and Dad, just, like, how to reframe me doing things on my own as new opportunities for friends and stuff."

I absorb her words. I've been so caught up in this election, in all the drama of my own making, that I not only accepted that I was doing all of this for me instead of her, but I also just . . . completely lost track of what she's been doing. I've seen less of her now that she goes to my school than I did when we were separated. I'm relieved, but I'm also horrified.

"I've been totally obsessed with myself," I say to myself, aloud.

She laughs. "Totally," she agrees, mocking me. "But you've at least had a reason to be. Before this year, you kind of did things only for me."

"Yeah . . ."

"I used to think that . . ." She avoids my eyes. "I used to think that maybe you were depressed because of me. Because you hated me and had to spend time with me."

I stop her, a hand gripping her shoulder. "Connie, no. Never. *No.*"

"I know that now," she says, nodding. I'm not reassured. "I know that, but back then, I thought it. So I tried to be super happy and to make you happy—"

"That's not your job. That's my antidepressant's job." I pull her into my side and squeeze. "Despite it all, I love you. It's impossible not to. Okay?"

"Okay." She nods again, with more confidence this time. "I love you, too."

We continue walking.

"I'm good," she says out of nowhere. "Please know that. I'm fine. Do this whole student council thing for you. Win this for you—and me, and everyone—but mostly you. I'm really good here."

"I'll try." I offer a smile. "Thanks."

"You're welcome."

I bite my lip. I know deep down I shouldn't ask, because I'm not prepared for the answer, or her enthusiasm, but it's going to bother me if I keep it to myself. "Can I get your advice on something?"

"I'm nothing if not an endless well of wisdom, wise beyond my years."

"In your fanfics, what happens when the main character

messes up? Like, do they just not get a happy ending?" It's been a while since I read one of Connie's completed works to give her feedback. I wasn't very good at it, so I think she gravitated toward other writers she found online to beta for her, but I remember being so impressed that she could pull these stories, these whole entire worlds and people, right out of her head.

"Messes up how?"

"With . . . the best friend, or . . ." I lower my voice and say, "You know, with the *love interest*."

She practically chokes on her own excitement. "*No*, oh my god. They do a grand gesture! They show their loved ones they're sorry and that they're willing to change and admit fault and all that stuff." She claps her hands together. "I'm so pumped; let me help you get this apology train in motion. Patrick will forgive you!"

"Don't get ahead of yourself," I say through a laugh. "I appreciate the help, but I think I need to get off the apology train at a station before Patrick."

"The Stevie Station?" she accurately guesses.

Yes. The Stevie Station.

Taking the long way home gives us tons of time to talk about my wrongs with Stevie and Patrick, and what I can do to fix things. I *hate* that Connie's right—and she loves it, of course. I'm constantly letting the people around me not only make decisions for me and pressure me into doing things I expressly do not want to do, but I'm basically nothing without them— and I use their influence on me like a shield; like, if I'm not the one coming up with the idea, then it's okay if I fail because it was *them* failing. I don't know how to make decisions on my own. I can come up with the idea in my head, of course, but when it comes to the action . . . if I don't have support, nothing gets done. And now that I'm back on my own again, I'm searching for help at the first moment I can. I worry that I'm not enough to win this election on my own. But do I even want to at this point?

My excuse for this whole thing, Connie, is finally free and thriving now that she's not living under my supervision. I was too scared to admit that this was more for me than her. Scared that it's possible I'm going for something, giving it my all, and might embarrassingly *fail*. But failure never stopped my mom, or Connie. It never stopped Patrick or Stevie. If I'm going to surround myself with these people, try to win them back, then I need to be at least as good as them, as determined. I have to show them who I am without them—and why we better each other.

Twenty-Four

In the name of continued irresponsibility, because Connie no longer needs me as a role model and I honestly just used that as an excuse to stay away from things I was afraid to do, I call off from my first shift ever in order to go to the store and buy Stevie a new phone. And a case. To protect it from future Ella meltdowns that I hope never occur.

The ease of online shopping has yet to kill the Best Buy on the Carlisle Pike, so I drive my mom's car there after a long-winded lecture from my dad on being reliable, among other things, and wait for my pickup order of the most expensive iPhone they have in stock. Yes, I could have walked in there and bought it in person, but I didn't want to get distracted by the iPad accessories I don't need and can't afford. I am here in search of forgiveness, not credit card debt.

With the windows cracked, I recline my seat and spend the next thirty minutes scrolling through @StevieSays's TikTok feed and re-falling in love with her. I was quick to play the "I'm too superior for social media" card when we fought, but Stevie's more than that. She doesn't just post gossip or paid advertisements; she opens herself up with weekly "one-on-one" talks as she cleans her room or gets ready for wherever she's going that feel more like a FaceTime call than something that has over twenty thousand views. She ends each of those videos with, "Stevie says be kind." People in the comments adore her, relate to her, cheer her on. In some of the videos, she even admits that she tries so hard, maybe too hard, to be liked by the people in her life. That she thinks if she can act confident enough, she'll be confident enough, though she feels anything but. I hope it's not too late for me to realize that I was a fool to her facade all along. She wasn't just using me for views and follows; she genuinely wants to make friends. She does it through growing her platform. As someone who hasn't been on social media, I didn't see it like that. I didn't get it. But I think I do now.

When I return to the car with way less money but way more determination, I plug Stevie's address into Maps and head over to her house, uninvited. It's not until I'm sitting in front of the two-story house I came to a total of one time in middle school that I worry she may have moved since then. I decide, *screw it*, and get out of the car anyway. I can't chicken out now. She typically does live streams from her house on Wednesday nights—a kind of midweek reset where everyone checks in on drama, homework, mental health status, etcetera—so, logically, she should be home right now, even though she doesn't have a phone to live stream from.

I release a sigh of relief when I spot the mailbox at the edge of the yard spelling out Hernández in looping cursive writing. Now, if she doesn't slam the door in my face, maybe I will return to an almost-resting heart rate.

I step onto the wraparound porch and knock on the red front door.

What sounds like an entire pack of miniature wolves starts barking and I instantly regret not just texting her to let her know I'm here.

"Back! Get back, you beasts!" I hear Stevie call from the other side of the door. The small bit of light shining through the peephole breaks, and then the door swings open. "What are you doing here?" Her voice is rightfully defensive, and her eyes narrow.

A Pomeranian and a dachshund—the said pack of wolves—jump past Stevie's legs and onto mine, over and over.

"Este, who's at the door?" her mother calls from somewhere deeper in the house.

"It's my friend Delaware," Stevie says over her shoulder.

"Oh," comes the delighted response, her mother still out of eyesight. "Welcome, Delaware! Can you stay for dinner?"

"Hi!" I say around Stevie. She's a parent pleaser . . . but I am, too. I raise an eyebrow at her in question. "I'm not sure I can, but thank you!"

Behind Stevie, two younger girls with the same dark, thick hair chase each other around the house, giggles spilling out of their red-stained mouths.

"Sorry," I say quietly. "This is a bad time. You . . . have company—"

"That's Luna and Mercedes." She says it like I should know—and I should. The last time I saw Stevie's mom, she was pregnant, with twins. "My sisters."

"Yeah," I say quickly. This is not going well. "Yes, I remember. And your older sisters are probably out of the house by now, right?"

Stevie smirks. "Well, not Carmen, and she's so pissed about it."

She closes the door behind her and guides me to wooden rockers near the door. "Gabriella is engaged."

Stevie isn't the baby anymore. She is the middle child. Suddenly, her thirst for attention, validation, companionship makes a lot more sense. Probably as much as my older-sister bossiness makes sense.

"Good for her," I say with real excitement. "Gabriella, not Carmen. Sucks to be Carmen."

"Sucks to be Carmen," Stevie agrees with a nod. "But Gabriella's man is a real piece of work, thinks he's going to write the next great American novel and yadda yadda yadda. All Carmen has to deal with is technically living in the same house as us. She has her own entrance and everything; it's really not that big of a deal."

There's a slight hurt tone to her words. Perhaps they couldn't come together as middle sisters over the years. It's not past my notice that I should know this about her. I've been so single-minded that I haven't gotten to know the person I've been calling my best friend. I'm more superficial than I accused Stevie of being.

I sigh.

She bites her lip. "So, what are you doing here? I don't have anything else for you to break but my spirit."

"That could never be broken."

She inhales through her nose deeply and then meets my eyes. "I'm sorry. I shouldn't have been using you for clout. When the views started getting higher, it's like I did, too. I was in a haze. That wasn't cool, especially when you told me no and I ignored you."

"I should *not* have broken your phone, though."

"No," she says through a laugh. "Be quiet. I haven't told my parents yet."

"I wondered why your mom was inviting me for dinner."

"Because you're Delaware!" she says with mock enthusiasm. "The other little girl with the weird name."

I blink. "Oh my god."

"Did you forget?"

"I guess I did."

The whole reason Stevie and I started revolving around each other when we were younger was because we were outcast for our names. Yes, we had friends—the kind who would just as easily stab you in the back as defend your life. We adapted, though. She became Este and I became Ella. But then she became Stevie, and I was still Ella, after all these years. It took me until today to really realize that. When I watched her Tik-Toks in chronological order, I started to see the big picture.

"I'm sorry, really," I say. "I shouldn't have broken your phone and I shouldn't have freaked out on you. You've been so helpful, and also—it's just been nice to have a friend. One who wasn't my little sister." I pull a face. "I gave her shit for having *me* as a built-in best friend, but all this time, it was *her*. *She* was *my* built-in best friend. My parents literally made her for me."

"I explicitly told my parents I did *not* want a new sibling and they gave me two." She smiles at me. "You could have just caught me tomorrow to apologize. I was fully prepared to corner you and shout 'I'm sorry' into your face."

"Oh shit, yeah," I say, pulling the Best Buy bag onto my lap. "I came here to give you this. It couldn't wait because you need to set it up."

She peeks inside the bag and her eyes go wide. "Ella."

"Don't act like I did something nice; I'm just giving you what I took from you."

She reaches into the bag. "This is much nicer than the phone I had, though."

"Consider it an investment into your future career. I'm a shark or whatever."

"Or a sugar daddy," she whispers, pulling the phone from its box and admiring the red color I chose. "This is expensive."

"I had money saved."

She looks at me and there are tears in her eyes. "This is really nice."

"No, it's not," I remind her forcefully. "Don't get mushy—"

She's already hunched over me with her arms around my neck. "Thank you. Even if you broke the last one, you didn't have to go above and beyond."

"You needed the one with the good camera," I mumble

into her hair. "I see what you've made online. I get it. You have friends there, people who really like your content. You're a great storyteller."

"I can't wait to take pictures and videos of you *with your consent*," she says, pulling away.

I groan. "That's another thing. Connie's too smart."

"What?" Already it's happening again; she can't keep her eyes off the phone.

"Connie was talking about boundaries." I tuck my hair behind my ear. "And communication."

"I promise I'm listening." The screen turns on and illuminates her face in the dying light of the day.

"I think that if I tell you when I'm mad or annoyed or whatever—and you do the same, of course—we wouldn't have any kind of resentment toward the other, and it wouldn't build up and then explode in the cafeteria in front of Courtland Academy."

"Yes. Good. Love this."

"And I think the consent thing goes along with that. I think it's okay for now if you film and take pictures, but let me have a say if they get posted?"

"Of course." Somehow she's gotten through setting up her phone already. She launches the camera app. "Makeup selfie?"

I try to hide my exasperated eye roll, but she catches me.

"Oh, come *on*."

"Fiiiiine," I say with a laugh. "Makeup selfie."

We commemorate our first and hopefully only fight with an Instagram post on both our profiles—because that's Stevie's love language. I get sentimental in mine, including a photo from middle school that Stevie pulls from the deep recesses of her Google Photos account, and Stevie fills her caption with all the reasons people should vote for me in the election this week, the top reason being that I right my wrongs.

Twenty-Five

My mother insists on driving Connie and me to school on Election Day. We detour for coffee and breakfast sandwiches, and she lets me pick the music for the whole ten-minute car ride, the three of us sitting awkwardly for the entirety of one never-ending ska song—and I see why Patrick's band idea never came to fruition. I won't make that music choice mistake again. That's what I get for being sentimental.

When we arrive on campus, my mom shoos Connie out of the car as soon as she pulls up to the sidewalk. With love, of course.

"Ella, wait," my mom says when I try to escape while I have the chance.

I turn back to her and plaster a smile on my face. "Yes?"

"Good luck. I believe in you."

"Thanks."

"Seriously. You'd make a great student council president. You have the best ideas and you really care about people, including them and making them feel protected and valued."

I blink, an actual sting of tears threatening my eyes. "I wasn't expecting this or I wouldn't have put mascara on this morning."

She laughs and pulls me in for a one-armed hug. "I'm just so proud of you for going after the thing you wanted. You've always been shy to admit you like things or want things, so I'm—I'm really happy for you. I know it can be hard with your depression and all your responsibilities. . . . Your dad and I want you to know that we're excited to alter your work schedule so you can fit in your new student council duties."

I roll my eyes but can't fight the smile. "I might not get it."

"If you don't, are you okay with that?"

Patrick immediately comes back to mind. Not the version of him with short hair and a perfect uniform. The messy chaotic version of him that let me take stupid pictures of him in an art gallery. The version of him that cooked me a homemade meal that I have been salivating over for weeks. Patrick, who hit a vending machine to get a lost soda for someone.

He's the reason I even ran for this position in the first place. He's a man of the people: charming, smart, caring, and kind. If I lost to him, it wouldn't be the worst thing. It wouldn't even be a bad thing. I trust that the version of him I fell for is still deep inside the robot his father created for nefarious means.

"I'll be okay. Patrick's a good choice, too. He's a good guy, and he cares." She nods and I continue, "I know there isn't an apprenticeship available, but he really deserves one. Is there *anything* we can do for him? He would love to work with you, and you would *love* him and his food. It felt like I'd never eaten before and each bite was full of flavor and feeling and—I know I sound silly. I don't know the words like you and Connie, but it made me feel happy and I could taste his passion."

She deflates, sighing. "I know how much that means coming from you, but the spots are filled, and things haven't gone to plan with Andrew and Taylor. They nearly flooded the kitchen the other night."

I fight past the exhaustion in her voice. "Maybe he could replace one of them, and you'd be helping your daughter be less of a liar?"

She rubs between her eyebrows, eyes squeezed shut. "That would not make you less of a liar; it would just make me an even nicer mom and chef."

"True. You're so nice. And such a great chef. Please. I think if you worked with him, you'd maybe start liking the apprenticeship again—"

"Fine."

"Fine? Fine meaning . . . ?"

"Meaning we'll work something out if he wants to. Weekends only or something, at least until graduation, and then I may decide to bring him on full-time if that works for him. But I can't just get rid of Andrew and Taylor to make space for him, even if they give me migraines. He might end up doing a lot of dishes—"

"He would be honored," I interject, grabbing her forearms excitedly. "I assume," I add, calmer. "Thank you. Thank you so much."

"If you hadn't nearly burned down the house trying to replicate his food . . ."

"I won't do it again."

"Better not." She pinches my cheek. "Get inside and vote for yourself."

"Voting doesn't start until lunch, but will do!"

"No voter fraud!" she calls as I shut the door behind me.

"We can only hope there's some in my favor!" I shout back, running inside the school.

Connie waits at my locker, which surprises me. She holds her fanfic binder tight against her chest and meets me halfway.

"Everything okay?" I ask. For once, the sight of her out of place doesn't send me spiraling into panic.

She nods, holding out the binder. "I was hoping you could read my creative writing assignment before I turn it in today."

There are about ten minutes until class, but this is such a rarity lately that I plop down right there on the floor and crack open the binder. Connie reluctantly joins me, tucking her knees to her chest. Our classmates hustle back and forth, occasionally ramming into the toes of our shoes with the toes of theirs, but no one trips or stops to yell at us.

I'm about three pages in—already emotionally invested in the growing relationship between the passionate but inexperienced protagonist who's running for city council and the flirty love interest who's the son of the mayor and always joking around to make her blush—before it all feels . . . familiar. The couple rushes through an art gallery before closing, turns a stuffy fundraising event into a rager, and—ultimately become enemies when the mayor's son runs for the same city council position as the protagonist.

It's hard to ignore the facts: this little brat wrote about *Patrick and me*.

"Connecticut!" I smack her with the binder, my finger keeping my place inside. "What the hell?"

"Took you long enough," she says with a laugh. It earns her another smack. "What? I changed the names!"

"You need to change all of it! Your teacher will know you're writing about us and send you to a padded cell for our protection."

"Okay, realistically, what should I change? I only have study hall to work on it. It needs to be minor changes, and I think I did a really good job at making it *thickly* veiled."

I groan, flipping the binder open. "For starters, you can't have the whole plot start with an abrupt overturning of previous election results, which is *exactly what happened on our first day*." I skim the rest of the pages. "Thickly veiled, yeah right—"

"Clearly it's *somewhat* innocuous if you didn't realize right away."

I pause on the final page. "Cali," a.k.a. "California," a.k.a. *me* does the hard thing and apologizes to Percival, a.k.a. *Perk*, a.k.a. Patrick. She admits to never intending to fall for him, admits to never wanting to hurt him. She thought she was doing what was best for her sister with a perfectly normal name (*what the hell?*) and the other community members. Percival had to understand that there are few things in this world more important to Cali than her sister, and that love and responsibility often get in the way of sense and reason.

Connie watches me close the binder.

"It's not your fault that I messed things up," I say. The crowd of students stopping at their lockers has begun to grow and louden around us. "You didn't need this—I did. You don't even care what people think about you. You've been given more than enough reasons to hide yourself and you refuse to."

She shrugs a shoulder. "Well, it's not my job to make people accept me. I don't need to change for them."

"No. You don't." I pull her into a hug like my mom did to me a few minutes ago. "But you *do* need to change this story before turning it in."

She laughs, staring at the binder in her lap. A piece of the corner is peeling away from the cardboard underneath. "I guess I could make it, like, Cali wants into a really hoity-toity book club or something, make it less political."

I try to hide my twisted expression. "Sure."

"You don't like that?"

"I think if you wrote it, I would." I stand, and then pull her to her feet. "But you have to change the ending. Because it's not *Carrie*'s fault, and because there's no happy ending."

"Maybe you're just not at the end of the story yet."

I stare at her for a minute, disgust pulling my mouth into a grimace. "Ew. Go to class." I shove her gently in the direction of the freshman halls.

Over her shoulder, she says, "Good luck with your closing remarks."

I had been trying not to think of them. Every candidate will have a few moments to speak one last time to the school before voting begins, and it's a great opportunity, but I don't know what to say that I haven't already. So . . . Connie and I decided during our brainstorming session last night that I would use my time for her beloved grand gesture.

I feel sick.

The ding of the crackly announcement system rings through the halls, stalling everyone's movements.

"Would the following students please report to the auditorium: Patrick Logan, Delaware Parker-Evans, Tana Smith, Todd Carlisle, Dean Hammond, and Kat Simms."

Fingers tingling with nerves, I make my way slowly to the auditorium. I try to rehearse snippets of what I'll say: *I'm sorry, you made me better, I understand why you did everything*—

It's about halfway there that I see the signs that I'm doing the right thing.

The literal signs.

The first reads: VOTE FOR ELLA. THINGS NEED TO CHANGE.

The handwriting is sloppy and the color scheme clashes. It's not one of the signs my team or I made. It's followed closely by another sign, just as haphazardly made, that says: ELLA PARKER-EVANS HAS A NICE RING TO IT. ALMOST . . . PRESIDENTIAL.

Number three: IT'S NOT UP FOR DEBATE. ELLA FOR PRESIDENT.

Four screams: IF YOU DON'T CARE ABOUT THE ELECTION, THEN IT DOESN'T MATTER IF YOU

VOTE FOR ELLA. (I find it to be slightly insulting, but the intent is apparent in the skinny, squished words and little fingerprints of paint on the edges of the posters.)

I don't want to get my hopes up that they were made by who I think they were. Patrick has no reason to suddenly support me aside from maybe wanting to call things even between us. He may have admitted to feelings, or feelings in the past tense, but that doesn't mean he would make me posters. Surely, some other well-meaning person with an encyclopedia of quips and charm spent a whole several minutes working on these and then taping them up on the exact path that will lead everyone to the assembly and then the voting booths (because Courtland has the funds and the dramatic flair to do such a thing instead of having us fill out paper ballots in class and turn them in to the teacher, but not enough funds and flair for an annual theater budget).

But . . . if it *was* him . . .

The universe is kind of telling me that everything will be okay. Connie is good. I have a friend again in Stevie. My mom is on the same page as me and Connie now. And Patrick might have a shot at his apprenticeship.

When I open the auditorium door, I see I'm the second person to arrive. Patrick sits on the edge of the stage, waiting for me.

Twenty-Six

"He thinks you might win," Patrick says without preamble or greeting. Definitely not the words I expected after our last interaction, or the posters I just saw. I'm a mix of emotions—my stomach churns with scared apologies and excited butterflies—and my heart pounds in my chest as I drink in his appearance. He wears his uniform casually, shirt untucked and tie loose, like he's not giving a second thought to the closing remarks that we're both supposed to deliver in mere minutes.

"Who?" I hurry toward him.

"My dad." He slides from the stage and meets me. "He's worried."

"Why? What changed?" I'm not sure if I mean "what changed between us" or "what changed that your dad is finally afraid of me."

"I think my fight with his fanboy shook him. Thomas is telling all his friends not to vote for me now."

I blink. "But then they would have to vote for me?"

He starts walking toward the stage stairs at a leisurely pace. I struggle to walk slow enough to keep next to him.

"No, they could still abstain," he says.

"But that would be like voting for me anyway."

"I don't really care." He pauses on the last step and looks over his shoulder at me. He clarifies, "I don't want those guys in my corner anyway. That was just what my dad wanted."

"It's okay," I say quietly. It's *not*, but it is. "If you do this for your dad, I mean. I get it if you had to change who you were in order to get his approval for school. It's a messed-up situation he put you in, though, so if you change your mind at any point today, tomorrow, in a million years . . . I'm here for you, as your friend."

I take a calming breath as he processes what I said, his face a confusing mess of emotions. I wasn't expecting to have a moment to speak to him before my supposed grand gesture and I hope I'm not making it worse.

"I'm sorry that I had such a meltdown over your choice to run," I say. "And I'm sorry that I lied about the apprenticeship opportunity. I talked to my mom and she's agreed to take you on during the weekends as a start—if you still want that. I told her about your eggplant Parmesan. I nearly burned my house to the ground trying to make it myself because I loved it so much."

He finally comes back to his body and opens his mouth to respond, but then the full auditorium lights slam on and the doors open to reveal our other classmates in the student council running, along with Principal Logan.

We have no chance to speak further before we are all corralled to different sides of the stage and Principal Logan explains once again the rules of the microphone. In no subtle feat of discrimination, Principal Logan puts Kat, Tana, and me on the same side, with Patrick, Todd, and Dean on the other. Dean put in nearly zero effort during this election, so I'm actually surprised to see him show up. I assumed he had dropped out.

I get to gauge the crowd's openness to change through Kat's speech on budgeting and organization. They stir as Tana talks about her desire to expand the student council with committees, to better hear the wants and needs of the school and make sure issues see follow-through. Dean's and Todd's answers show no growth, no passion, no vision.

As Tana and Todd exit the stage to their opposite sides and hand the microphones off, I meet Patrick's eyes. He mouths "I'm sorry" and then marches onto the stage when his name is called.

At first, I'm ecstatic that we're no longer fighting—but then I consider that maybe he's apologizing for *not* apologizing, for not disowning his father. Saying sorry for what he's about to do: rip me to shreds in front of the school. I step out a moment later, delayed by this sudden fear, and blink against the bright lights. I feel like I'm doing this for the first time, and I'm even more nervous because this time will be harder. This time, losing will be devastating.

Maybe winning would be, too. Winning might mean taking away Principal Logan's approval of Patrick's passion.

Principal Logan lofts a question at Patrick to get our final words going: "Why should you be the Courtland Academy student council president?"

"I'll go first," I say suddenly. I raise my microphone to my mouth and repeat the words so I can actually be heard.

No. I was wrong. This is not like the first time.

Patrick nods, silent.

"Thanks." I glance into the darkness of the quiet and captive audience before us and release a shaky breath. "I think the most important quality for a student council president to have is . . ."

Do I say what makes me look good, or do I say what Connie and I rehearsed? It's hard not to get caught up in how I played dirty to get Thomas removed from the running, how I failed to point out to Patrick that my mom had sworn off apprenticeships, how I literally broke my best friend's phone instead of just *talking* to her clearly about my feelings.

"Integrity," I finish. "But I'm not sure I have that yet. I'm only seventeen and something like that has to take a lot of fucking time to achieve, right?" Someone chokes out a shocked laugh, and I dare to look at Patrick. It was him. He watches my every move with wide, concerned eyes that scream, "You're blowing this!"

"Ms. Parker-Evans," Principal Logan hisses.

I push on quickly, talking over any further interruptions. "Sorry—I make a lot of mistakes. I've lied. I've—" I stop myself before saying I've cheated because, while true, it's not helpful, and something that would bring Patrick down, too. "I've failed people—failed *friends*. But I don't want to, I don't want to be someone who does that, and I think that's important.

I'm growing, I'm changing, I'm hopefully becoming better, and that's what I want to do for Courtland, because I think the potential of this place is a lot. I want to make this school the best it can be and that starts on the student level. You shouldn't elect someone because they're nice or because they play favorites. You should elect someone into a position of power because you think they'll do the job the right way, with integrity. I'm not sure you can go wrong with whoever you choose today, but if you vote for me, I promise that I will never forget that I am your voice and I will make sure I'm heard, in the lunchroom, at student council events, school functions, Board of Directors meetings. You can trust me to be there for you—everyone, even the people who don't vote for me or talk to me or even like me."

I let the arm holding my microphone fall to my side, indicating I'm done. My skin buzzes with nerves, and I don't chance even a brief glimpse of Patrick after the mention of board meetings.

"That didn't exactly answer my question—" Principal Logan starts, speaking directly into his microphone.

"I agree," Patrick says, cutting him off. "We can trust Ella. She cares. She'll make this school better every day that she serves as president." He glances at his dad; his face has turned bright red and there is no way to hide it in the stage lighting. "She won't only hear people out when they offer her something in return. She follows through on her word no matter what. She knows the key to being a good president—a good person—is not in the end results, but the intentions." He smiles to himself. "But the results matter to her, too."

His words remind me: I came here today to make a grand gesture and thus far, I've just bragged about myself. What an end result.

I hold my hand out to stop Patrick from saying anything else, no matter how nice it would be and how good it would make me feel. Our classmates and teachers must think we're unhinged up here the way we keep volleying compliments back and forth.

"Patrick will be an excellent president. He's just . . . excellent, in general. We met on my first day here and he very quickly became my best friend. His presence brightens a room, his jokes make me laugh so hard that I cry, and the attention he gives me, and everyone, is so admirable and respectable. He cares about the people here, especially those in the minority. He wants to be everyone's voice. I just want him to . . ." I can't say the words I planned to say. They're too cheesy. *Be mine.* "Have your votes."

The student body can't contain its whispers. A few teachers shush the crowd, but their demands go ignored.

He smiles at me, then the audience. "Well, as sweet as that is, *I'll* be voting for Ella. She's the best thing to happen to me—to this school. If you're smart, you'll vote for her, too. We need someone who won't put up with the same old bullshit, someone who won't back down from a fight, and someone who tries to make everything right for everyone in the end."

Well, I suppose there is no way I can be punished for swearing without *Patrick* being punished for it, too. *Well played, Trick.*

Principal Logan's face splits into an expression of pure outrage as he stalks onto the stage. Patrick turns and walks away, completely disregarding his father, the now-loud chatter of our classmates, and my torn expression. I . . . don't even know what to do. What to say. How to feel.

I take a deep breath and speak into the microphone. "I believe we have some more time allotted for this." I motion for Kat and Tana to join me, and then—reluctantly—Todd and Dean. I mimic Patrick's casual position at the edge of the stage from earlier. "Let's talk, Courtland."

Twenty-Seven

I don't have a chance to speak to Patrick again before voting begins. He's nowhere to be found in the cafeteria or the halls; Stevie reports that he didn't show up to chemistry. I've snuck into the bathroom to text him, but my messages have gone unanswered. I wonder if his dad has him locked in his office to lecture and make sure he doesn't do anything else rebellious. Certainly, by now, Patrick regrets advising people to vote for me, ruining his opportunity for culinary school and the chance to ensure his dad keeps his job with no bumps in the road.

I shuffle forward in the line of seniors waiting to vote on one of three iPads set up inside privacy shields in the cafeteria. As Patrick mentioned earlier, students can abstain from voting entirely if they don't want to vote for either of us. It's possible that even though Patrick basically pleaded with the students to vote for me, and Thomas's crowd has vowed not to vote for Patrick, I still don't win because enough people don't vote for me. I have to get at least fifty votes across every grade to make my presidency official at Courtland. While that's only like an eighth of the entire school population, I feel like I'm standing in front of all my classmates and begging them for the chance to be rejected one last time. I stopped myself from doing the mental math of counting sure votes a few minutes ago because it just leads me to second-guessing my friendships and discussions I've had over the last month.

The girl in front of me turns around—I was in such a fugue state that I hadn't realized I was right behind Nadia.

I take a half step back. "Hi."

"Hey." She smiles, cautiously but warmly. "I'm voting for you."

"Thanks." I'm not sure what else to say. I'm not sure how to even feel. "I appreciate it."

She twists her fingers together. "I hope you didn't break up with Patrick because of me—not that I could break you two up or anything," she adds quickly. "I just mean . . . things with him and me weren't good when we dated. We didn't mesh like the two of you do—did."

I wish it were Patrick saying this to me and not his ex who he lied to me about.

"He didn't tell me about you," I say reluctantly. "I found out about it. I felt kind of . . . lied to, but I was planning on letting it go. Things just didn't go according to plan. It wasn't your fault."

"I think he's used to people giving up on him. I hope you won't."

I *thought* I was going to give up on him. I certainly tried. I thought it was what was right for me to do, to respect myself and focus on the campaign. But whenever I thought about leaving Patrick in the past, I wanted him in the present. When I saw him alone, I wanted him with me.

"I won't. I don't think I can."

The conversation kind of awkwardly ends there, and true to her word, she steps forward and votes for me. With a thumbs-up, Nadia leaves me questioning everything and everyone. This wasn't the best time for a Patrick epiphany, but when would it have been? The world doesn't get an ending all wrapped up in a bow like it would if Connie were writing it. It's messy and inconvenient, and sometimes it leaves you with more questions than answers. Sometimes you plan a grand gesture to try to be friends again, and then sometimes you talk to an ex-girlfriend who gets you more determined than ever to win him back.

I take a deep, steadying breath and push all the cluttering thoughts to the back of my mind. Stevie's across the room, having run into the cafeteria and been first in line to vote for me. She was so excited, she told me, that she almost forgot to vote for Tana and Kat. She records me on her phone and when I make eye contact with her, she throws her free arm up in a fist pump. Lila does the same with both arms, nearly taking out a girl walking in front of her.

I sit in front of the iPad where a plain white screen with black text asks me to decide my secretary/treasurer choice. I pick Kat. Then the vice presidential candidates. I pick Tana.

Then it asks me to choose myself or Patrick.

I know that *not* clicking Patrick does not mean I'm giving up on him.

It was not an easy journey here, but it's an easy choice.

I choose me.

It's announced before the final bell, like a hurried afterthought, which I'm sure is Principal Logan's intention. First, to drag it out and keep me on edge all day. And second, to make me and the election feel smaller than we are. This has been on my mind since the first day of school, and if I win this presidency, it'll be on my mind until I graduate. I've never been more excited for responsibility, though. I've also never felt so much like a live wire, buzzing with nerves and energy, ready for something to do.

"In the secretary/treasurer role," the administrative worker says into the crackly speaker, "Kat Simms, junior."

My stomach drops and a laugh bubbles out of me. *Oh, Kat.* Their mom will be so happy.

"In the vice president role . . . ," she continues.

I can't let myself get confident. Kat winning does not guarantee—

"Tana Smith, senior."

I don't dare release my breath. I am not a sure bet. The presidency will automatically go to Tana if neither Patrick nor I has over fifty votes—and that would still be great! But, admittedly, I would cry. Probably a lot.

"And your new Courtland Academy president . . ." She wouldn't announce this part if Patrick or I didn't get enough votes, right? The school would just say there was no president assigned. "With three hundred and four votes—the most votes for a student council position since Courtland Academy's establishment in 1969—"

The classroom screams "nice" so loudly and unexpectedly that I nearly miss when she continues to say . . . my name.

"Delaware Parker-Evans is your new student council president."

There was more excitement for a played-out 69 joke, but the classmates around me *do* applaud. Not loud enough that I can't hear Stevie's scream from the hall. But it's applause. For me. For what I did. I made *history* at this school. I activated my classmates and overthrew the (local and very specific) patriarchy. I made a difference for Connie, for me, for the rest of my classmates, and I won't take this duty lightly.

The bell rings shortly after and I leave the classroom on cloud nine. It floats me to my locker in a daze, where Stevie, Lila, and Connie meet me to crush me in a group hug that breaks my bones, but I can't feel it. I am numb with shock and happiness and confusion. As we head toward the exit, people pat me on the back, tell me "good job," say they voted for me. Every single time they tell me, I reply that I believe them, because three hundred and four is not an insignificant number when there are around four hundred students in the school. I'm sure if I had mentioned my—apparently ridiculous—bout of self-doubt to Stevie or Connie earlier, they would have done the actual math to assure me I'd be winning today, but saying that I was afraid I wouldn't secure such a small amount of votes after all this time was like breathing life into the fear.

When the final group of well-wishers leaves us, we head for the exit door just past the band room—gentle plucking of guitar strings and the familiar hum of a song pulls me to the doorframe. I stop and lean in, waving Stevie and Lila off so they can get on their way to Lila's after-school away game. I want to speak to Patrick, but I also don't want to disturb him. There's a reason he hasn't reached out to me yet. I don't know where we stand. I don't know what these election results mean for us, for his future.

But.

He's playing my favorite song, the one I mentioned to him so briefly all that time ago.

And it's an invitation if I ever heard one.

When I knock on the door, his body, once slung over his guitar, tongue poking between his teeth as he concentrated, snaps ramrod straight. He meets my eyes, the trace of a smile already on his face, like he was expecting me, calling me to him. My little cloud carries me over and deposits me into the seat next to him. Connie lingers at the door.

"How long have you been playing this song on the off chance I walked by to hear it?" I ask, elated that he's playing it at all, but especially right now.

He silences the guitar with a skilled hand. "Why do you think it's for you?"

I smile.

He smirks. "Hi."

"Hi," I say back. My cheeks do the thing that they're known to do when Patrick Logan looks at me.

"Congratulations."

I play up my shrug, aiming for humble but landing on smug. "I had some help."

"A team victory, then." He looks over my head at Connie. "Hey, Connie. Could I have a moment with Ella?"

She rolls her eyes. "Just say you're going to make out like an adult, Patrick."

I whip my head toward her. "Wait down the hall, Connecticut."

"I'm going to head home, actually." She waits at the door, hands gripped on her backpack straps. Nervous.

"Okay." I stay firmly in my seat. I'm determined to let her do this and to not worry about it. "Be careful."

"I'll share my location and find someone to walk with," she adds. The tension works out of her shoulders and she releases her straps.

"Text me when you're home, please."

"Obviously. I want to know everything that happens as soon as possible." She turns, but says over her shoulder, "I've got a sequel to write."

"What?" Patrick asks with a bemused smile.

Connie walks away without another word, thankfully.

"I'll explain later." Or never. Most likely never.

"Too busy to do it right now?"

"Well, I *am* Courtland Academy's new student council president, and that seems to come with a lot of work."

He sets his guitar aside. "You're not wrong. Like apparently delivering grievances from the student body to the Board."

I sigh. "I wish we had gotten to talk about that more before this morning."

"I put the pieces together." He bites his lip. "Then my dad

spent a good two hours chastising me for ruining his career."

"*He's* responsible for his career, not you! Maybe if he were a better principal, his students would be happy with him and he wouldn't have to rig his contract renewal." I settle into the seat a little more. "But I am sorry that he's not helping you with culinary school anymore. He's not, right?"

"Oh, he made that abundantly clear." He shrugs, his face blank. "You were right. I don't want his support if it comes with strings attached like that."

"I'm so sorry."

"I'm sorry, too." He turns to me. "For not being more open. I was *so* embarrassed about the Nadia thing, and it only got worse the more I—it got worse when I realized I had feelings for you and we were only in a fake relationship to get you votes against her new boyfriend. I just felt really weird. It was complicated. I felt like I wasn't worth a real or fake relationship. I know that's on me—"

"I'm sorry. I was too harsh. You didn't need to share, and I should have been way more understanding that you would rather get your father on board with your passion than continue to piss him off for me."

He releases a long sigh, and slips a little in his seat. "I'm so glad you won. I couldn't keep up with the charade anymore. It made my skin itch."

"Mine, too. It was like you were body snatched."

"The only body I want to snatch—"

"Trick."

"Ella." He looks deeply into my eyes and it feels like he has a literal grip on my heart.

"Yes?"

"You get me like so few people do."

"It's not hard," I say quietly. "Do *not* make a joke about that."

He grins again, teeth clamped down on his bottom lip to keep his comment to himself. "I just mean, everyone says I'm too much when I'm not even trying to be, so I just lean into it. So I didn't have to feel bad about it anymore. But with you, I'm at ease. It's never an act."

He hesitantly laces his fingers through mine and rests our hands on my thigh. "I want to be your real boyfriend, no tricks. And no campaigning, lies, or strip trivia—well, maybe strip trivia—"

"*Patrick.*" I squeeze his hand.

"Do you feel the same?"

"Yes, similarly," I say, mocking his catchphrase.

"Even about the strip trivia—"

I close the space between us, connecting our mouths in what feels, finally, finally, finally, like *our* first kiss.

Twenty-Eight

The first student council meeting begins with attendance, as every important and life-changing meeting should. It's always good to take note of who is present when history is made and the future is rewritten.

"Secretary/Treasurer Kat Simms?" I ask, even though they're sitting right next to me to jot down minutes with one of those thick multicolored pens.

"Present." They click open a new color.

"Vice President Tana Smith?"

From my other side: "Present."

"And I'm here, as well. Ella Parker-Evans, president." I shuffle the four copies of my one-page agenda in my hands. Sure, black words on a white page would have been easy and more sensible—not to mention an email, which would have been even better—but creating a colorful template on my iPad for us to reuse for each agenda, so that they have a cohesive look in the binder I'm making for preservation purposes, felt more on brand for me. I pass them to Kat to hand out. "Let's begin the discussion of—"

Patrick clears his throat. All three sets of our eyes flick to him, the only other person in the room. He sits on the opposite side of the table, offering a patient smile. "What about me?"

"What is your job title again?" Tana asks with amusement, tapping her baby-blue nails on the table.

"Liaison to the principal."

"And your position responsibilities?" Kat poises their pen above their notebook.

"I'm here to ensure any and all changes will annoy my father."

"Ah, yes," Kat says, jotting it down. "Noted."

"I'm also the First Dude. I make food to keep you all fueled, shake hands with douchebags, and handle any dirty work that is beneath the council—it's hard for people to say no to me. I think we'll have a successful year. What's first on the agenda?"

I tap the agenda Kat placed in front of him with a finger. "I want to talk about the Senior Supervisors program."

Tana frowns. "I've never heard of it?"

"It's new," I say with a confident tilt of my head. It's hard not to get dreamy thinking about this. "An Ella Parker-Evans creation."

The program is pretty simple, actually. It will require some volunteers, but, as Patrick said, it's hard for people to say no to him, so I imagine he'll find enough students in a day. Plus, it's an extracurricular, like Stevie being my welcome guide. People will gravitate toward it to bulk out their college apps, and the mission of the program will entice them to stay and encourage others to join.

"We get senior volunteers to—in exchange for college application padding, obviously—become mentors of sorts for freshmen, and then even sophomores and juniors eventually. They'll have a scheduled time each week to hear out the freshmen's grievances, answer questions, form bonds. And then that would lead into the mingling of the grades. Hallways, classes, lunches." All three of my friends—my student council—nod along. "I just don't want there to be such a separation. There shouldn't be. Plus, the freshmen could end up helping the seniors out. Give us new perspective on things, help us see the problems we've grown used to, and open our minds to the possibilities."

"What possibilities, exactly?" Kat asks.

"I don't know, but they're there, okay?"

Patrick smirks. "You're spending too much time with Connie."

"Well, that's not my fault. You're so busy *working with my mom* now."

His smirk breaks into a full-on grin. "That's *your* fault."

Tana clears her throat. "How about we focus, lovebirds? I only have five minutes until my tutoring session."

"Yes, you're very busy and I won't waste your time," I say sheepishly, to laughter. I lightly kick Patrick under the table.

Embarrassed, but only a little, I go into more detail about the Senior Supervisors and how this program/committee/ whatever we want to call it could make a huge difference in not only the social aspects of the school, but the actual learning and curriculum. I ask the three of them to imagine study halls and extracurriculars and electives with a diverse and inclusive group of students learning together. Picture how that can broaden a student's point of view. It will also work as a means of earning privileges (that are no longer just for seniors).

We end the meeting scheduling our time to talk next week. We hope to loop in our senior volunteers and Connie, as the freshman liaison, then, and discuss the homecoming dance. The new election pushed back the planning process a bit, but I have trust that this group can get a lot done in a little bit of time, and Stevie is eager to help on the planning committee.

Afterward, Patrick and I dawdle through the school, holding hands, and make our slow way out to his car. We both have shifts at Ashes tonight and he doesn't want to be late. I, on the other hand, would not care if we maybe dedicated ten minutes to kissing before we got there.

"Your mom said I can take leftovers home tonight."

I snort. "How magnanimous of her."

"You laugh now, but you'll be sorry when I don't share any of my Have It Three Ways Cake (Patrick's Poor Attempt) with you."

I grab his arm before he can open the passenger door for me and tug him close. "Don't forget me when you're famous," I mumble into his polo.

"I could never."

I pull away, just to interlock our fingers and stare at them as a means of distracting him from my warming cheeks. "Okay," I say quietly.

"I'm serious, you know," he says, tipping my head up with

a finger under my chin. "I'll never forget you, no matter what happens with cooking or college or anything. Because I have a trick for that. That's why they call me Trick."

"Let me guess . . . you make a song for each of your exes or something? A seven-minute travesty of trumpets and guitar?"

"*No*. But that is a good idea." He brushes some of my wind-blown hair back and presses me against his car, arms caging me in. "The trick to not forgetting you is to not let you go anywhere, and I won't either. We'll stick together."

I nod. "That sounds pretty good."

"As good as my food?"

"Better, somehow."

He nuzzles his nose against mine but pulls away before letting our lips connect. The little tease. "Now let's get in the car. I don't want to be late. And my ears are freezing."

"That's what you get for putting them on display like that."

"First on *my* agenda is growing my hair out again, followed by taking you on a date where I don't have to cook, forcing you to listen to me butcher your favorite song on guitar, letting me kiss your cheeks whenever they get all red and cute like that—"

I cut him off with a kiss, planting both my hands on the sides of his face and pulling him closer again. We do not get in the car. In fact, with his hands on my waist and a quick jump, I am *on* his car. The cold hood of his SUV stings the bottom of my thighs, but the rest of me is warm—practically on fire—at his touch. He rests between my legs, kissing my mouth, biting my bottom lip, and traveling to my neck, but then someone *rudely* clears their throat.

We break apart, dazed, to spot Thomas walking to his bright red Acura. "What a class act you two are," he mutters in disgust.

"You know what," I say, then bark out a laugh, "you're right for once, Thomas."

"Classy is exactly the word I would use to describe us," Patrick says, nuzzling back into my neck.

I laugh, pushing him the tiniest bit away, but he clings tight and huffs out warm air onto my neck, shooting tingles down my sides. In a whisper, he restarts his list of all the things he wants to do, and I continue turning into a tomato. I pull back to kiss him at the same time he leans in to kiss me, and yet . . . we both miss spectacularly. We course correct, and then naturally we're late to work. But it's okay, because there's no rush, no end date to us, and we can accomplish a lot in a small amount of time, the two of us. We're a class act.

Acknowledgments

Like a student council president, I would be nowhere without my cabinet. I'd like to thank the editors who worked on this book with me: Stephanie Stein, Sophie Schmidt, and Sara Schonfeld. They had the difficult task of helping me whip this book into shape, and I hope I did their valuable feedback justice.

Thank you to the Harper team who worked behind the scenes to produce this book: Mikayla Lawrence, Gweneth Morton, Jessie Gang, Meghan Pettit, Allison Brown, and Audrey Diestelkamp.

To my agent, Katelyn Detwciler, thank you for jumping on this train even though it was going full speed ahead.

A special thanks to my best friends who put up with me doubting myself during every part of the process to publish this book: Rachel Lynn Solomon, Marisa Kanter, Carlyn Greenwald, Sonia Hartl, Annette Christie, Andrea Contos, Auriane Desombre, Susan Lee, and Jennifer Dugan. Thank you to Ellen O'Clover, Emma Ohland, Sierra Elmore, Elizabeth Lynch,

Jenny Howe, Hannah Whitten, Maggie Horne, and many others for small talks, laughs, and commiseration.

Thank you to my POA coworkers for embarrassing me at every opportunity and announcing to crowded rooms that I'm an author.

To my mother, Wendy, for always telling Young Kelsey that she was so creative.

To my sister, Nicole, for asking me to proofread your college papers when I was in high school.

To the love of my life, Dylan, for always being ready to say something hilarious and unexpected.